CANDLELIGHT ECSTASY SUPREMES

- 69 FLIRTING WITH DANGER, *Joanne Bremer*
- 70 ALL THE DAYS TO COME, *Jo Calloway*
- 71 BEST-KEPT SECRETS, *Donna Kimel Vitek*
- 72 SEASON OF ENCHANTMENT, *Emily Elliott*
- 73 REACH FOR THE SKY, *Barbara Andrews*
- 74 LOTUS BLOSSOM, *Hayton Monteith*
- 75 PRIZED POSSESSION, *Linda Vail*
- 76 HIGH VOLTAGE, *Lori Copeland*
- 77 A WILD AND RECKLESS LOVE, *Tate McKenna*
- 78 BRIGHT FLAME, DISTANT STAR, *Blair Cameron*
- 79 HOW MANY TOMORROWS?, *Alison Tyler*
- 80 STOLEN IDYLL, *Alice Morgan*
- 81 APHRODITE'S PROMISE, *Anne Silverlock*
- 82 ANOTHER EDEN, *Dallas Hamlin*
- 83 PLAYERS IN THE SHADOWS, *Donna Kimel Vitek*
- 84 AGAINST THE WIND, *Anne Stuart*
- 85 A LITTLE BIT OF WARMTH, *Jackie Black*
- 86 HIDDEN CHARMS, *Lee Magner*
- 87 DOUBLE OR NOTHING, *Lynn Patrick*
- 88 THE BEST REASON OF ALL, *Emily Elliott*
- 89 MORE THAN SHE BARGAINED FOR, *Lori Copeland*
- 90 MAN OF THE HOUR, *Tate McKenna*
- 91 BENDING THE RULES, *Kathy Alerding*
- 92 JUST FOR THE ASKING, *Eleanor Woods*
- 93 ISLAND OF DESIRE, *Antoinette Hale*
- 94 AN ANGEL'S SHARE, *Heather Graham*
- 95 DANGEROUS INTERLUDE, *Emily Elliott*
- 96 CHOICES AND CHANCES, *Linda Vail*

A GLIMMER OF TRUST

Alison Tyler

A CANDLELIGHT ECSTASY SUPREME

Published by
Dell Publishing Co., Inc.
1 Dag Hammarskjold Plaza
New York, New York 10017

Copyright © 1985 by Alison Tyler

All rights reserved. No part of this book may be reproduced or transmitted in any form or by any means, electronic or mechanical, including photocopying, recording or by any information storage and retrieval system, without the written permission of the Publisher, except where permitted by law.

Dell ® TM 681510, Dell Publishing Co., Inc.

Candlelight Ecstasy Supreme is a trademark
of Dell Publishing Co., Inc.

Candlelight Ecstasy Romance®, 1,203,540, is a registered trademark of Dell Publishing Co., Inc.

ISBN: 0-440-12913-3

Printed in the United States of America

First printing—November 1985

To Our Readers:

We are pleased and excited by your overwhelmingly positive response to our Candlelight Ecstasy Supremes. Unlike all the other series, the Supremes are filled with more passion, adventure, and intrigue, and are obviously the stories you like best.

In months to come we will continue to publish books by many of your favorite authors as well as the very finest work from new authors of romantic fiction. As always, we are striving to present unique, absorbing love stories—the very best love has to offer.

Breathtaking and unforgettable, Ecstasy Supremes follow in the great romantic tradition you've come to expect *only* from Candlelight Ecstasy.

Your suggestions and comments are always welcome. Please let us hear from you.

> Sincerely,
>
> The Editors
> Candlelight Romances
> 1 Dag Hammarskjold Plaza
> New York, New York 10017

CHAPTER ONE

Jackie Archer kicked off her shoes. The white tile floor of the tiny bathroom was freezing cold, but her feet hurt too much for that to matter. They'd been aching for the last five days straight. She peered at her small, heart-shaped face in the mirror. Her bright-green eyes looked especially large with her long brown hair severely pulled back in a tight chignon, a ridiculous black cap trimmed with white lace perched on top. Her gaze moved down to the tight, excessively starched white peasant blouse that flattened her full breasts against her chest, the wide, gold-braided cummerbund that dug uncomfortably into her narrow waist, and the black-and-gold print skirt layered with petticoats that gave an illusion of ample hips—an illusion Jackie could have done without.

"Jackie Archer," she said to herself, "you must be in there somewhere." She laughed. It was one of her saving graces. At five feet two inches, weighing almost one hundred and five pounds—after a good meal—she decided she looked more like a painfully wanting and misshapen Kewpie doll in this preposterous getup than she did the sixteenth-century French handmaiden all of the waitresses at the chic Côte d'Or were supposed to resemble.

The bathroom door opened, letting in a blast of hot air from the restaurant kitchen. Monique Gilbert, another handmaiden, stepped inside. Unlike Jackie's her tall, broad frame carried off the costume quite well. She looked much like the real McCoy until she lit up her cigarette.

"Pelouze is on the rampage. You'd better hurry." Monique leaned in toward the mirror, closely examining a faint blemish on her chin.

"Isn't he always?" Jackie sighed. The head chef of the three-star Paris restaurant, Hubert Pelouze, was an intense, volatile martinet who seemed to exhale fire rather than air. Behind his back, the waitresses all made fun of *La Grande Gueule*, the loudmouth. But when the lumbering ox of a man set his narrow gray eyes on any one of them, they positively trembled.

Jackie forced her sore feet back into her shoes. It wouldn't do to have *Le Grande Gueule* breathe fire down her neck. She needed this job too badly. Not that carting heavy trays around a restaurant fourteen strenuous hours a day had exactly been one of her fantasies back in Middleton Corner, Ohio. Three months ago she'd walked into the administrator's office of the Middleton Corner Main Library—a definite misnomer, as it was the only branch in town—and handed in her resignation as head librarian. Donald Winston had stared aghast at her. Jackie had practically lived in that library since she had started reading. Why, she'd started working there as soon as she was tall enough to see over the book-checkout counter. The only time Jackie had ever left Middleton Corner was to go to Ohio State University to get her degree in library science.

"Jackie," Donald had said that crisp October day, "this isn't like you. Not like you at all."

That was where Donald Winston was wrong. For nearly twenty years, ever since she'd seen the movie *April in Paris,* Jackie had nurtured a secret dream of running off to live in the City of Light. For her tenth birthday she'd insisted the only gift she wanted was a five-record set from the Berlitz language school which advertised that anyone could learn conversational French in ten easy lessons. Mrs. Archer had tried to talk her shy, reticent daughter into dance classes instead, preferring that Jackie do something more outgoing than sit alone in her room saying, *"Parlez-vous Français?"* to a record player every afternoon; but Jackie was adamant. She always had been a stubborn and persistent child, as well as a dreamer.

After mastering the first set of records, Jackie sent away for the advanced course and then continued her studies from books and French newspapers. Paris was her dream, all right, but no one ever took her seriously. Jackie had been born and bred in Middleton Corner and, sure enough, she'd likely die there someday.

Even when she bid her not-so-fond farewells to the folk back home, they had little doubt that

Jackie would be returning soon enough. Most chalked up her strange behavior to being close to thirty years old and still unmarried; in Middleton Corner the modern single career woman was merely a fancy tag for "spinster." Not that she hadn't had her chance. Tom Coopersmith would have gladly put a gold ring on her finger had Jackie shown a little more interest. But, said Donald Winston to Jackie's sister, Gwen, the day Jackie left for Paris, Jackie was too busy dreaming of French knights in shining armor. The girl was a romantic fool. And this job in Paris, France, she'd taken, translating torrid French romance stories into English, wasn't going to help matters any.

Jackie had seen the ad for a translator in one of the overseas career newsletters she received each month. She didn't tell a soul she'd applied until she had landed the position. Four days after receiving the letter offering her the job, she was on a flight for Paris.

Claude Marigny, the publisher of *Toujours Amour,* was a living, breathing prototype of the sensual heroes strewn across the pages in the romances Jackie translated. He was not only tall and darkly handsome, he exuded that special aristocratic assurance and cool, languid manner of the nobility—or at least Jackie's fantasy of nobility. She was intrigued by him, and if Marigny wasn't exactly swept off his feet by Jackie, she had the feeling he found her quaintly amusing; certainly different from the tall, lanky blondes he escorted about town in his apple-red sports car. However, Jackie's fascination with Claude Marigny lasted all of nine weeks, at which time *Toujours Amour* came to a very unromantic end. Marigny's style turned out to be his downfall. Aristocratic good looks and languid airs alone did not pay the bills.

When the small publishing house went bankrupt, Jackie came face to face with her first hard look at unemployment—in a foreign city, no less. After a solid month of pounding the pavement Jackie went to see Marigny in desperation. Oh, Marigny was pounding the pavement as well, but he was doing the rounds in his shiny red Porsche while Jackie was wearing out her last pair of black leather pumps.

Jackie finally elicited her former boss's assistance after she flooded him with a proliferation of tears, breathless entreaties, and loud sniffles. She'd mustered up these theatrics only after her inept stab at charming the suave Marigny had fallen hopelessly flat. Not that some of those tears hadn't been real. If Jackie didn't get her hands on some money soon, she was going to be thrown out of her less-than-elegant attic flat in the rue de la Jonquière, on her not very well padded derrière. She was two months overdue on her rent and the only source of income she had left was a return ticket to Ohio. As much as she swore she'd never use it, she was nervous about cashing it in.

Marigny used his still considerable pull to get her this job at the Côte d'Or. It wasn't exactly her dream come true, but the work would keep her living—if not in style, at least intact. Another week and she'd be able to pay her landlord, Jean

Guillaume, the rent money. She might even manage to eke out enough francs to resume painting classes with Yves Jérôme and enroll in the nineteenth-century French literature seminar at the Sorbonne. After all, she hadn't come to Paris to dress up in a costume that made her look like an overripe pear and lug laden trays of food around a restaurant—three stars notwithstanding.

Jackie tipped the frilly cap farther back on her head and tugged free a few tendrils of brown hair from her chignon, softening the pinched look about her face. *Très bien.* She nodded to herself in the bathroom mirror, mimicking the suave Marigny's languid smile of assurance. Monique, still busy with her cigarette and blemishes, ignored Jackie's *"A tout à l'heure."*

The kitchen, heady with the aromatic scent of garlic, was a madhouse of activity and noise. The chef, Pelouze, was busy ranting at one of his assistants, chastising a waitress for not being quick enough about picking up her orders, and stirring a delicate *beurre blanc* all at the same time. Still, he gave a moment's pause to glare contemptuously at Jackie's skewed bonnet. Gritting her teeth and hastily reminding herself of all the francs she hoped to rake in tonight, Jackie readjusted her cap. She caught his look of sheer disgust as she headed for the swinging doors. It was obvious he considered her a poor waitress at best, which was true enough. But Jackie was well aware that his deeper resentment had to do with the fact that she was an American; even more so for being an American who spoke French with

"IF THIS PLAN IS ANYTHING LIKE YOUR SCHEME TO GET OUT OF PAYING YOUR TAB AT THE RESTAURANT, FORGET IT."

"Stop griping," Peter replied, "and point out your windows before I freeze to death."

Jackie aimed at the top story. "Fourth floor—the penthouse suite, you could call it." She gave him a bemused grin. "Are we thinking of a heist?"

"We are." He arched his brow. "Are you game?"

Jackie shrugged. "Well, if we get caught, at least I'll have a roof over my head and three meals a day. Then again, a prison cell in Paris isn't exactly the place I'd want to call home."

"Can you whistle?"

"Like a champ."

"Good. Keep your big green eyes open and your lips puckered to warn me if someone comes by." He paused before stepping onto the bottom rung of the fire escape. "This better mean you'll forgive me for costing you your job."

Seeing the smile that graced his mouth and lit his deep-blue eyes, Jackie wondered if she wouldn't forgive him just about anything. . . .

such astounding proficiency as to fool many of the staff and customers.

The contrast between the clamorous, steamy kitchen and the cool, grand, old-world elegance of the formal dining room still, after five nights of work, threw Jackie off kilter for a couple of moments. She stood a few feet from the swinging doors surveying the scene. It was close to ten P.M., but the French enjoyed late dinners. The room was nearly full. Jackie had learned earlier of the anticipated arrival of the Marquis and Marquise de Ternaux. She'd been duly prepped, as she would be the waitress serving them. Henri Bouchard, the austere and pompous maître d' of the Côte d'Or, had not been too pleased about that, but Jackie was filling the regular station of a waitress who had taken ill that morning.

Monsieur Bouchard was ushering in the de Ternaux, a rather plain-looking, middle-aged couple, showering them with an obsequious attentiveness reserved for the rich and famous. The strikingly handsome, dark-haired man accompanying them was, no doubt, of the same vintage. Close to six feet, with dark, sensual blue eyes, chiseled features, and a lean build, he reminded Jackie of her ex-boss, Claude Marigny. They displayed the same cool elegance, easy confidence, and simmering attractiveness. But where Marigny's style was languidly restrained, this man's manner seemed to burst with an energetic aggressiveness.

Jackie chastised herself for taking those romance novels she'd translated too much to heart.

She ought to be concentrating less on the man's fiery good looks and more on how to induce her special customers to leave her a generous tip. She watched Bouchard lead the threesome to one of the best tables in the house and bow ever so subtly from the waist as the marquis nodded his approval. With yet another subtle gesture Bouchard motioned to the wine steward, who strode gracefully to the marquis's side.

Jackie took a deep breath as she waited her turn to move to the table dotted with nobility. She was determined to carry this off with style, despite her inexperience—and despite feeling utterly ridiculous in her voluminous outfit.

Peter Santiago cast a blank gaze at Jackie when she walked over. His mind was still swimming over the cost of the bottle of 1966 Perrier-Jouet champagne the marquis had just ordered so nonchalantly from the steward. Peter hoped the marquis and his wife had less expensive tastes in food or he would be blowing every franc he had in his wallet, since the de Ternaux were his guests for dinner. The marquis had suggested the Côte d'Or as a pleasant dining experience, and while Peter was savvy enough to plan on a classy, high-priced joint, he wasn't expecting de Ternaux to get the ball rolling with a bottle of bubbly that cost more than Peter had spent on the last few months' groceries. No doubt de Ternaux assumed a wealthy American vintner like Peter Santiago would drink only the finest wines.

Peter started praying. This all-out effort of his to entice de Ternaux to invest in his project had better pay off or he was not only going to be up a creek without a paddle, he'd be sans the rowboat.

The waitress had finished taking the marquise and marquis's orders, which Peter barely managed to decipher. While he had never made it past high-school French, his fluent knowledge of Spanish helped him over most rough spots. Right now it was helping him to note that the marquis and marquise were intent on a soup-to-nuts spread that was not only going to leave his wallet naked, but was going to leave him in the kitchen washing dishes. Not exactly the image he was banking on making if he had any hope of interesting de Ternaux in financing his lifelong dream.

He felt the waitress's stare and looked up, paying attention to her for the first time. She had incredibly large green eyes, which, he decided, were her only distinguished characteristic. That, and the fact that she looked like a comical waif in that dumb getup. He forgot his financial dilemma for a moment and found himself smiling at her.

"That outfit must weigh more than you do." He spoke in English, not really expecting her to understand. It was obviously said more for the amusement of de Ternaux and his wife, both of whom smiled.

The irritating man continued grinning up at her. Provoked by his ridicule, Jackie forgot about that big tip she needed so badly and fixed him with an icy stare. She was mimicking one of Pelouze's famous royally disdainful looks, hoping she carried it off half as effectively as the imperial chef invariably did.

The subtleties of French-style intimidation were lost on Peter. He assumed the waitress was annoyed because he was holding her up with her orders. His grin faded into a mildly apologetic smile as he misread her look. "What do you recommend this evening?"

His French was stilted, but his voice was deep and melodic, and his smile was far more attractive than the mocking grin it had replaced. Jackie could also detect a twinkle of amusement in those dark-blue eyes. She held on to her subtle look of disdain as she rattled off a long list of possibilities in her most rapid French, none of which, she felt confident, the gentleman even vaguely comprehended. Then, feeling she had paid him back for making her the object of his mockery, she smiled demurely and waited.

The marquis came to the rescue, suggesting the *terrine de veau* for an appetizer and Pelouze's renowned *quenelles de poisson* as the main course. And, of course a bottle of vintage '78 Chateauneuf-du-Pape with the meal itself.

"That sounds wonderful," Peter said with an easy laugh. Now that he knew for certain there was no way he was going to be able to pay for this meal, he decided to relax. *What the hell,* he thought philosophically, *if I'm about to go down the tubes I might as well enjoy my last feast before I start falling. Or scrubbing pots and pans, as the case might be.*

The veal terrine was excellent. So was the bottle of wine. And wine was something Peter knew. Wine was, in fact, the very heart of the reason he was sitting in this overpriced, stuffy restaurant trying his utmost to sell de Ternaux on his plan to establish a new and unique vineyard in Labarde, right in the heart of France's Haut-Médoc wine country. The marquis, whose English was only a little better than Peter's French, was having a difficult time understanding much of what Peter was saying.

To add to Peter's woes he was still trying to come up with some face-saving solution to the problem of the hefty tab that the funny little waitress with the big green eyes was going to present to him at the end of this illustrious meal. It was an awkward predicament, but Peter Santiago had come through too many tight spots in his thirty-three years ever to give up without a fight—or at least without an alternative plan.

Jackie herself provided him with the solution quite by chance. She was carrying a large tray, laden with four silver-covered dishes, to the next table. Peter hadn't noticed her, as he was too busy struggling to get across his ideas to de Ternaux, until he heard a low gasp directly behind him. Turning his head, he saw that the petite waitress who had given him the haughty stare had accidentally hit her elbow against the back of his chair.

"Excusez-moi." He pulled in his seat. Peter was unable to stifle a momentary laugh at her comical efforts to steady the silver-domed dishes, which were sliding wildly across the tray. Jackie was furious, but she couldn't pause to communicate her feelings as she was too busy trying to keep all

the food from tumbling to the floor, or worse still, over the customers.

When she had managed, albeit not too gracefully, to get things under control, she glared at the gentleman who seemed to find her appearance and performance so amusing. Her temper getting the best of her, she was about to say something not very flattering when she caught the maître d's hard stare. Forcing back her irritation, she turned away and set the dishes down in front of the four customers who had been too nervous about getting drenched in *bouillabaisse à la marseillaise* and *boeuf bourguignon* to be amused. Bouchard scurried over, offering profuse apologies. It was at that moment that a plan began forming in Peter Santiago's devious mind.

Meanwhile, Jackie finished serving the food, feeling her cheeks redden from anger and embarrassment. To make things worse, the obsequious maître d' was called to the side of the man who had been amusing himself at her expense. He explained that the entire matter was his fault for keeping his chair too far from the table. Of course, Bouchard immediately broke into a new set of hushed apologies, implying clearly enough that Jackie's clumsiness was to blame. Then, to top it off, as she turned away, Jackie accidentally skimmed the back of Bouchard's head with the edge of the empty tray. She made a hasty retreat before he had a chance to react. However, she wasn't fast enough to miss the gush of laughter behind her. She did not have to guess where it came from.

Jackie Archer rarely took an immediate dislike to people. She decided to make an exception tonight. Little did she know that at that moment, her negative feelings toward Peter Santiago would shortly intensify to an alarming degree.

Le grand dénouement came along with the dessert, an opulent, overflowing *soufflé à l'orange au Grand Marnier.* Jackie had managed to regain her poise by this time, helped by the fact that Bouchard had other fish to fry and seemed to have grown weary or bored with glaring at her. She had even reclaimed her sense of humor about her brush with disaster, admitting that she must have presented a funny sight counterbalancing that overloaded tray of dishes.

A moment later all humor deserted her. She was almost home free, having carefully avoided any obstacles as she maneuvered the soufflé and her full petticoats across the crowded dining room. Then, just as she was taking her final step to the marquis's table, preparing to present the dessert with a grand flourish, a leg shot out.

Peter made a grab for her as both she and the soufflé went flying. He'd only intended to get her momentarily off balance so that some of the dessert would splatter a bit. This, under the watchful eye of the maître d', who would be mortified, would be enough to allow Peter to insist that the meal be on the house.

Monsieur Bouchard did exactly that. It was the least the flabbergasted maître d' could do, considering that half the soufflé had landed right in the

Marquise de Ternaux's lap, the rest of the rich dessert decorating her husband's navy suit jacket.

Peter's clever maneuver, however, sent the aristocratic couple storming out of the restaurant, leaving little doubt that de Ternaux would be pleased to forget both the humiliating incident and Peter Santiago's vineyard. To top things off he'd also managed to get the poor little waitress with the enormous green eyes fired on the spot.

Jackie, her fingers sticky with soufflé, smudged her face as she wiped at the tears of outrage running down her cheeks. Her eyes burned with fury as she insisted she had been tripped.

"Really," Peter said to Bouchard in her defense, "it was all my fault. I had a cramp in my leg and foolishly stretched it out just as the waitress arrived with the soufflé. She's certainly not to blame."

"I'm sorry, monsieur. Believe me, this was not the first problem we have had with her. Do not trouble yourself further. *C'est fini.*"

Bouchard turned away, the discussion no longer of interest to him. He wanted only to get through the rest of the evening and then forget this madness had ever occurred. He could feel the eyes of every customer follow him across the room. His one consolation was that he would not have to see the small American when he arrived at the Côte d'Or tomorrow night.

Just when Peter thought the waitress was going to crumble into a thousand pieces, she tore off her funny little cap, threw it into his cup of coffee, and stormed off to the kitchen. Peter Santiago remained in his seat, watching the lanky, blond-haired busboy energetically clean up the remaining debris. Before leaving with the tray of broken crockery, the young man glanced awkwardly down at the lace-trimmed cap protruding from Peter's cup. *"Un autre café, monsieur?"*

As rotten as he felt about this whole fiasco, he had to laugh. "No. *Merci.* I think I've had enough."

He stood up and started toward the door. Then, halfway there, he turned abruptly, much to Bouchard's distress, and headed directly for the kitchen. Peter realized that the least he could do was apologize again to the waitress who had lost her job because of him.

Jackie had practically torn her clothes off in the tiny dressing room next door to the employees' bathroom. She pulled on her jeans and, not even stopping to button her blouse, tugged on her loden jacket. Amid the hushed silence and curious stares of everyone in the kitchen, Jackie strode across the room and out the back door to the street.

Just as the staff were about to explode into gossip, Peter Santiago burst into the kitchen, followed by a frantic Henri Bouchard, who was insisting that customers were not allowed in this area. Peter saw the back door close on a small figure and, ignoring Bouchard's increasingly angry protestations, took off after her.

He didn't have to chase her very far. Jackie was sitting on a back step a few yards down in the dimly lit street. She watched with large, sullen eyes as Peter drew closer.

"I'm sorry," he said softly. Getting no reaction, he attempted some fragmented French. *"Je suis regrette. Excusez-moi."*

He sat down beside her. *"Vraiment,"* he added, at a loss for any other words of apology.

"Go away."

Peter did a classic double take. "You're American. Why the hell didn't you say so? Here I am, struggling to remember what little French I learned in high school and you—"

"I certainly don't owe you any explanations. But you owe me one, I should think. Why did you do it? Are you some kind of perverted degenerate who simply takes pleasure in turning those of us in the working classes into laughingstocks? Or do you have something against me personally? Do you think I dressed up in that ludicrous outfit purely for your amusement? Frankly, I find nothing amusing about it at all."

"I only meant to get out of paying a bill I couldn't cover. I never dreamed you'd go flying like that. I did try to grab you. All you had to do was spill the smallest glob on one of us and everything would have worked out fine."

"So this is all my fault, is it? I'll say one thing for you, mister, you've sure got audacity. Maybe you should have let me in on your plan so I could have done something a bit less dramatic. Do us both a favor, will you? Next time take your swank pals to McDonald's."

"Isn't there something I can do for you?" he asked contritely.

"Oh, you've done quite enough already, thank you."

"Come on. You can't sit here all night. I'll take you home."

She laughed dryly. "Home for another couple of days, anyway. If I'm lucky. I've been promising the landlord the back rent for the past month." She shook her head forlornly. "I would have had it too." She stood up and cast her eyes down at him. "If I were a few inches taller, I'd take one hell of a slug at your jaw. In one short evening you've managed to ruin my entire life." Tears fought a battle with her rage.

"I'm a lot smaller than you while I'm sitting down. Go ahead. I deserve it." Peter tilted his chin up and closed his eyes. Nothing happened. He opened them again to see her racing off down the street. He rushed after her.

"Hold on," he said, grabbing her sleeve. "I feel lousy about this."

"This may come as a surprise to you, but I really don't give a damn about your feelings right now. I'm broke, I have no job and no one left to turn to for help. I'm likely to find my luggage sitting on the front steps of my building—" Her voice caught. "My feet hurt, I smashed my knee against the blasted marquise's chair when you tripped me, I have no idea what I'm going to do now, and you tell me you feel lousy?"

"Look, how about if I give you enough money

to keep your landlord off your back for a few more days? It's the least I can do."

"No. I can't take money from you. I don't know you. I don't even like you."

Peter grinned. "Are you always so quick to tell a man where he stands?"

"Go on. Keep laughing. My whole life is disintegrating and you want to play games."

"No, I don't. I want to help you out. But you're not making it easy."

Jackie sighed wearily. "All right. I'll borrow a few francs from you—strictly as a loan. And only because this is all your fault. Maybe Guillaume will settle for a partial payment. I'll have to convince him I can come up with the rest within a few days, though. Exactly how I'm going to manage that remains to be figured out."

Jackie took the money, getting Peter's full name and address and carefully writing out an IOU for the amount of the loan.

Peter looked down at the note, then tucked it into his breast pocket. "Good luck, Jackie Archer."

"Well," she said with a small smile as she slipped the francs into her purse, "thanks for the money. I'm glad you were simply a guy in over his head rather than a perverted degenerate." She walked away. *"Mais, tout de même, je ne vous aime pas,* Pierre Santiago."

"What does that mean?" he called after her.

"I still don't like you." She turned her head around and gave him a curious grin.

Peter decided Jackie Archer had a fairly attractive smile to go along with her big green eyes. He caught up with her. "I'll like myself better if I see you home safely."

CHAPTER TWO

Peter was lost a couple of sentences into the heated conversation Jackie was having with the concierge. But he didn't need to be able to translate the words to get the picture. The concierge, a slovenly man in his fifties with deep bags under his watery eyes and a thick stubble covering his slack jaw and paunchy cheeks, looked as if he had heard a hundred hard-luck stories in his day and hadn't been moved since the first or second one. He certainly wasn't touched by Jackie's tale of woe or her three hundred francs.

Peter had to admire Jackie's persistence as well as her wide variety of techniques. She was very talented. In effortless French, she switched her manner from winsome charm, to disbelief, to outrage, to tears of desperation. As the concierge turned his back, took a few steps from his desk into his private office, and slammed the door on Jackie's tear-streaked face, her rage surfaced anew.

Peter had to calm her down before he could get her to speak coherently in English.

"He won't give me my key. He's locking me

out of my apartment. I can't believe this. He won't even let me get any of my things. Nothing . . . until I pay up in full. He can't get away with this," she fumed, ready to barge into his private domain.

Peter held her back. "That's not going to help."

"I suppose you have a better plan," she hissed, her green eyes narrowing.

He knew she was thinking this was all his fault. He could have argued the point since, job or no job, the concierge had clearly intended to lock her out of her flat until she came up with the back rent money. Still, he couldn't shake feeling responsible—or feeling sorry for her. If that dissipated slob of a concierge wasn't moved by Jackie's powers of persuasion, Peter had to admit she had definitely gotten to him.

Grabbing her hand, he tugged her toward the front door. "As a matter of fact, I do have another idea."

Jackie turned up the collar on her jacket as they stepped outside again. January in Paris was a far cry from April in Paris.

"If this plan is anything like your little scheme to get out of paying your tab at the restaurant, forget it."

"Stop griping," he said, leading her to the narrow street at the side of the building. "Point out your windows before I freeze to death."

The light dawned. Jackie stepped into the street and aimed a finger at the top floor of the four-story building, giving Peter a bemused grin. "It's right up on top. The penthouse suite, you could call it." She crossed her hands over her chest. "Are we thinking of a heist?"

"We are." He arched a dark brow. "Are you game?"

Jackie shrugged. "Well, if we get caught, at least I'll have a roof over my head and three square meals a day. Then again, a prison cell isn't exactly the place in Paris I'd like to call home."

Peter's eyes scanned the rickety metal fire escape that ran up the side of the building to the top floor. Then he cast a rueful glance down at his black cashmere coat that had cost him half a fortune. His coat was part of the elegant image he needed to cultivate. As was the Paris-tailored, navy silk and wool suit he was wearing under it. Just as Jackie had been forced to don her getup at the Côte d'Or, Peter had his own costume he was required to wear for special occasions.

He took off the coat and the suit jacket and handed them to Jackie.

"You'll freeze," she argued.

"If I ruin these duds I might as well throw in the towel." He laughed. "I'd strip off the trousers as well if my innate sense of modesty didn't interfere."

"Not to mention risking arrest for indecent exposure if we get caught," Jackie said.

"Your part of the job is making sure we aren't nabbed. Keep those big green eyes of yours peeled to the street. Can you whistle?"

"Like a champ."

"Good. Keep your lips puckered and send out a warning note if someone decides to stroll by or our cheery pal inside comes out for a breath of night air."

Jackie caught hold of his wrist. "I can't let you go up there. This is my problem. I'll do the breaking in." She tried to hand him back his clothes, but Peter was already busy tugging the rusted fire-escape ladder down low enough to get a firm grip.

Before he stepped onto the bottom rung, he gave her a quick smile. "This better mean you'll forgive me." He paused for a moment. "Don't worry. I won't be long. I've had a bit of experience in this area."

"Now, that doesn't surprise me." Jackie grinned.

She listened to the creaking of the metal rungs as Peter made his way up the fire escape to her apartment. Placing his clothes on the top of a trash can, she dug into her purse to tally up her meager cash on hand. With Peter's loan thrown in, she'd be able to find herself a cheap hotel room for a week or two. After that . . . well, she really didn't want to think about after that.

The sound of Peter's footsteps on the metal stairs ceased. Jackie, on lookout, peered up and down the side street. No one was coming; not surprising, as it was close to midnight. A light drizzle was descending from a black sky. She stepped further out from the edge of the building, looking up to see if Peter had made his way inside the apartment yet. It wouldn't be a cinch. Unfortunately, she had never had occasion to unlock her windows because it was always too cold to open them for fresh air. Anyway, the area was short on fresh air, being a block away from a factory that bottled olive oil. A marvelous aroma in small quantities, but definitely cloying by the hundreds of barrels full.

Jackie didn't mind. It was just another scent of Paris, another reminder that she was no longer little Jackie Archer, head librarian of the Middleton Corner Main Library. Never again, she swore to herself, would she go back to that life she had so abruptly and resolutely severed. Here, in Paris, she was the free spirit she had always dreamed of becoming. Even being homeless, jobless, and practically friendless did not make her despair. Maybe it dampened her spirits a bit, but she'd just have to find herself an umbrella.

She heard the muffled sound of glass breaking and nervously looked around, hoping no one else had heard. So far, so good. What felt like an eternity later, but probably no more than ten minutes, she heard Peter's footsteps moving faster as he descended the old fire escape.

"Here, catch," he whispered, tossing a duffle bag over the first-floor fire-escape platform and then scooting down the ladder.

"This is all you took?" She stared at him in disbelief.

Peter hastily slipped on his jacket and coat, wrapped a handkerchief around a cut finger, and was now carefully examining his trousers. He totally missed the note of distress in Jackie's voice. "Don't tell me you wanted me to cart down those canvases covered in colorful scribbles," he said offhandedly.

"Those scribbles happen to be the result of two hundred francs worth of art lessons, thank you. For your information, Yves Jérôme, a noted French artist and teacher, considers me to be someone with a great deal of potential."

Peter, having spotted a rip in the right-hand seam of his trousers, was in no mood to be tactful. "Yeah, especially if you keep dishing over the francs. Some people will tell you anything to keep their pockets full."

"I suppose you're some kind of art connoisseur," she snapped.

"Look," he said with an exasperated sigh, "you've got some clothes to put on your back for now. It's more than you had twenty minutes ago. Let's get out of here while the going's good." He shivered, trying to get warm again.

"What about Gogo?"

"Run that by me again?"

"What did you think I'd do, leave the poor thing to die? Or let that bastard Guillaume impound him? He'd probably feed Gogo to Gaspard for Sunday dinner." Jackie dropped the duffle bag on the ground and headed for the ladder. Even with it pulled down, there was no way she could reach. "A boost, *s'il vous plaît?*" The "please" was not tacked on for politeness.

"Who the hell is Gogo?" Peter demanded, offering her no assistance. "And who, for that matter, is Gaspard?"

Jackie gave him an impatient grimace. "Gaspard is a mean old alleycat that Guillaume dotes on. Gogo is my parakeet. He was sitting right on my kitchen table. How could you have overlooked him? Or are you too callous to bother about the life of *un petit oiseau?*"

"I didn't see your *oiseau*. I happened to be too busy packing your panties and bra-seaus to stop by the kitchen. I'll tell you one thing, though, he ain't much of a watchbird."

Jackie's grimace changed to a grin. "Too bad. He might have bitten you."

"Move away from there." He gave her a not-so-gentle nudge to the left. "Never let it be said that Peter Santiago left a *oiseau* to perish at the hands of a—*un chat*, I believe is the word for mean old hungry alleycat."

"A partial translation, anyway. But I'm impressed." She laughed.

Peter grabbed for the ladder.

"If it wouldn't be too much trouble"—she tugged on his sleeve—"could you just stick the one still-life that's on my easel under an arm? I have a special fondness for that particular bit of scribbling."

Jackie met his look of exasperation with a beguiling smile.

"I hope," he said, shaking his head in rueful resignation, "you're better with a needle and thread than you are with a loaded tray of dishes." He slipped off his coat and tossed it to her, but he left his jacket on for this run, as he was still freezing cold. "By the time I finish these little missions of mercy, I'll be lucky if my suit won't have to get tossed into a Salvation Army deposit box."

"I'll do a first-class stitch job. *Je promets*—I promise," she pledged, raising her right hand. Then she carefully draped his cashmere overcoat across the trash-can cover and gave Peter a boost up. "Oh, and don't forget Gogo's food. It's in a bag beside the cage."

"Anything else? Perhaps some dishes, a throw rug, maybe some of Gogo's favorite toys—the kitchen sink?"

Jackie tucked a damp strand of hair behind her ear. "I could use some of my paints and brushes," she said blithely, "but I wouldn't want you to risk spotting your fine clothes."

"You're so considerate."

Jackie was about to throw back another snappy retort when the front door to the building squeaked open. Peter jumped off the ladder and pressed himself and Jackie against the wall, edging them into the cover of a side doorway. They held their breath. Jackie took a quick peek out as a man passed by. She was relieved to see it wasn't Guillaume snooping about. It was Monsieur Valmy, who lived in the studio flat one flight below her. As he passed the opening to the side street, he took a casual glance inside. Probably keeping a desultory eye out for muggers or winos. Noticing neither, Valmy continued at a leisurely pace up the block.

Christophe Valmy worked the night shift at the Naboulet factory down the street. He was a reasonably attractive man in his mid-thirties who had made a halfhearted pass at Jackie when she'd first moved into the building. But the scent of olive oil that seemed to permeate the air around him made Jackie queasy, thus causing her to rule out immediately all possibility of an *affaire de coeur*. Besides, the rather rough-looking factory worker was not her type.

Valmy seemed less than bothered by her rejection, which, Jackie admitted, did hurt her ego— an ego already suffering from the suave Claude Marigny's lackadaisical response to her feminine charm. But then, how was she expected to break hearts in a city filled with scores of exquisite, chic Parisian women? Even the poorest clerk seemed to have a certain panache that Jackie recognized but felt at a loss to imitate. She'd never been terribly involved with fashion, never really paying much attention to what enhanced her figure, what colors heightened her tawny complexion. No matter what she wore, what she tried to do to her long, thick hair, she still stood out like a plain librarian from Middleton Corner, Ohio. But, she told herself on many occasions, that was only on the outside. The inner Jackie Archer was someone else altogether.

Once the danger passed, Jackie became acutely aware of Peter Santiago's hip pressed against hers, his breath warm at her ear, so that she felt a shivery sensation course down the middle of her back.

"I think the coast is clear." Her voice was a bit husky.

He looked down at her and then stepped back.

If the nearness of her body had affected him in any way, his face didn't show it. He merely looked relieved. "That was close."

And then they heard footsteps again. Peter grabbed Jackie's hand, dragging her farther down the street for cover.

It was Christophe Valmy again. This time he turned into the street, heading right for the black cashmere coat still draped over the trash can. Jackie heard Peter's muffled curse as they watched the factory worker greedily examine his find. Faster than either Peter or Jackie could ever have anticipated, Valmy snatched up the coat and the duffle bag and tore off down the street. When Peter recovered from the shock and raced after him, it was too late. Valmy had rounded the corner and was nowhere to be seen.

As upset as Jackie was about Valmy absconding with her clothes, she felt much more upset for Peter, whose obviously very expensive and much valued cashmere coat was now warming the lucky factory worker's olive-scented body. "I'm really sorry, I feel just awful."

Peter gave her a wry smile. "There goes a good chunk of my current assets—and you feel awful?"

Jackie sighed. "This hasn't been a lucky night for either one of us, has it? I'll give you back your loan if it will help."

"It will only pay for a new sleeve. Besides, that creep just sashayed off with all of your clothes. You're going to have to buy a whole new wardrobe."

"Well, they probably weren't worth more than

the two sleeves and maybe a pocket of that coat of yours. I'll manage," she said with a weak smile.

"Something tells me we'll both come through this. Pucker those lips."

For a fleeting moment Jackie thought Peter Santiago was preparing her for a kiss. She admitted she could use one just about now and was not unhappy about the prospect of receiving it from Peter. But he was already heading up the street toward the fire escape when it dawned on Jackie the pucker had to do with that championship whistle of hers. She swallowed her flash of disappointment, consoling herself with the fact that Peter was rescuing Gogo and hopefully her *Oranges and Pears on a Lacy Cloth*. Yves Jérôme had proclaimed that her best painting to date. Of course, Peter might be right about Jérôme praising anything that meant a few more francs. But Jackie thought it showed a nice sense of color and balance, even if it never would get to hang in the Louvre.

The drizzle was fast becoming a substantial rain shower when Peter returned from his second sojourn. He looked like an unlikely and bedraggled Santa Claus; a covered birdcage in one hand, a cumbersome painting wrapped in newspaper under the same arm, and a pillowcase filled with sundry gifts tossed over his shoulder.

His suit—well, it stood every chance of being rejected by the Salvation Army at this point.

Jackie took the birdcage from Peter and peeked under the cloth. *"Mon cher Gogo, triste*

Gogo," she murmured soothingly. "I'll find you a nice warm home, don't fret."

"That sounds like a good idea for all of us," Peter grumbled. He had a sick feeling that the paint was leaking from the canvas onto his jacket. Not that it mattered much anymore.

"There are a few hotels in the area," Jackie said as they hurried out of the side street. "Here, I'll take the rest of my things." She smiled as she heard the clatter of jars in the pillowcase. "You really didn't have to cart down my paints, but I do appreciate it."

Peter held on to her meager possessions. Shaking his head from side to side, he pursed his lips. "Come on. You can stay with me for the night. I can't see you walking into a hotel with a birdcage, a canvas dripping with paint, and a sackful of artist's supplies. Not to mention that you look ready for the spin-dry cycle of a washing machine."

"I can't go home with you, I—"

"I know. You don't know me. And you don't like me. On the other hand, you're nearly broke and a hotel room is going to cost you."

"So could staying with you," Jackie retorted.

Peter gave her a condescending smile. "Will it help matters if I promise you that you're not my type? I guarantee you the invitation is purely one of expediency. Besides, a plan is starting to brew in here." He pointed to his temple.

"Oh, no. Not another plan." Jackie smiled wryly, meanwhile telling herself that his promise should have been reassuring rather than so bruising to her pride. The problem was that she no longer considered Peter Santiago a stranger. She was even getting to like him. He'd gone a long way toward retribution for the disastrous consequences his outstretched leg had caused.

"Listen," he said, leading her by the elbow toward the métro, "I have an idea that just might get both of us out of debt. I'll tell you all about it after we get a good night's sleep." He caught her wary glance. "I'll sack out on the couch. You and your pal Gogo can take the bedroom."

Jackie Archer realized she had come a long way from Middleton Corner as she stepped into the Paris métro with Peter Santiago. She had promised herself that she would be open to new experiences once she came to Paris, but she hadn't quite planned on one so unique. Still, Peter was right about a hotel room being a strain to her pocketbook. And though his pledge about her not being his type was a disappointment, she did believe he was telling the truth. Wounded pride notwithstanding, she decided she could trust him.

She didn't start feeling uneasy until Peter led her off the métro at the Avenue Victor Hugo, a posh Parisian thoroughfare that ran from the tree-filled oasis of the Bois de Boulogne to the famous Arc de Triomphe in the center of the Place de l'Etoile. This was a section of Paris reserved for tourists and the very rich. So what was a man who couldn't pay for his dinner doing with an apartment in this exclusive district?

Besides feeling tense, Jackie felt like a complete fool trudging along the elegant boulevard with her arms wrapped around a plastic-covered birdcage. Peter appeared equally awkward about his mismatched luggage. At least it had stopped raining; when they arrived at his building on the corner of the Avenue de Malakoff they were no longer totally waterlogged.

The doorman must have seen many strange sights over the years. He didn't even bat an eyelash as he held the door for them.

"Bonsoir, Monsieur Santiago."

Peter nodded, nudging Jackie toward the elevator. She was growing more and more hesitant about having so cavalierly accepted his invitation to spend the night.

"What's this all about?" she asked, once they were well past the doorman. "If you're so broke, how can you afford to be living in a place like this?"

"It's a long and complicated story. I'll tell you about it in due time."

Jackie eyed him cautiously.

Shifting the pillowcase farther over his shoulder as he pressed the button for the elevator, he said, "Unless you want me to leave you, your sack, your bird in its gilded cage, and your scribbled canvas here in the lobby."

The elevator doors slid open. A striking blonde with flawless skin, blue eyes, and a lithe body wrapped in a silver fox fur stepped out with her perfectly groomed, honey-brown standard poodle. Gogo, possibly sensing the dog or merely responding to the warmth, woke up and started chirping away. The poodle immediately broke into a paroxysm of barking. The sleek blonde tugged the leash, urging the dog along and grimacing in disgust at the same time.

Jackie wrinkled her nose, squared her shoulders, and got in the elevator with Peter, whose gaze remained on the departing blonde until the doors slid closed. Gogo settled down.

"Your type?" Jackie quipped.

"I prefer German shepherds." He winked. "But the blonde wasn't bad."

Jackie gave him a dirty look that was a pretty good imitation of the one the blonde had bestowed on her. It was wasted on Peter, who was busily examining the paint stains on the side of his jacket.

For a man who worried over a little spilled paint and where his next meal was going to come from, Peter Santiago fretted in style. His apartment, while compact and unpretentious, was a study in understated elegance, with its cream walls, mauve leather couches, marble tables, and thick brown carpet.

"So this is how the other half lives," Jackie said, arching a brow and setting the birdcage on the counter that led to the kitchen. Lifting off the cover, she peered down at her bird. "Well, what do you think of your new quarters, Gogo? Quite a step up from the rue de la Jonquière, *n'est-ce pas?*" She glanced over her shoulder at Peter, who was moving toward what was more an alcove with a bed than an actual bedroom.

"When do I hear the fairy tale about the rich little poor boy?"

Peter was rummaging through a drawer. He glanced over at her, then lifted a sweatshirt and a pair of running pants out. He tossed them on the bed. "This is the best I can do for you tonight," he said, pulling out a pair of pajama bottoms for himself and closing the drawer. "At least you'll be warm and dry."

Jackie was still wearing her jacket. She slowly unbuttoned it and slipped it off. Peter went toward her to take it from her hand, only to come to a dead stop a few feet away. Jackie Archer might not be his type, but a full-breasted woman standing before him with her shirt open almost to her navel made a very tempting sight nonetheless.

Jackie's gaze followed Peter's. "Oh," she muttered, her face reddening. "I—I was in such a—a rush to get out of the restaurant." Her fingers clasped the material closed.

Peter tugged the jacket from her clenched fist. "I'll hang this up. Then I'll change in the bathroom. Call out when you're ready."

Jackie nodded mutely. When she heard the bathroom door click shut, she quickly undressed and pulled on Peter's sweatshirt. It came down to her knees, making the pants superfluous, but given the situation, she stepped into them anyway. She had to roll up the cuffs several times, which solved the problem of the extra length but did not deal with the good eight inches to spare around her waist. She was trying to figure out a way to keep the pants from slipping down her narrow hips when Peter called out.

"Are you decent?"

Jackie gave herself a brief survey in Peter's full-length mirror. "That's debatable."

He stepped into the room. Jackie could see he was making an effort not to laugh. She'd certainly managed to display herself at her varied worst this evening.

"Don't just stand there holding back a chuckle," she snapped, trying to ignore his broad and naked chest. "Find me something to keep these things up."

He found a ball of heavy twine in a kitchen drawer. When he went to tie a piece of it around her waist, Jackie grabbed it from him. "I can manage."

She knotted the twine securely and then moved to the mirror, pulling out the pins from her hair. "Did you get my brush?"

Peter rummaged through the sack he'd set down in the hallway. "Here you go." He tossed it at her. "A touch of home."

Jackie brushed the tangles from her hair, feeling a bit more human now. She braided it with a quick, adept motion, fashioning a single plait that reached midway down her back. She caught Peter's curious gaze in the mirror. "What's the matter?"

He came closer, his study more blatant and thorough. "You aren't all that bad," he said matter-of-factly. "With a few alterations I bet you could look quite attractive."

"I've gotten better compliments from my worst enemies."

"No, really. All it would take—"

"Hold it right there," Jackie cut him off. "I don't like the look in your eye, Mr. Santiago, or the sound of your voice. Don't tell me you're some kind of Svengali who lures bedraggled maidens up to his palace for perverse remodeling jobs." She cocked her head, a rueful smile curving her lips. "No, maybe that isn't it. Wait, I know. You're *un coiffeur*—a demented beautician who goes mad when he sees a head of hair badly in need of a restyling."

Peter grinned. "No question that a good haircut would do a lot for you, but I'm lousy with a pair of barber's scissors. No, princess. I'm not Svengali or Charles of the Ritz." He made a sweeping gesture with his hands. "But all of this is a fairy tale. A fairy tale that comes to a finish at the end of two months and four days, to be precise. After that I either step into a new fairy tale in which my dream comes true and I live happily ever after—or I have to hustle up a new dream pronto. Every last centime I own is invested in this operation."

"Just what is this dream of yours?" Jackie asked cautiously. "And where do I fit in?" she tacked on.

Peter grinned, resting his hands on Jackie's shoulders. "I have a proposition for you, mademoiselle. A business proposition, of course." His dark-blue eyes sparkled. "Tell me something, Jackie. Did you ever see *My Fair Lady?*"

Jackie's gaze grew more cautious. "So you want me to play Eliza Doolittle. Transform me from an out-of-a-job waitress into—into what?"

"Into a lovely, refined young woman who looks like she comes from money—lots of money. A new hairstyle, some classy outfits, the proper makeup, and no one would recognize you."

"I grant you," Jackie said acidly, "I have not looked my best tonight. But, surprising as you may find it, I don't happen to want to be made over."

"Look, Jackie. You need a job, *oui?*" Not waiting for a response, Peter went on. "I need a partner—temporarily. And that partner has to be quick-witted and gutsy, but attractive and oozing with class. She also has to speak French like it was her first language. I need someone who can help me woo people like the Marquis and Marquise de Ternaux."

"I don't think I wooed them tonight."

"That's because tonight you were a waitress in an oversized clown costume. Give me a week, Jackie, and you'll have those aristocrats eating out of your hand." He lifted her palm. "After a good manicure." He grinned.

Jackie tugged her hand away.

"If we team up we could pull this thing off," he persisted.

"Just what are we pulling off?"

"Nothing illegal, if that's what you're worried about. I need you to help me find some people who are willing to invest in a vineyard that's come into my hands somewhat unexpectedly. I've always dreamed of my own vineyard, although I wasn't planning on it being situated in France. I had my eye on a nice spot in the Napa Valley region of California, which I called home until a few weeks ago. But I have a fantastic idea that could turn a particular parcel in Labarde into a real gold-star operation. Besides, I've never been one to stare a gift horse in the mouth. In my world opportunities don't knock all that often. How about you, Jackie? Are you the type to pass up a golden opportunity?"

"Exactly what do I get out of this partnership?"

They shared a knowing smile of understanding. "I'll give you free room and board, get you a wardrobe that will dazzle those big green eyes of yours, and, if we're successful, a whopping pocketful of francs—enough to keep you from having to set foot in a restaurant, except for a good meal, for many months to come."

Jackie studied Peter Santiago thoughtfully. "Since we find ourselves in need of each other's assistance, I'll make you a counteroffer. I say we enter into a less temporary partnership. In short, I'll play your Eliza Doolittle, Professor Higgins, for a cut of the operation—modest, of course, since I know very little about the wine business, although I guarantee I'll learn fast. Like you, I don't believe in passing up golden opportunities, but they have to be truly golden. If I'm successful in helping you achieve your desired dream, I have no intention of ever again having to play the role of comic waitress. No, being a partner in a French vineyard fits my particular dreams far better."

CHAPTER THREE

"I prefer the Louis Gérard. It's a bit daring," Peter said with a teasing smile to the saleswoman, a young, exotic, ebony-haired beauty dressed in skintight, gray velvet slacks and a hot-pink silk blouse that was tantalizingly sheer, "but then that is its appeal, no?"

"Oui, monsieur, exactly. The cut is perfect for mademoiselle's small frame. The dropped neckline gives just a gentle hint of sensuality. And the color—*magnifique*."

"A gentle hint?" Jackie bristled. "Only if I give up moving. The slightest bend and the subtlety is obliterated. I can't wear this."

Peter, ignoring her completely, was busy selecting a silver choker to go with the shimmering, sapphire-blue cocktail dress.

"Of course," he was saying to the saleswoman as he slipped a necklace around Jackie's throat, "something has to be done about her hair. But that will be taken care of tomorrow afternoon."

Jackie grabbed away the choker before Peter clasped it. "Do me a favor," she said hotly, "and pinch me."

"What?" Peter, seemingly paying attention to her for the first time, stared at her in confusion.

"You must think I'm some kind of store mannequin. You obviously need a reminder that I'm flesh and blood—with a mind of my own." She swung around and stuffed the silver necklace into his hand.

Peter smiled.

"What's so funny?"

"You're right about the subtlety getting lost when you move in that dress."

"Oh, you're impossible," she said in exasperation. She started off, but Peter firmly gripped her wrist.

"How about the black jersey dress instead?"

"It's better than this one," she responded tightly. Then her expression softened a bit. "It's also more expensive."

"You're worth it."

Jackie gave him a reluctant smile. "The black, then." She plucked the choker from Peter's hand. "This will go very nicely with it, no?"

"Oui." He grinned.

Jackie was relieved to get back into her jeans. These past three days of shopping had proved more exhausting than toting trays at the Côte d'Or—and equally filled with tension, though of a different sort. Jackie found it increasingly disturbing to have Peter, on the one hand, pay such constant and intense attention to her, and, on the other hand, not really relate to her at all. He was completely immersed in his self-appointed task of making a new woman out of Jackie Archer. In the process she was left feeling like a piece of chuck steak getting camouflaged with gravy so that Peter could pass her off as filet mignon.

"Let's concentrate on shoes this afternoon," he said as she came out of the dressing room.

"Let's concentrate on eating," she retorted. "Flesh and blood, remember? I do require sustenance every once in a while."

She moved ahead of him toward the door, letting out a little cry as she felt herself get pinched.

"Just checking." Peter gave her a wicked grin as he stepped alongside her.

They left the small, chic Left Bank boutique on the rue de Grenelle. This area was dotted with many smart shops catering to those with haute couture tastes but ready-to-wear purse-strings. The boutiques offered a compromise. Well designed, authentic copies of famous labels were available at half the cost. Peter was quite pleased with their purchases to date. He had been right about Jackie. In the proper clothes she gave off a definite spark of class. And she was plowing at record speed through those books on wineries he'd lent her. Jackie was a fast learner. She was right about that.

Jackie slipped her shoes off as she sat down in the tiny, crowded bistro. There was lots of noise and bustle, but they had managed to grab a table toward the less frenetic back of the restaurant.

A waiter handed them menus, impatiently hanging about for their order. The bistro was too busy to allow the customers much time to make their decisions. Understanding only too well what it was like to hustle for tips, Jackie hastily ordered a cassoulet, a rich, aromatic stew of beans and meat, while Peter opted for the ever-popular *steak frites*, a thin sirloin and french fries.

"Well"—he looked across the table at her after the waiter had hurried off—"I think, princess, we should be ready for a practice run Friday night. We don't have a chance in hell of getting Troyan or Juillet to come up with the cash to invest in the vineyard—rumor has it they have their hands full trying to keep from going under themselves—but they are the right types. It will give you a chance to test out your skills."

"And a chance for you to decide whether Eliza Doolittle has truly been transformed to your liking," she said caustically.

"What's the matter, Jackie? Don't tell me getting a little dolled up is so painful. If this works out, you'll have a ten percent share of a first-class French vineyard. And after you help me secure the necessary shareholders you won't have to lift another finger. If you recall, you were the one to drive the hard bargain. But," he added, shrugging with a good-natured smile, "I think you really are going to prove to be worth it."

Jackie leaned back in her chair, crossing her arms over her chest. She thought for a moment before she spoke. "I've discovered from my reading that the art of wine making is quite fascinating. It's also a lot of hard work."

"I'm a tireless worker when I'm doing what I want. And owning my own vineyard is most definitely what I want."

"I'm a hard worker too," Jackie said pointedly.

Peter gave her a scrutinizing study. "It's a one-man operation, Jackie. That's the way I want it. I know myself very well. I don't like having to explain my actions. I've done it for too long. I paid my dues—and now I intend to reap the benefits."

"According to what you've told me about the Château Cardinet, it's going to take some time to get the vineyard back on its feet."

Peter's dark eyes sparkled. "That's where my 'dues' come in. Have you ever heard of the Louis Morgan Winery in Napa Valley? It's one of the leading producers of Gamay and Zinfandel wines in America."

"I've seen Morgan wines in the States," Jackie said. "Is that where you worked?"

Peter's smile darkened. "Louis Morgan taught me everything I know. Everything my father might have passed on to me, had he been around while I was growing up."

"I don't understand."

Peter shrugged. "It's not important."

"What happened to your father?" she persisted. Jackie was beginning to get a glimmer of the man behind the glib façade and she wanted to see more.

"I was named after my father," he said in tacit surrender. "Pedro Santiago. He made his way from the poverty-stricken hills of Sonora, Mexico, to Napa Valley as a teenager, working as an itinerant laborer up the coast. He arrived at the Morgan Winery when he was seventeen. Started by picking grapes during the harvest season and ended up twenty years later as Morgan's cellar master. And a fourth cousin by marriage—which did not sit too well with the Morgan clan."

He smiled mysteriously, a smile devoid of humor. "My father was a brilliant wine master. He loved the business, every aspect of it. He always dreamed of buying into the winery, but there again, a Santiago from Mexico was not a name the Morgans wanted to see on their letterhead stationery. Oh, Morgan kept promising, kept dangling him on a string. My father died with his dream. I was eleven years old."

"And now you will make his dream come true?" Jackie asked softly.

"My dream as well. After my father died, Morgan took his poor cousin Helene and her half-Mexican son, myself, under his wing. It was the least he could do, considering my father worked himself to death for the Morgan Winery. My mother died a few years later in an automobile accident. Louis was stuck with me. He clothed me, educated me, taught me all the refinements of life, got me out of a few jams, and eventually let me into the business—up to a point. I was never allowed to forget that I was a poor relation."

His laugh was bitter. "Well, that situation is soon to be rectified. Louis is partially backing this vineyard for me. If I find enough shareholders to get the Château Cardinet off the ground, he's agreed to sign the property over to my name alone. And provide at a modest cost enough Zinfandel grapevines to enable me to be the first vintner in France to produce the now uniquely American Zinfandel wine. It's about time the French wine-growing aristocracy was shaken up a bit—which, admittedly, is part of the problem we have finding investors. But I'm banking on the fact that someone with money and vision will see that a new, full-bodied, yet relatively inexpensive country wine so popular in the States will intrigue enough of the French wine lovers to create a stir and produce ample profits. Especially as Zinfandel, like Beaujolais, is delicious drunk young, so that we won't have to wait years to see some cash come in. And whatever isn't grabbed up by merchants here in France can be exported via Morgan's shippers to the States. Louis Morgan, who never gives without receiving twofold in return, stands to gain whether I sink or swim."

"How's that?" Jackie asked as the waiter brought their food.

"If I succeed, he makes that much more money. Our agreement is that he gets a large percentage of whatever sells back in the States."

"What does he gain if you fail?"

Peter hesitated. "Part of the deal is that, no matter what happens, I don't go back to Morgan Winery or, for that matter, to any other winery in the Napa Valley."

"Why is he so desperate to keep you away?"

Peter didn't answer, concentrating for a few moments on his steak, cutting up some pieces, but not making any attempt to eat. "He's desperate," he said finally, in a low voice, "to keep me a distant cousin and not a son-in-law. Let's just say my lineage doesn't meet his standards."

Jackie felt chilled to learn more of the real story of how Peter had managed to come by his "unexpected windfall."

Her expression must have communicated her feelings. "What's the matter, princess? Did I dash your fantasy about what makes Peter Santiago tick? I told you the other night, opportunities don't come to the son of a peasant laborer too often. There was no way I was going to wind up like my father, killing myself working only to have somebody else's name appear on those bottles of wine. This is my one chance to see the name Peter Santiago, Proprietor, on a label. *Excusez-moi. 'Propriétaire,' n'est-ce pas?*"

"I wonder how Louis Morgan's daughter felt about you taking this 'golden opportunity'?" Jackie remarked crossly. Her new insight into Peter as a cunning opportunist jarred painfully with her growing image of him as a romantic figure. There was nothing romantic about choosing to be bought off.

Peter leaned forward. "Pam Morgan is twenty-three years old—a stunning and passionate girl who will certainly find a new outlet for her youthful desires with no difficulty—and with only a few pangs of regret."

Jackie glared at Peter across the table. Part of her shock was in realizing how little she knew about this man whom she had so impulsively taken up with. For three days she had shared his home and planned strategies for his business. If he had been annoyingly preoccupied with her makeover, Jackie had kept in mind that he was also the man who had destroyed his best suit to rescue her bird. She was drawn to his wit, his mocking tenderness, his drive and determination to get what he wanted. But then she hadn't known just how much he had been willing to compromise in order to reach his goals.

She stood up abruptly, shoving her food away. "I was right in the first place," she said, grabbing her purse. "I don't like you. And I don't care to have any further dealings with you or your vineyard. Find yourself some other mannequin to dress up and use. I should think you'd have no trouble. You've already been quite successful at using innocent people." She walked off.

Jackie didn't realize tears were running down her cheeks until several shoppers gave her curious stares as she strode along the narrow street. What a mess. She was once again jobless, homeless, and now friendless. The last hurt the most, she admitted.

She felt suddenly very young, very naive—very Middleton Corner, Ohio. Even a brief pang of homesickness swept over her. But she took a deep breath, brusquely wiped away her tears, and told herself this was all part of the belated process of growing up and wising up that she had missed the opportunity of learning in Ohio. Missed opportunities. Jackie smiled ruefully to herself and headed for the métro. She would have to take the train back to Peter's apartment to get Gogo and her few belongings. Peter would either find someone else her size for the new purchases, or exchange them for others.

The doorman wouldn't let her into Peter's apartment, despite the fact he had seen her exit the building with him the last three mornings. Jackie walked for a few blocks along the outer perimeter of the Bois de Boulogne. It wasn't safe to wander through the park when there were few other strollers about. In the winter the cold kept most Parisians indoors. In the springtime, Jackie pondered, it must be quite wonderful in the park. Turning back toward the Avenue de Malakoff, she made up her mind that she would find some way to survive so that she would be able to experience April in Paris.

Jackie's own feeling of desperation tempered her bitterness somewhat when she met Peter's gaze as he opened the door to his apartment.

"I came for Gogo."

Peter stepped back from the door and let her in.

"That's a funny name for a bird," he said casually as he watched her cross the room. "Very rock and roll . . . I know, you were a secret go-go dancer back in Ohio. Prim librarian by day, flashdancer at night."

He made her laugh.

"*Gogo* is a French word," she said, stopping at the counter and turning back to Peter. She cocked her head, her expression sober. "It means 'greenhorn.' Apt isn't it? For both me and my bird."

"Jackie, can't we talk about this?"

"You probably think I'm a fool. Here I am, in a foreign city, without resources, being handed a 'golden opportunity,' and I'm willing to throw it away because . . . because I happen to believe the ends don't always justify the means. I don't want to reap benefits from something I can't feel proud of being a part of."

"I didn't love Pam Morgan, Jackie."

"That makes it worse," she said, not holding back her anger and disappointment. "What was it, Peter? Another one of your grand schemes? Pursue the owner's daughter, get her to fall madly in love with you, and then hit her father with one of your business propositions? Or should I call a spade a spade—blackmail?"

"Hold on a minute," he said, a sharp edge to his voice. He made it across the room in five large strides. "For the record, princess, I didn't pursue Pam. She pursued me. But, just so I won't ruin your condemning image of me, I didn't ignore the come-on. Pam had been going to school in Switzerland from the time she was a scrawny kid of fourteen. When she came back to California she was a dynamite-looking twenty-three-year-old. I found her very appealing—from afar. After all, we are vaguely related, and I hadn't spent all those years with Morgan not to know my place," he said bitingly. "But Pam Morgan was a woman with a mind of her own. No." He smiled wryly. "I guess the truth was she enjoyed stirring up her father. I did too. There, that should hang me in your eyes. Yeah, I liked seeing the old man getting nervous. I liked him worrying about the fact that his daughter had set her sights on me."

Jackie turned away, but Peter cupped her chin, forcing her to meet his gaze. "But there was no grand scheme. A good month before Morgan ever offered me the deal, I had made it clear to Pam that I was not in love with her and had no intention of getting hitched, to her or anyone else for that matter. And—whether you choose to believe me or not, Jackie—if I had wanted to marry her, no deal in the world would have been sweet enough to tempt me."

"If you weren't going to marry her, why did Morgan offer to stake you to the vineyard?" She pulled his hand from her face, her expression puzzled but still guarded.

"Morgan is a man who doesn't believe in taking chances. He's also the father of a girl who has managed most of her life to get everything she's ever wanted. Louis figured Pam would work her persuasive powers on me in the end. And he was worried about my integrity. After all, I might decide, love or no love, that marrying Pam would be a very smart move."

Peter's lips turned up slightly, his eyes expressing a glimmer of amusement. "Maybe it would have been a smart move. But, although I'll confess I'm far from perfect—no doubt quite imperfect from your perspective—I also happen to believe, like you, that the ends don't always justify the means. On the other hand"—his smile broadened—"when cousin Louis offered me this deal, I said to myself, why argue? Why try to convince the man that I'm no threat to him? Louis was anxious to get me away, and not only because of Pam. I reminded him too much of my father. I reminded him too much of his own guilty conscience. You want to talk about using people? Well, Louis Morgan is a pro at that. He used my father, kept him clinging to a promise he never meant to keep. And, until Pam came back home, he was perfectly happy to use me in the same way. That's okay. I was using him too. I stepped into my father's shoes, but I had no intention of spending my life working for cousin Louis. I was saving my money, keeping my eyes peeled for a nice piece of Napa Valley land, and learning every angle of the business at Morgan Winery."

"Then why didn't you stick to your plan?" Jackie asked, her expression softening a little as she began to understand Peter better. "Wouldn't it have been a cleaner, neater move?"

"Ah, Jackie. They must have a bunch of real nice guys in Middleton Corner, Ohio. Clean, neat guys. Sure, I could have continued saving my pennies and biding my time. But I'm going to be thirty-four years old next month. Life is short, princess. Too short. I think you can understand that. That's why you ignored everyone's shocked reactions and hopped a plane out of Ohio for Paris. That's why you took me up on my offer. Come on, Jackie. You didn't want to spend your life playing by someone else's rules any more than I did."

"No. I suppose you're right," she said slowly.

Peter's hands pressed lightly on her shoulders

as Jackie watched Gogo flutter from one trapeze to another. She tried to ignore the sensations Peter's touch continued to provoke. Never once in the three days and nights they'd spent together had he made the slightest advance. She wasn't his type. Well, he wasn't hers either. At least not the cool, calculating, opportunistic part of him. Maybe that was due to the fact that she recognized some of the same qualities in herself. Still, she was drawn to him. He was unlike any of the men she'd known in Middleton Corner, Ohio. He was the kind of man whose very presence generated excitement. He was daring, willing to take big risks, and he was extraordinarily sensual. It could prove very frustrating, she admitted to herself, to stay involved with Peter Santiago. And very disappointing.

"Jackie." His voice was low. "I don't want you to do anything that really goes against the grain. I'm not going to pretend I'm Mr. Goody Twoshoes. I have my faults." He grinned. "You haven't seen half of them. But I truly believe I made nothing more than a smart business deal with Louis Morgan. And I don't want to fail." He touched her cheek. "Since you've been here, I've been feeling—more optimistic. More inspired. Stick around. Please?" He leaned toward her, at the same time gripping her shoulders tighter and drawing her to him.

Before he kissed her, he held her gaze for one brief moment. It was long enough, though, for Jackie to pull away if she wanted to. Instead, she tilted her head up as they bridged the distance between their heights and his lips found hers, warm and responsive.

It had been a clever move, she thought when he released her and she managed to get her breath back. Now she couldn't claim he had in any way taken advantage of her. She had wanted the kiss. It didn't, however, alter the surge of anger that rose to the surface.

"Don't ever do that again," she said tightly.

Peter's hands dropped to his sides, his eyes narrowing in confusion. "Why?"

"I don't ever want to feel that you're using me, Peter. Ever. We're talking about a business arrangement here. Nothing more. I'm not your type, remember? Well, then, don't pull a stunt like that again. I may come across as naive and very small-townish, but I'd like to believe you have more respect for me than to think you could manipulate me in that way."

Peter felt off kilter. He stepped away. "I—I wasn't pulling a stunt, Jackie. I don't know why I kissed you." He shrugged, then flashed a smile. "It was pure impulse. I wanted to kiss you. I liked it." He held up his hands in mock surrender. "But you're right. We're talking business and I should have kept my impulses under wraps. I'm sorry. I'll behave."

Jackie didn't know what to say next. Her feelings were in turmoil. She started across the room toward the front door, deciding she'd made more than enough impulsive decisions lately.

"Where are you going?"

Jackie stopped for a moment. "I need to think this through—alone. I'll get a room. I'm just not sure what I want to do."

"What about Gogo?"

She turned to face him. "Would you take care of him until I decide? He seems very content here. I've never heard him sing so much."

"I'm growing attached to your *oiseau*." He grinned. He wondered with a rush of discomfort if he wasn't also getting attached to Gogo's owner. He hastened to reject the notion. At the same time he made no effort to walk Jackie to the door, afraid his impulses might get the best of him again.

"I'll call," she said.

"What about your clothes?"

"They don't belong to me."

"They're part of the deal."

"Well," she said, one hand on the doorknob, "I'll be back if I decide to sign on again. We may have to renegotiate the terms, though." She opened the door.

"You've got that hair appointment at three tomorrow afternoon."

Jackie looked back at him. "That's part of the renegotiations. I prefer to make my own decisions about my metamorphosis, and that includes what I do to my hair."

Peter shrugged good naturedly. "Okay. I wasn't too thrilled about sitting around a Parisian hair salon anyway."

"I would have thought it a great way to meet

someone like the blonde with the poodle we bumped into at the elevator the other night. That salon you picked is where the very rich and the very chic hang out."

Peter walked over to her then, his impulses no longer at issue. "Let's get something straight, Jackie. I'm not looking for a woman—of any type. I have only one goal in mind right now, and that's to get the Château Cardinet off the ground. I'm not only investing every last cent I own in this operation, I'm giving it all my time and every ounce of energy I possess."

"I get the message," Jackie said, not sure how she felt about it. Peter's sweetly tender kiss had left its mark. Despite her anger and her worries about being manipulated by his smoldering sensuality, she had to admit she found Peter disturbingly appealing. Even though he wasn't perfect.

"What about Friday night? We have dinner reservations at Vergennes."

"My trial run," she said with a brief smile. "I don't know yet, Peter."

He slipped his hand into his pocket and brought out a key. He tossed it to her. "I had this made for you. I'll be down in Labarde Friday afternoon. If you want to come back to visit Gogo, or dress for dinner . . ."

She pocketed the key. "Vergennes isn't quite the Côte d'Or, but it's supposed to be a nice little restaurant. At least you should be able to pay the bill."

"If you join us"—he raised his right hand—"I

promise not to trip the waitress. Besides," he added as she started out the door, "I do owe you a good meal."

"I'll keep that in mind."

CHAPTER FOUR

"*Oui*, Gogo." Jackie propped her elbows on the counter and studied her delicate green-and-yellow parakeet reflectively. "*C'est moi.* I've come back."

She gave the tiny trapeze inside the cage a gentle swing. When Gogo flew over to catch a free ride, Jackie smiled. "What have we gotten ourselves into, my fine feathered friend?" Gogo left the trapeze and landed on the edge of his food dish. He pecked away eagerly, unconcerned by Jackie's presence. "I see Peter feeds you well," Jackie said, observing him for a moment.

She stood straight up and gazed about the room. "I wasn't going to return." She cast a winsome smile over at the bird. "Oh, I would have come for you, of course. Though something tells me, Gogo, you might be fickle. I think you've fallen under the spell of the cunning Monsieur Santiago. I may be in the same predicament. So what do I do, Gogo? Play Eliza Doolittle out to the end? Ah, but Eliza won the stodgy Professor Higgins over in the final act. I don't think I'm likely to reach the same happy ending. Then again, do I want to? How silly I've become. It must be the Parisian air. I certainly had a head on my shoulders back in Middleton Corner."

Jackie laughed. "Well, maybe not," she reflected. "I was good at pretending . . . until it suddenly dawned on me that my life was passing me by and if I didn't do something drastic, I would probably have nothing but dreams to take to my grave someday." She walked over to the small closet and pulled out the black jersey dress. She held it up in front of her and studied her image in the mirror.

She still had difficulty getting used to her new look. Antoine Fouquet of the elegant Philippe David Salon had been less than kind about her braid. She panicked when he picked up his gleaming scissors, afraid he would lop it off in one fell swoop. But in the end he'd done far less than she had feared. Antoine had trimmed her hair to shoulder length, cutting into the natural wave, gave her a soft rinse to bring out the rich chestnut highlights, and showed her several ways to wear the new blunt cut for different occasions. He left it falling soft and loose over her shoulders, sweeping just a few strands away from her face with an ornamental barrette. He had been quite pleased with the results, feeling that a simple style was necessary so as not to overpower Jackie's delicate features. Then a young, stunning redhead named Nicole had spent nearly an hour instructing her on the art of using makeup so that it heightened her own natural coloring.

Jackie unsnapped her jeans, stepped out of

them, and unbuttoned her blouse. She swept her hair up and then let it drop back down around her shoulders, a few shimmering locks falling sultrily over one eye. *The birth of a siren.* She grinned at the thought.

Her blouse fell to the floor. She was standing in her lacy bra and panties when she heard the muted sound of scraping metal. Then came the click of the tumbler in the lock. She was halfway across the room, racing for the bathroom, when the door swung open.

Peter walked in. For one long moment they stood staring at each other in surprise, Jackie foolishly pressing a much-too-small toss pillow against her body for cover. Peter was holding his newly pressed suit in his hand and when he went to hang it on the coat rack, he missed, his eyes on Jackie and not the task at hand.

"You're supposed to be in Labarde," she said awkwardly.

Peter regained his equilibrium first. "I came back early to get my suit. You did a good seamstress job on those rips." He had picked up the suit from the floor, being more careful to hang it up this time. "I'm glad you're here," he said, turning his attention back to her.

Jackie finished her dash for the bathroom.

"I like your haircut," Peter called out.

"You might have told me you'd be coming back," she shouted through the closed door, ignoring the compliment.

"I had no way of reaching you. I suppose I could have sent Gogo after you as a kind of homing parakeet, but I didn't want to take the chance."

"Very funny." She turned on the shower. "Bring me my dress, will you?" One hand came out from a slit at the doorjamb. "Hand it to me."

Peter caught hold of her hand. "Manicure too. Nice."

"The dress." She peered out with one eye. "I may be sorry about this in the morning."

Peter laughed. Jackie flushed. "I thought the only thing you ever had on your mind was your vineyard."

"Give a guy a break. What do you expect me to have on my mind when I walk into my apartment and find a voluptuous naked lady with a dynamite new haircut standing in the middle of my living room?"

"I wasn't naked."

"I should have walked in a couple of minutes later." He laughed.

Jackie slammed the door shut. But she was smiling. "I'll be out in a little while."

"We could save time—and water," he teased, not surprised that Jackie didn't answer.

After a few minutes he heard the water stop. Peter came close to the door again.

"Jackie?"

"What?"

"Listen. I, uh, I was thinking that the most effective way to get some of these Frenchmen to be interested in our operation is for them to believe that you're one of them. You know the French, they're so nationalistic. I have the feeling they're going to be too threatened by a pair of hotshot Americans moving onto their turf. But if they think you're, say, Jacqueline Armand . . . a wealthy French aristocrat who's been living in Switzerland the past few years . . . and who is so excited by the prospect of this vineyard that you've decided to become involved in its establishment . . . they might be more amenable to doing the same. We could see how it goes tonight with Juillet and Troyan. A practice run. You'd have no problem pulling it off. Jackie, are you listening?"

"I should have known you'd have something more up your sleeve."

"What do you think of the idea?"

"I think it's dishonest," she snapped. "I thought you'd gotten my message clear the other night. I don't want to be involved in a shady operation. And I don't want to feel any more alien from the old Jackie Archer than I already do."

"Jackie, I'm only asking . . ." His sentence trailed off as Jackie opened the door and took a few steps out of the bathroom. Her slightly clammy hands slid over the soft black jersey that fell clinging over her hips.

Peter looked even more stunned than when he'd walked in on her half naked.

"You look—incredible."

Jackie gave him an ironic arch of her brow. "I know. You would never have recognized me."

He laughed. "You're right. It's amazing, though. Nothing really drastic has been done, and yet, you . . . well, you exceed my fantasies, Jackie. We can't lose now."

"You mean as long as I complete the transformation and become Jacqueline Armand."

He came closer. "Look, princess, you came back here tonight because you obviously decided to play the part. You certainly look it. Don't go small-townish on me again. If we're going to do this thing, let's go all the way. We handle it right and we both stand to gain. That is the point of this whole deal, isn't it? You want to make your dreams come true as badly as I do."

Jackie walked over to the mirror and gazed at her reflection. She saw a striking young woman with a delicate oval face, bright-green eyes, silky chestnut hair, and a finely shaped mouth with the faintest curve downward at the corners revealing her ambivalence.

Watching her, Peter felt a flash of arousal, but he hastily doused it, remembering that Jackie's enthusiastic participation in his negotiations was the prime consideration here. He stood behind her. He saw her gaze transfer itself to his face and smiled gently. "It's an adventure, princess. How many adventures did you have in Middleton Corner? I bet you'll find it a lot of fun to play Mademoiselle Armand, back home in France from Lausanne, Switzerland. Think of it, Jackie. Think of all the secret dreams you nurtured in Ohio."

"What do you know about my dreams?"

He let his fingers caress her shimmering hair. "I know you were never meant to be stamping books at some library in Small Town, U.S.A., for the rest of your life. Look at yourself, Jackie. You've got style, class, brains . . . and beauty. Don't tell me you want that all to go to waste." His hand fell to her shoulder. He turned her gently around and their eyes met.

Jackie gasped sharply. "Dammit, Peter. You are a terrific manipulator. Was that what you were doing when you told me about Morgan and his daughter? Was there a word of truth in that tale?"

"I wasn't lying, princess. But, I guess you're going to have to decide for yourself whether you're going to trust me."

"I don't know you well enough."

"I know." He grinned. "And you still don't like me."

"That's the problem," she answered with a sigh. "Why do you think I came back here tonight?"

"Because you couldn't walk away from the opportunity of a lifetime . . . and because I have a certain charm," he said, his eyes bright with amusement.

"Jacqueline Armand, huh?"

"*La belle* Jacqueline Armand."

Jackie walked over to Gogo, stared at him for a few moments, and sighed. "Well, *mon petit*, relax. We'll be staying awhile longer."

"What about your hotel room?" Peter asked, rummaging in the closet for his good shirts.

"It was very reasonably priced, but not too classy. Turns out the rooms rent more frequently by the hour than they do by the night. Very noisy. I did receive several interesting propositions"—

her eyes sparkled—"but none of them came close to matching yours."

Peter walked over to her and put his hands on her narrow waist. "I like you, Jackie."

Jackie felt her heartbeat speed up as she looked into his incredibly blue eyes. She wet her dry lips nervously. Peter's hands pressed harder.

"I have an impulse to kiss you again, Mademoiselle Armand."

Jackie shook her head. "Mademoiselle Armand is make believe, Peter. I'm still Jackie Archer from Middleton Corner, Ohio. And we have a dinner appointment to keep. You'd better get dressed."

Peter let his hands slip from her waist. "Right."

Philippe Troyan set down his café au lait and dabbed his lips, his eyes ever vigilant on the charming woman beside him. Jackie, whose own coffee was growing cold as she waxed eloquent on the glories of the Zinfandel grape, was pleased at how well she was doing tonight.

Yves Juillet had kissed her hand with courtly grace before leaving a few minutes earlier, despairing that he did not have more time this evening to discuss the exciting enterprise Jacqueline had been telling them about. He would certainly love to meet with her again, he'd said eagerly, then corrected himself, nonchalantly including Peter. Kissing her hand once more, he had commented that he believed he knew of her fine family . . . had been honored to have met Monsieur Charles Armand, the noted financier, many years ago, although he might not remember . . . Jackie had caught the twinkle in Peter's eye as she smiled up at Juillet. She'd tried her best to keep a smirk from creeping into her own expression.

Peter now watched the thin, energetic Philippe Troyan, observing the way the middle-aged aristocrat with the receding hairline leaned closer to Jacqueline as she spoke, his brown eyes, magnified by gold-rimmed glasses, taking her in with greedy delight. Peter doubted that Troyan was paying the least attention to what Jackie was saying, being too busy studying her big green eyes, the delicate blush of her cheeks, the way her silky hair fell softly and provocatively around her slender shoulders, and the way her black jersey dress clung in all the right places.

Troyan took Jackie's hand for a moment and said something low and throaty. She smiled, her jade eyes bright. "Peter," Jackie addressed him in a voice filled with the lyrical tone of French even though she had switched to a somewhat bastardized English. She'd almost forgotten for a moment that English was the second language of the aristocratic Jacqueline Armand. "Monsieur Troyan has been kind enough to invite us to his château in Margaux next weekend. On Friday evening, *une petite soirée* . . . a little party, you know. Then a pleasant few days to meet some of Monsieur Troyan's friends and neighbors. We will be delighted to accept, *n'est-ce pas?*"

Now it was Peter's turn to work at keeping a straight face. Jackie Archer might have been resistant at first about her acting debut as Mademoiselle Armand, but now that she was into it, she was giving an Oscar-winning performance.

"Certainly." Peter gave Troyan a reserved nod. "We will be delighted."

Things were going better than Peter had expected. At Troyan's château he'd get a chance to hobnob socially with just the kind of people he'd been angling to get close to all these weeks. He could see that Jackie, too, was elated by how well they were doing tonight. *Come on*, he thought to himself, *be honest, Santiago. You aren't the one charming the pants off the ogling aristocrat.* Jackie was the one pulling all the weight tonight. She certainly seemed to thrive on it.

Funny, he reflected as he watched her animated conversation with Troyan, the little mouse really had turned out to be a princess in disguise. It was true he'd been the one to see the potential, but he realized now that he had underestimated much of Jackie's unique appeal.

Jackie Archer had an exuberance for life that came across in her every word and gesture. That quality, far more than the new clothes, hairdo, and makeup, gave her a vitality and allure that many women who were more beautiful on the surface completely lacked. It provided that added sparkle, that special sensual excitement, tinged with just the right touch of vulnerability.

Peter could clearly see that Troyan and Juillet had both responded to that vibrant essence in Jackie. He had no doubt that his two guests tonight would have lingering fantasies of the enticing Jacqueline Armand. Peter's sense of exhilaration faltered briefly. For some odd reason which he did not wish to ponder, he found the notion of his two guests' fantasies somewhat disquieting.

When the waiter brought over the check, Peter and Jackie shared a private smile. No tripped waitresses this evening. He pulled out some bills and set them on the table.

The three of them walked out of the restaurant together.

"Can we drop you somewhere?" Peter asked, glancing up the boulevard for a cab and trying not to shiver as the cold night air whipped through his jacket. He was still looking for a good price on a new cashmere coat. The outlay for Jackie's outfits had taken a good bite out of his dwindling resources. He didn't want to spend any unnecessary francs.

"Monsieur Troyan has invited me to join him at his club," Jackie said, pulling her jacket closed as Troyan muttered something to her. "He says he's dying to teach me baccarat." She smiled. "Don't look so concerned, Peter. I'm not a reckless gambler. We'll be glad to drop you off instead," she offered as Troyan's chocolate-brown Mercedes sedan pulled up to the curve. The parking-lot attendant leapt out and held the passenger door open for Jackie.

Peter stared sullenly at the car and then at Jackie and her late-night date. He felt like a third wheel. The feeling didn't please him one bit. Nor was he thrilled by the notion of his naive young partner going off with Troyan to his private club, where the old goat more than likely kept a room for his city visits.

"We've got a hectic day tomorrow, Jackie. Are you sure you don't want to come home and get some sleep? You know, these past two nights you haven't gotten much rest." He gave Troyan a subtle wink. "It was my fault."

Jackie did not appreciate Peter's far-from-subtle innuendo. She was also confused as to why he was doing it. He should have been elated that his investment was paying off. She might be able to make some valuable connections at Troyan's private club. Peter's remark could cause Troyan to reconsider the invitation if he thought there was something more than a business partnership going on between her and Peter.

The attendant was beginning to appear impatient. Jackie gave Troyan a bright smile. "Peter has been kind enough to let me use a room in his apartment. The hotel I was staying at got my reservations wrong and I had to find new quarters in a hurry. Peter felt badly because he was the one who had booked me at the hotel."

"I understand perfectly." Troyan smiled, taking Jackie's hand.

She turned to Peter. "I feel wide awake. Don't worry. I promise not to let my evening plans affect my work tomorrow. I'll be very quiet when I return. If you prefer, I could take the couch tonight and you can have your bedroom back."

She gave Peter an innocent and fetching smile, then focused back on Philippe. "Shall we go?"

Troyan nodded eagerly, his lips curved in a

broad grin that showed well-capped white teeth. Jackie took his enthusiastic response as a sign that she had effectively nipped in the bud any concerns about her and Peter being intimately involved.

Troyan pressed the palm of his hand against the pit of Jackie's back, urging her toward the car. She paused before stepping inside and looked over her shoulder at Peter. "Coming?"

"No, thank you," he said archly. "I wouldn't want to take you out of your way."

Neither Jackie nor Philippe Troyan argued. They hurried into the warmth of the running Mercedes, leaving a sullen Peter standing in the street. A cab pulled up. Peter waved it away and walked down the block to a small bar where he hoped to rectify his chill and his foul mood.

It was exactly four thirty-seven A.M. on Peter's illuminated digital watch when he heard his front door open. He shoved his hand back under the covers and closed his eyes.

Jackie listened for a moment at the door, then slipped out of her spiked heels and tiptoed across the living room. As she passed the couch, she came to a halt. It was empty. She picked up Peter's steady, rhythmic breathing and glanced over to the alcove. So, he'd taken her up on her suggestion, she thought ruefully, and decided to leave her the couch tonight.

She still couldn't figure out what had irritated him this evening. In fact, she'd hoped Peter would still be awake so that she could tell him all about the club, the people she'd rubbed shoulders with, and Troyan's invitation to take her to lunch Saturday afternoon.

To think that last week she had been a hopelessly inept waitress struggling to make ends meet, and tonight she'd danced under crystal chandeliers to a six-piece band, played baccarat, sipped the finest of champagnes, and felt like the belle of the ball. Never in her twenty-nine years could Jackie remember a man looking at her in quite the way she'd been looked at tonight. And not just by Philippe Troyan or Yves Juillet; there had been many admirers at Philippe's club, leaving her little doubt as to her newfound appeal.

She smiled to herself as she unzipped her dress, shrugged it off her shoulders, and let it fall to the floor. Then she took out the small silver barrette and shook her hair free, delighted by the sensation it produced across her shoulders. She didn't miss her braid for a moment. With a languor that came from knowing Peter was asleep, she unhooked her bra, tossing it carelessly on the coffee table, and slowly slipped off her pantyhose, her body moving to the silent strains of the last tune she and Philippe Troyan had danced to. She did a silly little pirouette.

That was when she discovered that she was no longer the only one wide awake in the room.

"You obviously had a pleasant night," Peter said, his arms across his chest, his head propped up on his pillow.

Jackie took a dive behind the couch. "You've been watching me the whole time. Why did you let me think you were asleep?" she demanded, aghast.

"I was asleep," he lied. He certainly wasn't about to tell Jackie he had been tossing and turning here since midnight worrying about her, thinking about her—having disturbing fantasies about what she had been doing until four-thirty in the morning. "You woke me up."

"You could have had the decency to pretend to stay asleep. Why is it you seem to get such a kick out of humiliating me?" she asked hotly.

Peter got out of bed and reached for Jackie's robe. It was draped over one of the bedposts. He carried it over to her as she moved to sit on the couch, her black dress crunched against her breasts.

"Here. Put it on." He sat down beside her, dropping the flannel robe on her lap, trying to ignore the pulsating arousal she had caused. "So, you had a good time," he stated more than asked, not bothered in the least by Jackie's contorted attempts to keep herself covered as she struggled to get her arms into the sleeves of the robe.

"I had a fabulous time, no thanks to you."

"What's that supposed to mean?" he asked contentiously.

"It means you almost blew it. Why, for heaven's sake, did you want Philippe to think we had —something going on between us?"

"I was trying to protect you," he said, punctuating each word.

"Protect me from what?"

Peter sighed loudly. "The guy was practically drooling over you in that restaurant."

"You're disgusting." She dropped her dress on the floor as she closed her robe and knotted the tie.

"And you're pathetically naive." He grabbed her by the shoulders. "This is the big city, Jackie. People like Troyan are very entitled. They see what they want and they go after it. Just like he went after you tonight."

"What makes us any different?" she snapped, unable to free herself from his grasp. "We're playing the same game, aren't we?"

Peter stared down at her, his expression hard and intense. "I didn't mean for you to play it in the bedroom."

"Is that what you think I was doing tonight?" Her voice was so tight it cracked. "I hate to ruin any of the perverse fantasies you've obviously been overindulging in all night, but Philippe Troyan was a perfect gentleman this evening. We had a wonderful time at his club. He was kind enough to introduce me to several people who might be interested . . ." She let the sentence drop, too angry at Peter to share any good news. "For your information, despite my small-town upbringing, I'm not as naive as you seem to think. I know it may come as a surprise to you, but I have had men come on to me before. And I've never had any difficulty dealing with the situation —in whatever way I decided. Am I making myself clear?"

Peter sighed, a sheepish smile on his lips. "Now

I'm the one who feels humiliated." His hands slid lightly across her shoulders to the base of her neck. His voice was very low. "I'm sorry, princess. I guess it was just that you looked so ravishing tonight—"

"That you thought I'd end up getting ravished." The peevishness was gone from her tone now that Peter's expression was contrite.

"I can't honestly say I could blame him," Peter continued, "if that's what he was thinking—even if he didn't make any untoward advances. He's probably smart enough not to move in too fast." His breath held for a second, then he slowly lowered his face to hers, planting a whisper of a kiss on her lips. "I'm not that smart." Then he pulled her closer and put his arms around her. This time his kiss was long and fierce, his tongue parting her lips, the warmth of her mouth sending a tremor through his body.

Jackie's head was swimming. As Peter's lips moved to the crook of her neck, she murmured a weak protest. When his hands traveled down her spine, her words turned into a soft moan. She let her fingers move tremulously up his chest, conscious only of the luxurious feel of his skin and of her own desire—a desire that had been warring with her common sense practically since her first outrageous encounter with Peter Santiago.

He looked down at her. Jackie lowered her eyelids self-consciously. Peter had made it perfectly clear she wasn't his type and that he wanted no intimate involvements. What was she doing letting herself get carried away like this?

She met his gaze finally. "Weren't you just warning me a couple of minutes ago about situations like this?"

He laughed softly. "I also warned you that you looked ravishing tonight."

"Maybe this business partnership of ours wasn't such a good idea." Her heart was racing, but her mind was clearing a little. She tugged at Peter's wrists, freeing herself from his grasp. "I'm afraid I've let too many champagne bubbles go to my head tonight." She gave him a knowing smile. "And something tells me you had a few nightcaps since we left the restaurant."

"Only a couple. I'm not drunk, if that's what you're thinking."

"We're both feeling lightheaded. I am, anyway. I think we'd better get some rest." She paused. "Oh, by the way, I have a date with Philippe for lunch tomorrow . . . and dinner on Sunday."

Peter's tender expression abruptly chilled. "Oh. I see. Well, then, absolutely, princess. You need your beauty sleep. All these nights on the town . . ."

Jackie gave him a sly smile. "It's great, isn't it? Things are going so well. Troyan knows just about everyone worth knowing. We couldn't have dreamed of a more successful trial run." She gave his shoulder a quick pat. "Well, you were the one who believed in my potential. You must be feeling mighty proud of yourself." She grabbed a pillow and blanket off the armchair and dumped them on the couch. "I'm feeling pretty good myself."

CHAPTER FIVE

Anyone who knew anything about wine knew of the tiny village of Margaux in the southwest of France. Some of the finest Haut-Médoc vineyards were to be found there, yielding hardy, complex wines famous throughout the world. Jackie had never heard of the place until a couple of weeks ago. Now, under Peter's tutelage, she had not only learned about the wine-proud town and tasted the exceptionally delicate and richly aromatic Médoc *vin* with its lingering aftertaste of violets, she had come to experience much of Peter's excitement about the whole Bordeaux region. In the even tinier village of Labarde, southeast of Margaux, Peter hoped to make his dreams come true at the Château Cardinet.

During the long drive from Paris, Jackie had been doing the talking, Peter responding with a nod or a clipped word or two. For most of the trip she pretended to ignore his sullen mood. They had been invited to a château for the weekend and she was too excited by the prospect to let him get her down. She had wanted to stop in Labarde to see the Château Cardinet, but Peter had been surprisingly insistent in his refusal.

"You look so grim," she said finally. "Are you worried that the weekend won't be successful?" At this point she really didn't expect a reply and simply continued a running monologue. "Philippe says you're undertaking a monumental task. He says it takes decades, not to mention vast amounts of money, to get an idle vineyard restored. And he thinks you're making a mistake about the Zinfandel. Or at least you ought to consider cultivating some of the local Médoc vines as well. He was encouraging about Labarde in general, though. He says it's a fine wine-growing town as well as good hunting territory. He's promised to take me out shooting during the season."

She laughed softly at Peter's scowl. "I don't know what you have against the man. I grant you he's a bit pompous—the self-important aristocrat —but he's generous, charming, and filled with helpful information. Maybe he's right about cultivating more varieties. He's offered to come out to Château Cardinet and give us whatever assistance he can." Jackie checked the map. "Labarde is so close. Maybe we'll take a ride over on Sunday."

"No. Not Sunday."

"Why not?" she asked peevishly. "When do I get to see this place you plan to turn into a first-class vineyard?"

"You'll see it," Peter retorted obliquely.

"And when is that going to be?"

In answer Peter gave her one of his uncommunicative grunts. Jackie stared out the window in frustration.

They were driving along the west bank of the Gironde River, a flat and rather uninteresting terrain.

"It's hard to imagine that this region boasts such fame," Jackie said after several minutes of silence. She refused to succumb to Peter's somber mood. "Philippe told me the other night that it's the river itself, or more precisely the sand and gravel, that the Gironde tosses onto its banks that gives the soil a uniquely anemic quality so perfect for the production of the Haut-Médoc wines. Not that I know what that means exactly, but I love the sound of it. He says that in the summer, at first glance, the vineyards here resemble endless rows of billiard tables. Only when you look closely do you see the deep gravel beds in which the Haut-Médoc vines flourish." She sighed. *"Mon Dieu,* there's so much to learn. But it's unbelievably exciting. Philippe says I have a natural affinity for the wine business."

"You certainly seem to have a natural affinity for the wine itself."

It was the first full sentence of more than three words he'd uttered all afternoon. Jackie decided she preferred the silence.

"What's that supposed to mean?" she asked self-righteously. "Philippe was merely trying to teach me to discriminate among three different wines from Bordeaux. Maybe we got a little carried away." She grinned. "After a while, I admit, I lost track of the subtleties."

Peter's scowl deepened.

"Is that what this grim mood of yours is all about? Are you still angry about the other night?"

"Which other night?"

"Take your pick, actually. Last Friday night, when I returned from Philippe's club or—"

"That was Saturday morning, if I recall. Approximately four-thirty in the morning."

"Or Sunday night—excuse me, Monday morning," she went on. "Or perhaps last night."

"I don't know what you're talking about. I'm not angry about any of those occasions. As you said yourself, Troyan is a fabulous contact. And, obviously, a remarkable teacher. You're just filled with tidbits of information and advice. And look how well the two of you have hit it off. How can I be angry when you're doing so well?"

"That's a very good question. If you deny it's because of Troyan, then what is it? Something's bothering you. You've been morose, distant, irritable, and unreasonable for the past week."

"You're just getting to know me better, princess. I warned you I had my faults." He produced his best wry smile.

"Don't play games, Peter. We're in this thing together, and if something is the matter, I think I have a right to know what it is."

"Is that what you think?" His smile vanished and his expression became serious. "Well, I guess you've gone and hit the nail on the head about what's getting my goat. Look, I thought we had our signals straight, but I guess we don't."

They were coming around the bend along a vineyard road. Peter pulled off onto a dirt shoulder, barely missing a sign reading ROUTE TOURISTIQUE DU MÉDOC NORD. He pulled the emergency brake so abruptly that Jackie lurched forward and then fell back with a jolt.

"What is the matter with you?" she snapped.

"I'll tell you what's the matter. You're the matter. You talk about my vineyard as though it was your vineyard."

"Ten percent of it is." She glared at him. "Or are you reneging on the deal?"

"A ten percent share. That's it. That's all it is. Not fifty percent, Jackie. I made it clear to you from the start that you are not a part of the business. Your ten percent does not entitle you to start thinking you can move in on the operation. I told you before I don't want that kind of a partner."

"I see. Well, if I gave you the impression that I intended to move in on the operation, as you call it, I apologize. I did get your message, Peter. In fact, I got all of them. I won't deny the notion of being a part of the business intrigues me. Your excitement has rubbed off on me. I've become enamored of the idea of turning a broken-down château and its badly neglected vineyard into a proud, wine-producing estate."

"I never told you the place was a disaster."

"Isn't that why you don't want me to see it? Aren't you afraid I'll be discouraged and that my disappointment will affect my enthusiasm for pushing your cause?"

Peter ran a thumbnail over the leather steering wheel. "Okay. The place has seen better days." He gave her one of his more endearing grins. It was one she hadn't seen in the last forty-eight hours. "A lot better days."

She smiled back. "You are a tough man to contend with sometimes, Monsieur Santiago. You have too much damn pride."

"I come from a line of proud Mexican peasants. We need pride. We often had very little else. My father made it out of the bottom rung. He was proud, hardworking, and determined. He overcame every obstacle in the books to get ahead. I'm going to follow in his footsteps, only I'm not stopping like he did, even if I have to tread on some people's toes. Forget your fantasies about the château, Jackie. The reality is going to be blood, sweat, and some long, tough years."

"What about the tears?"

"Yeah. Tears too. But only mine. I'm sorry, Jackie. But that's one thing I am not going to change my mind about."

"I'd still like to see Château Cardinet. For my ten percent I deserve a peek."

Peter laughed. "You're a pushy lady. But I guess that's why I'm putting all my francs on you to come up with those investors."

"There may be a few of them at Troyan's place this weekend. Speaking of which, hadn't we better get going?"

He nodded, turning the key in the ignition. But

his hand lingered on the emergency brake. "Maybe after the weekend we can stop off in Labarde on our way back to Paris. But only if I have your promise to abandon your fanciful ideas about becoming a vintner."

Jackie smiled. "As for my fanciful ideas, if it weren't for them I would never have come to Paris. You would never have met me, and we'd never be on our way to Troyan's château. I'd still be stamping books in Middleton Corner. And, as for this particular fanciful idea about growing grapes, I'd like to remind you that you aren't the only fish in the sea, Monsieur Santiago. Or should I say, the only vintner in France?"

"Well, princess, take some friendly advice," Peter said laconically as he pulled out onto the road. "Troyan has gone through two wives already and has almost gone through a vineyard that, thirty years ago, was one of the finest in Bordeaux. Be smart and set your sights on someone with fewer excesses. And less well-meaning advice," he tacked on.

"I'll keep your advice in mind. As well as Philippe's. Who knows?" she said with equal aplomb. "Someone might be just around the corner. Someone who might be eager to have a hard-working, quick learner on his team. I may not have known a Burgundy wine from a Médoc a week ago, but give me a few months and I'll go head to head with you on the economics of wine growing. That's one thing about having been a librarian all those years. I have a healthy respect for research and acquiring knowledge. And for the first time in my life, I've come upon something I really want to master. I'm beginning to realize that running off to Paris was only the start of my dream."

"Just remember your priorities, Jacqueline Armand. We have a deal, *n'est-ce pas?*"

"I'm clever enough, monsieur, to work on more than one deal at a time."

"You know something? I think you probably are at that. Just don't go getting yourself in trouble."

"I'll take the proper precautions," she said lightly, keeping her eyes straight ahead, her expression one of barely suppressed amusement as she caught Peter's disconcerted glance in her peripheral vision.

Then he laughed, shaking his head. "You got me there, princess."

"While you're at it, why not admit that you have been out of sorts because of my dates with Troyan?"

He shot her a wry smile. "Only because he's not the kind of man you ought to be dating. Don't get any fanciful ideas that I was jealous or anything."

"There you go again with my fanciful ideas." Jackie smiled, leaning her head back. "How could I have any about you? You've made it perfectly clear I'm not your type. And even if you started having second thoughts about that, don't worry, Peter." She folded her hands primly in her lap. "You aren't my type. I like a man who isn't afraid of permanent partnerships."

He gave her a bemused look. "I didn't realize

before today that you were in the market for a permanent partnership. It's a good thing we aren't each other's type. Happy hunting, though."

"*Merci*," she said, an impudent and saucy smile curving her lips.

The truth was, this desire for a permanent partnership proved almost as much of a revelation to Jackie as it did to Peter. She hadn't consciously thought about finding herself a partner, permanent or otherwise. Not that she was against the notion for any philosophic reasons. She had, after all, indulged in a few fantasies about her ex-boss, Claude Marigny. But he'd never given Jackie enough of a real glimpse of himself for her to get those fantasies off the ground. That was certainly not the case with Peter.

In two short weeks Peter had revealed enough for Jackie to feel enraged, delighted, stunned, nervous, and disturbingly attracted to him. Peter was a man who provided ample opportunity for Jackie's fantasies to flourish. Which was precisely and dismayingly what was happening to her. She wanted to be more than a working partner in the Château Cardinet. The idea of an intimate partnership with the fiercely opinionated and independent Peter Santiago was becoming increasingly enticing. He was far more her type than she could ever admit to him at this point. Given his outlook on intimate relationships he would have bolted on the spot, deal or no deal.

Of course, it wasn't fashionable these days for women to have such mundane aspirations as to want to snare a man, but then, until Peter came along, Jackie had never been part of the fashionable times. Until Peter came along, Jackie admitted, the notion of Mister Right hadn't seemed very promising. No one in Middleton Corner had come close. Given his faults, all of which she would have been the last person to deny, Peter came as close as any fantasy she'd ever conjured up of the kind of man she could imagine falling in love with.

"We're here," Peter announced, braking the car in front of a pretty, ornamental wrought-iron gate. He hopped out. The gate wasn't locked. Troyan had either left it open for the arrival of his guests or the lock had broken and he'd never bothered to repair it. It creaked loudly as Peter swung it open.

"Needs some oil," Peter said. "Maybe I should offer Philippe some advice about the upkeep of his gate. I mean, after all, he's so generous with his advice."

"Maybe you ought to get yourself out of your nasty mood, *mon cher.*"

"Touché."

Peter drove past a good-sized parking area at the side of the château and pulled up at the front entrance. During the summer, when visitors came here to take the guided tour through the winery, the lot was probably filled. The Château Vauvilliers, Jackie had informed Peter in one of her many discourses today, had a tradition of opening its doors for viewing and wine tasting that dated back to Napoleon III. On this crisp day in late January there were only four cars in the lot. Peter noted two Rolls-Royces, a sleek silver Porsche, and a flashy, royal-blue BMW sports car as he stepped out of his rented Renault. He had that old familiar feeling of being the poor relative again, but he fought it off, reminding himself that his time would come.

As they walked up the wide stone steps to the house, Jackie was pleased to observe that the Château Vauvilliers showed little of the decline Peter claimed it had suffered at the hands of Philippe Troyan. It was a long, low, elegant château. Claret-colored shutters decorated the windows of the honey-hued stone building. Philippe had told Jackie that the original château dated back to the sixteenth century, but that it had been renovated in the late eighteen hundreds. Twenty years ago Philippe had installed modern plumbing and electricity, much to the distress of his elderly grandfather.

Jackie felt a little like Cinderella as they were greeted solemnly at the door by a respectful butler. He wasn't decked out in full livery, but his polite, correct manner more than made up for it. She didn't notice, as Peter did, the bare flick of a brow as the butler spied the little Renault in the driveway.

Peter dropped the key in the man's hand as they stepped into the hall. "The luggage is in the backseat," he said, knowing full well the butler would figure out the meaning of his words whether he spoke English or not.

Philippe Troyan came down the sweeping and

dramatic grand staircase into the large hall decorated with finely carved wainscoting. Two impressive old tapestries hung on the walls on either side of a wide doorway that led into the main sitting room. The wall beside the staircase was noticeably blank. Jackie wondered if a third tapestry had once hung there. Maybe Peter was right. It would be a shame if Philippe's circumstances were such that he'd had to resort to selling fine family heirlooms.

"Ah, I'm delighted to see you both." Troyan greeted them effusively in English, slipping a possessive hand on Jackie's elbow. "Most of my other weekend guests are already here." He bent low to Jackie, switching to an intimate French. "Some from the most notable families in the region, I might add." His eyes sparkled through his gold-rimmed glasses. He returned to a clipped English. "Come have a glass of wine and relax for a bit. I want you to taste a vintage Haut-Médoc from my private stock. Tomorrow I will take you for an extensive wine tasting. This way. You must see the exquisite view of the river from the sitting room."

He led them through the wide doorway, his hand still gripping Jackie's elbow, Peter a few paces behind. Troyan cast a quick glance over his shoulder. "I've been telling Jacqueline all about this old relic of a place. I find myself in Paris so much these days—business, you understand—that I'm afraid the château has suffered because of my negligence."

And, Peter thought snidely, *from all the price-*

less treasures you've already hocked to keep yourself afloat, you old goat.

Jackie gave Peter a warning glance. She knew exactly what was flashing in his mind. She, too, noticed more bare spots where antiques and paintings must once have adorned the salon. Still, it was a beautiful room, if a bit sparse and going to seed.

"The others will be down later. You will have plenty of time to rest and get ready for the party. It will be a small gathering. Some of the local families who I am sure will be delighted to learn of your acquisition of Château Cardinet. I would think one or two might have the available resources to invest in your enterprise, *mes amis.* Unfortunately, as I've already told Jacqueline, my investments are such right now that I cannot take on any additional burdens."

"We understand perfectly," Jackie said. "Philippe, this château is delightful. It brings back fond memories for me of summers in Beaune when I was a child, before Papa moved us to Lausanne. I remember how excited I would be to leave Paris and travel to Burgundy. We stayed with friends of Mama's in a lovely château on the hillside of Beaune. It was almost like a second home to me then."

"Please feel free to make yourself equally at home here, *ma chère.* After all, soon we will be neighbors." Troyan beamed at Jackie and bestowed a brief smile in Peter's direction. "So what do you think of the view?" he asked, leading them to the sweep of windows overlooking the water. "Centuries ago mariners would sail up the Gironde, their boats brimming over with wood to trade for wine. *'Baissez les voiles!'* they would shout." Troyan turned to Peter. " 'Lower the sails,' " he translated.

"I would love to have witnessed the sight," Jackie said dreamily.

Peter grinned. "You would have made a charming sixteenth-century maiden, I'm sure. I can picture you almost perfectly in the costume."

Jackie gave him a sharp stare. She needed no reminder of her brief spell at the Côte d'Or. Or of the farcical getup she'd worn there.

Philippe Troyan was pouring the wine when his butler appeared at the doorway announcing a new arrival.

"Excuse me while I greet my guests. I will be back in a few minutes." Philippe gave an aristocratic bow and an almost Germanic about-face as he left the room.

"So, mademoiselle, tell me more of your delightful summers in Beaune," Peter said.

Jackie shrugged. "You wanted me to play the part. I'm just trying to do a good job."

"And what about this business of being neighbors?"

"All part of the act," she said tightly. "Philippe likes the notion of my active participation in the château, and so I let him believe that is the way it is going to work."

"I know why he likes the idea."

"So do I," she answered blithely. "Who knows? Maybe it is you and I who will end up neighbors."

Peter opened his mouth to answer her, but Jackie cut him off. "I don't need to be reminded of your opinion of Philippe, Peter. I happen not to share it," she said curtly, turning her back on him.

Peter laughed softly.

"What do you find so amusing now?" she asked coolly, her back still to him.

Peter bent low and pressed his lips to her ear, completely disrupting her serenity. "You know something, princess? You are quite a little con artist. I don't believe for one instant that you really find Philippe Troyan appealing enough to move yourself into his crumbling château."

Jackie didn't answer. She knew anything she said at this moment, with Peter's warm breath against her ear, would probably give her away.

"Not a bad wine," Peter said nonchalantly after taking a sip. "What do you think now that you're becoming such an expert?"

"Oh, shut up," she retorted, taking too large a gulp and coughing.

"Slow down, princess. I guess Philippe hasn't yet taught you the fine art of wine tasting." He grinned as her cough faded. "Here, let me explain. First, you hold the glass by the stem, delicately . . . like a rare treasure. Swirl it gently, tenderly, observing the fine, rich color." He spoke in a soft tone, his lips curved in a provocative smile as his eyes met hers. "Then, we sniff, letting ourselves become captivated by the delicious bouquet. Now, a small sip. We hold the liquid in our mouth, letting the wine tumble about the tips and sides of our tongue, letting our taste buds become saturated, intoxicated, by the rare flavor." He reached out and cupped his hand over hers as she held the wine. Jackie looked up at him with her big green eyes as he gently tipped the glass to her lips. "You try it," he said in a husky voice that made no attempt to mask the seductive intent of his little lesson.

Jackie swallowed a taste of the wine and grinned at him. "I think I have the hang of it now. I hope I remember tomorrow when I go off with Philippe."

"I could always give you another lesson later tonight."

At the sound of voices in the hall Jackie moved away from Peter. She looked toward the doorway and froze as Philippe entered the room with his new guests.

"Jacqueline. Peter. Let me introduce you to three of my dearest friends, Jean-Louis Marigny, his wife, Madeleine, and their son, Claude. And these are our new neighbors, Peter Santiago from the States and the charming Mademoiselle Jacqueline Armand, a delightful Frenchwoman who has been residing in Lausanne, Switzerland. They have bought the old Château Cardinet in Labarde."

The elder Marignys nodded cordially. Then Claude Marigny walked over to her and Jackie fervently prayed that the floor would open beneath her and mercifully swallow her up. Her cheeks burned, her heart thumped double time. As soon as her ex-boss exposed her impersonation, Jackie knew that all the plans she and Peter had made to obtain backing for the vineyard would be ruined. No one in the community would trust them, and even if they found outside backing, it would be very difficult to establish the Château Cardinet as a reputable establishment. Peter and his grandiose schemes, she silently wailed. Why couldn't he have let her remain Jackie Archer from Middleton Corner, Ohio? But then, would Philippe Troyan have been interested in a small-town hick from the States? No more than he would a liar, probably.

Claude Marigny greeted Peter with a cursory nod and stood before Jackie. She held her breath as he gave her a lingering study for what seemed an eternity, his dark-blue eyes reflecting an open curiosity. Finally, he took her hand. It was trembling. He brought it to his lips. *"Enchanté,* Mademoiselle Armand. For a moment I thought we had met somewhere before, but I see now I would not have forgotten so lovely a woman."

CHAPTER SIX

Jackie now knew what it felt like when the condemned prisoner got one of those last-minute reprieves. The relief was stunning, but there remained that unshakable sense that the drama was not over, only on hold. How long could she fool Claude Marigny? She would have to endure an entire weekend of what was already proving to be his very attentive presence.

She managed to get through a glass of the vintage wine Philippe and the elder Marignys found so delightful. Claude took a few polite sips, his interest focused on learning more about the enchanting Jacqueline Armand, recently of Lausanne, Switzerland, a city, unfortunately, that he happened to know quite well.

In the midst of her crisis Jackie had to pat herself on the back for those long hours spent in Paris libraries reading tour books. She managed to answer Claude's questions with comforting accuracy, although her voice continued to tremble as she spoke. Claude seemed to find her tremulous style as appealing as her looks. For a rueful moment Jackie considered all those days and weeks at *Toujours Amour* when she would have given anything in the world to have the suave Claude Marigny dote on her every word and gesture as he was doing today. Now here she was wishing she were the original ugly duckling—or at least Jackie Archer from Middleton Corner.

Peter wasn't paying attention to his Haut-Médoc wine any more than Claude. While the youngest Marigny was intent on Jacqueline's charm and sensual attractiveness, Peter was intent on Jackie's sudden pallor and shaky voice. She had the look of a woman who feared she might have just swallowed a glass of poison instead of a vintage Bordeaux. He kept throwing her odd looks.

All Jackie wanted to do was escape. When Philippe suggested he show the guests to their rooms, Jackie was the first one to pop up from her seat. At last, she thought, a chance to regroup. She could feel a bead of sweat trickle down her temple. She quickly wiped it away, then glanced nervously around the room, trying to smile naturally as Claude walked up alongside her. She caught Peter's curious glance and Philippe's decidedly jealous one. It seemed clear that Philippe Troyan had not planned on Claude Marigny moving in on the young woman he was trying his utmost to court. It was enough he had to contend with the hot-blooded Mexican-American, although Jacqueline had insisted they were nothing more than business partners.

The lavish bedroom, with its striking view of the Gironde, was lost on Jackie, whose mind was busily trying to fabricate some excuse to remain upstairs all evening. She could come down with a migraine. With her blanched coloring and pained expression she would certainly have little trouble convincing her host of such an ailment. Tomorrow, she could claim still not to be feeling well, grab Peter, and hightail it out of there.

Her plan set, she began to relax a bit. A light rap on her door shattered her calm instantly. If it was Claude Marigny . . .

"Jackie, it's me, Peter. Let me in," he said, keeping his voice low. The elder Marignys were across the hall. Peter and Claude had been given quarters farther down the wing.

Jackie threw open the door and practically pulled him inside.

"We've got to get out of here, Peter."

He grabbed her by the shoulders and steered her over to the bed. "Slow down, princess. What's going on? You look like you saw a ghost downstairs."

"Worse," she gasped. "My ex-boss."

"Marigny?"

"Claude Marigny, former publisher of *Toujours Amour*. Where I happened to work eight or more hours a day for close to nine weeks."

"So?"

"So? So he's bound to put two and two together before the weekend is over. You heard what he said. He thought he knew me from somewhere!"

"He also said that it wasn't possible since he'd never forget you if he had met you before. You not only look completely different from that 'fresh from the hicks' Miss Archer—you have style and self-assurance. Marigny will never make the connection. He's too firm a believer in class lines."

"Oh, Peter, look who's being naive now. Can you honestly believe he isn't going to see through this preposterous impersonation? He'll be sitting downstairs at the dining table, swallowing his second escargot, and suddenly he'll look across at me and say, 'Aha, an imposter in our midst. This woman here, *messieurs et mesdames*, is not *la belle* Mademoiselle Armand, she's plain little Jackie Archer from Middleton Corner, Ohio!'"

Peter grinned at her. "Stop putting yourself down, Jackie. I saw something special in you even when you were Miss Small Town, U.S.A."

"And that's exactly who I want to be again. *Mon Dieu*, why did I ever listen to you? You'd think when I was the foil of that first little stunt of yours at the Côte d'Or, I would have been smart enough not to get set up again."

"Come on, Jackie. You've been having a ball as the enchantingly enticing Mademoiselle Armand. Will you just look around you? This boudoir Philippe chose especially for his favorite guest is what I would have to call overstated elegance. Every stick of furniture in here must date back at least a century or more. Your former garret would fit into a quarter of this space." He moved to a painting over the ornately carved headboard of her bed, a landscape of toiling peasants in a field. "This isn't some reproduction like they hang on a wall of a Howard Johnson's motor lodge, Jackie. This is an original . . ." He squinted his eyes, trying to read the signature, then shrugged. "Well, it's an original somebody or other. And this bed. My God, Jackie, think of all the history here. Courtesans might have slept in this very bed a hundred years ago. And tonight, you, princess, are going to sleep here. Think about it, Jackie. You've been wrenched from oblivion and mediocrity into the lap of luxury. This is your chance to have the kind of weekend you and all the folks back home in the midwest could only read about in books from your library. It's a dream come true, princess."

"The dream is turning into a nightmare. What's Claude Marigny doing here, anyway? I would have sworn nothing could have torn him away from his high-style Paris life, even for a weekend. He certainly never impressed me as the dutiful son."

"Maybe he needs money. It's amazing how dutiful sons become when they start running out of funds. And from what the father mentioned to me downstairs, he's got more than enough to help Claude out. He owns the Château Maiffret, which just happens to produce wines of legendary excellence. Not to mention that Monsieur Marigny has interests in several other vineyards in the area. And he happens to think Château Cardinet might be an interesting venture. He's one of the few vintners I've met who seem secure enough to consider the idea of introducing a French Zinfandel. Especially as the entrancing Mademoiselle Armand, who comes from a fine French family, is giving the vineyard her support and involvement. Don't you see, Jackie? It's just the right touch. Your participation gives the whole operation the *Good Housekeeping* seal of approval." He smiled. "If an aristocratic native daughter is so enthusiastic—"

"I am not an aristocratic native daughter, Peter. I'm a fraud. And I'm going to be found out. Claude is too bright and too perceptive to be fooled for very long. And when the jig is up, what do you think the eminent owner of Château Maiffret is going to say about investing in your vineyard? Peter, it's crazy to continue this impersonation. Now, listen to me. I have a plan. I'll pretend a headache tonight and tomorrow I'll ask you to take me home first thing in the morning because I am still not feeling well. Believe me, I won't have to fake it."

"Nonsense." Peter cupped her chin. "You are going to put on that smashing sequin gown we blew a thousand francs on for just this occasion. You're going down there tonight and wow every last Frenchman in the place, including Claude Marigny. Come here." He grabbed her hand and dragged her over to the mirror. "Now, take a good look at yourself, Jackie. No. Wait."

He left her standing there and rushed to the closet where the maid had already hung Jackie's clothes. He took the shimmering sequin gown off the hanger and brought it to Jackie. He placed it over a chair and started unzipping the back of her dress.

"What the hell are you doing?"

"I want you to see yourself in this gown and

then tell me you can't pull this thing off. If you honestly believe the reflection staring back from the mirror is that of Jackie Archer, I'll go downstairs and tell our esteemed host that we forgot to feed poor Gogo before we left and simply must return to Paris immediately."

"You're so amusing," she quipped. Then she stared at him in the mirror. "You did remember to feed him?"

Peter laughed. "Come on. Get that gown on."

"Not while you're standing here."

"I've seen you get undressed before." He grinned lasciviously.

"That was not one of the high points of our brief but tumultuous relationship. Now, turn around and don't peek. I happen to have a small-town sense of modesty, in case you haven't picked that up."

He turned reluctantly. "Believe me, Jackie. You have nothing to feel embarrassed about. You happen to have a beautiful figure." A moment later he laughed.

"And obviously a very funny one."

"No, no. I was just thinking about that first time I saw you. I thought you looked like a topless hourglass. Who would have guessed you had firm, full breasts where there seemed to be none and slender, curved hips where there seemed to be too much?"

Jackie glared at his back. "You are developing this habit of humiliating me into an art."

"What did I say? That you have delectable—"

"Shut up. And don't you turn around. I can do

without a descriptive course in anatomy, especially my own." Her voice was sharp, but her cheeks were flushed and she had to admit to herself that Peter's praise of her attributes was not entirely upsetting. It was his casual and forthright style that she found unflattering and unromantic. He might have been describing a particularly pleasing piece of melon.

She stepped into the gown, there being no other way to get the tight-fitting garment on. Underneath she wore only a skimpy pair of bikini panties. Anything more would have ruined the lines. "This is only a rehearsal," she said. "I haven't taken my shower, my hair isn't done, I have no makeup . . ."

Peter turned around and walked over to her. "It doesn't matter," he said softly, watching her look at herself in the mirror. "You really are beautiful, princess."

"No, I'm not." She swallowed hard. Then she tilted her head and flashed him a teasing smile. "But I have to admit I do look rather striking in an odd sort of way. Different."

"Most definitely unique," Peter said. "Most definitely not plain little Jackie Archer from Ohio, *n'est-ce pas?*" His hands skimmed her bare shoulders, the provocatively low-cut, strapless gown offering free access to his caress.

"C'est vrai," she murmured. "It's true." Jackie's pulsebeat raced as Peter bent down and started planting a row of kisses along her neck. She let herself lean against him as his hand came around her slender waist. She met his gaze in the mirror

and they exchanged the barest wisp of a smile before he turned her to him and took her in his arms.

His kiss was rough, demanding, unlike the others. The raw sexuality of his attack matched Jackie's response. She wrapped her arms around him, drawing him more tightly against her. When he slid down the zipper of the gown, she made no protest. His hands felt warm and intoxicating on her skin. The gown fell around her ankles. The next moment she was lifted up in Peter's arms and he was carrying her over to the bed. Her body trembled as he laid her down and bent over her, stroking, kissing, caressing her breasts. Her nails dug into his back, her lips parted in a low moan.

As he started undoing his trousers, Jackie whispered breathlessly, "Peter, this is crazy."

He silenced her with a deep, passionate kiss that made her feel even crazier, but no longer wanting to protest.

He was undressed and beside her in moments, his strong fingers sliding down her hips, pushing her panties off and exploring her body at the same time. A throbbing need seemed to be consuming her. She pressed her lips to his neck, darted her tongue out, and slid it down his skin. Her hips began to move, undulating, enticing, and she felt Peter shiver as his lips captured hers again.

There was a knock on her door. Both she and Peter froze. Jackie gasped as she heard Claude

Marigny softly call out her name. He said a few more words.

"What's he saying?" Peter whispered.

"He wants me to come down early and have a drink with him."

"Tell him you're resting, but that you'll be happy to join him a little later."

Jackie shot Peter a disgruntled look, but she couldn't think quickly enough to come up with an excuse and did what Peter said. When she heard Claude's footsteps fade down the hall, she said with annoyance, "Why did you want me to spend more time with him than is absolutely necessary?"

"Come on, Jackie. You convinced yourself you can carry this off. And Claude Marigny could be a big influence on his father."

Jackie felt naked. Of course, that was the true state of her appearance, but before that knock on the door, she didn't feel exposed. She reached for the *duvet* folded at the foot of the bed and drew it up around herself. "So that's what this is all about."

"What do you mean?" His state of undress apparently didn't bother him as it was now disturbing Jackie. He made no move to do anything but remain languidly reclined beside her.

She turned away. "You already had me convinced to play along, Peter. You didn't have to go through a whole seduction scene to keep me in line."

"You're crazy. That's not what I was doing."

"You are right. I am crazy. For letting myself

play the fool. Well, that's one role I don't think you can talk me into again. It's laughable, really," she said, fighting back tears. "You giving me speeches about Philippe Troyan being entitled. He doesn't hold a candle to you. Now, get out of here. I have a date with Claude Marigny and I'm sure you'll want me to look my best."

Peter sighed wearily as he got out of the bed and slipped on his clothes. "You've got it wrong, princess. In spite of your suspicions that I plot out every move I make, I had no preconceived thoughts of seducing you. It was pure impulse. Just like it was for you. I don't think you really understand yet just what a sensual person you are, Jackie. And," he said as he walked to the door, "I still think you'd better watch out for entitled aristocrats . . . including the handsome Claude Marigny."

"Sorry, Peter. Since you're throwing me to the wolves, you're just going to have to accept the results."

Peter grinned. "Aren't you the gal who lectured me about how certain ends do not justify the means? I would be quite surprised—and disappointed—to learn you don't practice what you preach. *Au revoir, ma chère.*"

He blew her a kiss and closed the door before Jackie could have the last word, but she was far from considering *la dispute finie.*

Philippe Troyan may have been going through some financial difficulties, but he knew how to give one of the most extravagant dinner parties around town. The meal made even the high-priced fare at the Côte d'Or seem paltry. Regional delights like *pâté de foie gras,* succulent oysters in oil, and dark, wild mushrooms known as *cèpes* were presented for appetizers. Then came such gourmet extravagances as *escalopes de poissons au soufflé de ciboulette,* roughly translated as thin slivers of fish with a chive soufflé, and an opulently sculptured *gigot d'agneau en croûte,* a leg of lamb encased in a pastry shell. All this served on the finest eighteenth-century French porcelain china, flickering silver candelabras adorning the Louis Quatorze dining table illuminated from above by a five-tiered crystal chandelier. Silver flatware gleamed with a rich antique luster. Philippe Troyan knew how to suffer hard times in style.

Jackie had a seat of honor to the right of her host, who presided at the head of the table. Both Claude Marigny and Peter were at the other end. Peter was wedged between Madame Marigny and a Mademoiselle Délecourt, a melancholy young woman in her early twenties. Her morose expression, Jackie decided, was largely due to the full and undivided attention which handsome Monsieur Santiago was giving Madame Marigny —leaving Mademoiselle Délecourt with the tedious task of listening to the near senile grandfather of one of the other guests.

Jackie had made up her mind, fueled by her anger and hurt, not to let her feelings about Peter spoil her evening. Peter wanted her to go on playing the part, and so she would—but she was going to write her own script from here on out.

She ate, with relish, what had to be the most elegant and delicious meal she had ever tasted. In between bites she flirted outrageously with Philippe. It was, she admitted, her way of killing two birds with one stone. She was striking back at Peter, who she knew expected her to charm the influential Marigny—not Philippe Troyan; and hopefully putting off Claude, who she judged would back away when he faced any real competition. She had already played it very cool during their brief drink together. This should cinch it.

Philippe was thrilled. He took hold of Jackie's hand. "You must promise me the first and the last dance tonight." The light from the chandelier was reflected in his glasses, giving his eyes a particularly unbecoming haze. "And in the middle I will take you on a private tour of the château. There are so many things I want to show you."

Jackie was pretty sure most of those "things" were in his bedroom, but she smiled sweetly and squeezed his hand. "You mustn't let me take you from your other guests, Philippe. But tomorrow . . ." Maybe by then she'd be able to convince Peter that they ought to leave.

"You look absolutely stunning this evening, *ma chère*. Every man in this room has his eye on you."

Jackie knew he was right about at least two men. Claude kept giving her his most sensual gazes, and twice, when she caught Peter's eye, he winked. Her plans weren't working. If she wasn't careful she would end up with three live birds and no available stones.

The dinner ended with a lavish *soufflé à l'orange*. Jackie couldn't help smiling when the pretty young servant carried the confection out of the kitchen and carefully made her way to the table. It would certainly liven up the staid group if Peter got one of those convenient cramps in his leg and accidentally tripped her. But Peter, having no tab to worry about paying, was busy with other pursuits this evening.

Dessert went off without any catastrophes. Afterward, Philippe took Jackie's arm and led the group into the smaller of the château's two ballrooms, designed for the master's more intimate soirées. A five-piece band played American mood music with a slight French lilt. It was all very subdued, very chic. In this kind of setting it was easy for Jackie almost to believe she was the fictitious heroine Mademoiselle Armand.

Philippe slipped his arm around her waist for the first dance. He was one of those men who danced as though the task were both difficult and urgently important, putting all of his energy into it, apologizing with breathy whispers and tightened grips whenever he lost the rhythm. Jackie didn't mind his ineptitude nearly as much as she did his attempts to make up for it. She was relieved when the music ended, even though she saw Claude walking over to her.

"Do you mind if I steal Jacqueline away for a dance, Troyan?" Claude didn't wait for an answer —from either Philippe or Jackie. He gathered her in his arms as if he were Fred Astaire. He danced, in fact, almost as well.

"I would love to show you the Château Maiffret sometime, Jacqueline. Perhaps next weekend? There is a magnificent fireplace in the sitting room. Really quite extraordinary. I will make you my special mulled wine and we will sit by the fire and become better acquainted. I would love to hear more about your plans for Château Cardinet."

"Well, they're really Peter's plans. I'm sure you would learn more from him."

He gave her a seductive smile. "But it is you I want to learn from. We are going to be neighbors, you know."

Jackie's body tensed. "I thought you lived in Paris."

He gave her a curious glance. "What made you think that?"

"I—I thought I heard somebody here . . ."

"I did live in Paris until a few weeks ago. Now I've moved back to the château. You could say I sowed my wild oats for a time and dabbled in some business ventures that didn't work out. I am now ready to take my place at Château Maiffret beside my father. It is my responsibility to carry on the fine family tradition." He grinned broadly. "So my father tells me—over and over again."

"You don't want to carry on the tradition?"

Claude shrugged. "I want, my lovely friend, to live well and have a good time. The wine business is very hard work. And my father, a very charming man, is a hard taskmaster. Our styles tend to clash. But a Marigny must reign at the helm and my father is not getting any younger. He has been at me to settle down. I have to admit I much prefer to drink a fine Château Maiffret wine than to oversee the making of it. But such is life. Anyway, now that you are going to be involved in the Château Cardinet vineyards, the notion of country life seems far more appealing."

The music ended. Claude held on to her for a moment longer, his eyes fixed on her with that curious look again. Jackie's nervousness returned. "Can I ask you a personal question, Jacqueline?"

She managed a nod, holding her breath.

"You and Peter Santiago, are you lovers or merely business partners?" He smiled at her shocked expression. "I believe it only wastes time to beat around the bush."

"I believe," Jackie said, her cool returning, "that people's affairs are their own business, monsieur." She flushed, realizing the implication of her choice of the word *affair* and continued more quickly. "Will you excuse me? I think I'll go freshen up."

Claude smiled, bowing slightly. "You look quite perfect, but I shall let you go for now, if you'll have lunch with me tomorrow? I know a charming spot in town."

"I'm not yet sure of my plans for tomorrow," she mumbled. Now she had two eager dates to contend with for the next day. She really had to convince Peter to leave in the morning.

Jackie, fully dressed at eight A.M. the next day, knocked on Peter's door. He didn't answer. She turned the knob and looked in. His bed was empty. On her way down the stairs she heard her name being called from above.

"Ah, Jacqueline. How delightful that you, too, are an early riser." Philippe hurried down the stairs to join her. "Come have some breakfast with me and then I shall take you on a private tour of the winery."

Jackie's only interest was in finding her errant partner, but she couldn't very well behave rudely to her host. When she asked Philippe if he had seen Peter, he shrugged. "Don't worry about Monsieur Santiago. You look a bit pale. Come eat."

They had fresh croissants and coffee in a sunny breakfast room. Jackie was not in the mood for Philippe's tour, but there was no way out of it. Reluctantly, she went upstairs for her coat, looked around in vain for Peter, and then finally rejoined Philippe downstairs.

"Of course, this time of year, there is little activity. Late summer, early in the fall—that's the time to see the place in full swing," Philippe said, leading her to a long shed with a sloped roof of sunbaked terra cotta tiles which he referred to as a *chai*. Inside were orderly rows of barrels stacked three high, running down the entire space.

The walls of the room were the characteristic pale-gold stone of the region. Light streamed in through clerestory windows and an enormous fireplace stood at either end heating the space, but there was still a cool, damp atmosphere in the room.

Philippe took Jackie's elbow and drew her closer to where a group of workers were busily filling a long series of oak barrels at one end of the room. "What are they doing?" she asked inquisitively.

"That is what we call topping off," Philippe explained. "This must be done to all the newly vintaged wines once or twice a week to keep the wine at the brim. It is vitally important not to let oxygen mix with the wine at this stage." He nodded to one of the men who seemed to be in charge.

The *maître de chaix* stopped his work and came over to greet Jackie and Philippe.

"Jacqueline, this is Monsieur Georges Alexandre, my right-hand man. He sees to it that everything goes like clockwork down here."

Monsieur Alexandre smiled. "I do my best. Unfortunately, nature and chemistry sometimes interfere."

Philippe scowled. "We have had a couple of bad seasons," he explained to Jackie. "Very frustrating . . . and costly. You will have to cope with such problems soon enough. Last season, for instance, we were counting on a hundred casks of vintage wine; but a freak hailstorm that lasted only minutes reduced it to fewer than twenty. The vines have a thousand enemies." He sighed. "But this season will be better."

Monsieur Alexandre did not look as optimistic

as Philippe, but he smiled politely and offered to show Jackie around.

"That's all right, Georges. You're busy. I'll give Mademoiselle Armand the grand tour."

After a brief while, as Philippe began taking her around, Jackie relaxed, finding herself entranced with seeing and learning firsthand so much about the art of making wine.

"Some of the vineyards have switched to steel vats," Philippe explained, "but I remain firm in my belief that oak is the divinely appointed wood for wine. There are some that have also turned to mechanical pumps for filling the vats. We keep the old ways. Everything is done by hand."

"It's all so fascinating, Philippe."

They were standing together near a row of barrels that separated them from the other workers. Philippe reached out and took hold of Jackie's hand. "It is you, *ma chérie*, who are fascinating. You know that I am very much attracted to you." He gave her a long, languid look, his palm uncomfortably moist as he squeezed her hand.

"We should be getting back, Philippe. Peter will be looking—"

"Peter is with Jean-Louis Marigny, trying to convince him of the merits of the Château Cardinet."

"Peter thinks he's quite interested," Jackie said, trying politely to remove her hand, to no avail.

Philippe moved closer. "I'm afraid he will be disappointed, then. Jean-Louis told me last night that he has his eye on another vineyard in Alsace.

He has already begun negotiations. I doubt he can be swayed."

Jackie frowned. "I think I ought to join in the meeting. Perhaps I can help persuade Monsieur Marigny of the advantages—"

"They drove off into town. I saw them leave from my window. Relax, *ma chère*. This evening Gérard St. Jacques, an old friend of mine, is coming for dinner and spending the night. He, too, owns interests in several châteaus in the region. And he is bringing his lovely daughter, Emilie, along. Your partner may be able to charm her into convincing her father of the merits of your château. Gérard is a widower and Emilie has a habit of getting whatever she wants from him." He captured Jackie's other hand. "Now let me see one of your beautiful smiles. You know I want to help you, Jacqueline. All you have to do is let me."

Jackie was trying to think up another excuse to leave when Philippe abruptly grabbed her and pulled her into his arms. A silent struggle ensued, Jackie too embarrassed to scream out in protest with Philippe's staff so close at hand.

"Ah, this is where the two of you are hiding. Monsieur Alexandre said you were still wandering about."

Jackie and Philippe fell apart and stared at Claude Marigny, who ambled over with a look of amusement on his face.

A flustered and irritated Philippe Troyan smoothed down his hair and readjusted his glasses. "What do you want, Marigny?"

"You are called to the telephone. Your stockbroker, I think. Anyway, it sounded urgent. I said I'd come track you down."

Philippe glared at Claude and turned to Jackie. "Please excuse me, Jacqueline," he said, regaining his composure.

Claude laughed as he watched Philippe go out the door. "You have to watch out for Philippe's private wine tours."

"*Merci,*" she said softly.

Claude turned to her and smiled. "Now, one favor deserves one in return. Come have that lunch with me."

"But Philippe will be expecting me to—"

"Don't worry about him. He'll be stuck on the phone for hours. Which is another reason why you must come away with me. I lied for you. His stockbroker didn't phone. It is his ex-wife, Nadine. I guarantee she's looking for late alimony and will give him a good earful. Philippe will be furious when he finds out I tricked him." Claude grinned.

Another prankster. It was all she needed.

CHAPTER SEVEN

"What are you smiling about?" Jackie looked across the linen-covered table at Claude. They were sitting in an intimate cafe in the village of Pauillac, eleven kilometers from Château Vauvilliers.

Claude cradled his wineglass between two hands. "You intrigue me, Jacqueline. I keep having this strange sensation that we have been together before. Do you know what I think?" His eyes grew dark and intense as he gazed steadily at her.

Jackie, who had spent the last hour with her ex-boss waiting and dreading the inevitable, swallowed hard. "What?"

He set down his wine and reached out for her hand. "I think we must have been lovers in a past life. Don't laugh, *chérie.* I believe in such things."

The radiance of Jackie's smile was pure relief, but it seemed to convince Claude Marigny that the notion appealed to her.

"That means, *ma chère*, that our meeting is fate." His other hand cupped her chin. "What do you think?"

"I think," Jackie said firmly, "that I've had too much wine and we ought to be getting back, Claude."

He motioned to the waiter, but instead of requesting a check, asked him to bring two coffees.

"Tell me how you became involved with the Château Cardinet," Claude said. He was a man used to taking the lead and Jackie knew they weren't going to make it back to the château until Claude was good and ready.

"It's a long and complicated story. Let's just say that Peter and I happened upon a golden opportunity and couldn't pass it up."

"What will your position be at the château?"

Jackie hesitated. As things stood now, she had no position. Once Peter had enough investors to begin operations, he still expected her to go off contentedly with her percentage of the profits and that would be the end of it. But Jackie had still not given up on the idea of convincing Peter otherwise.

"I'm not sure yet. That's something Peter and I are still sorting out. Anyway"—she smiled wistfully—"right now it's still a pipe dream. I may be back in Paris . . . or Lausanne," she hastily added, "if we don't find the backers to get the vineyard off the ground. I understand your father is tied up in negotiations for another vineyard. It's a pity he won't reconsider his choice."

Claude smiled. "Don't forget fate, *chérie.*" He gave her a sultry look and leaned closer. "I can't let you vanish before I discover what it was we once had—and have it again." His smile broadened. "Ah, Jacqueline, that is what is so rare about you—one half siren, one half . . . blushing maiden. It is a very appealing combination. You are very special." He planted a moist kiss on the palm of her hand.

Jackie would have been lying if she said she wasn't flattered by Claude's flirtations. It would have had more of an effect on her, however, had she not heard him say some of the very same lines when he used to talk to other "special" women on the phone at the *Toujours Amour* offices. She wondered what his reaction would be if she told him the truth right now. Would he still find her so alluring and desirable, or was it the mystery that kept him so interested?

She drank her coffee and tried to make small talk, but Claude was too intent on his game of seduction. He kept giving her knowing smiles, meaningful glances, and disturbingly provocative caresses.

"We really ought to get back, Claude," she said firmly, removing his hand from her arm. The strain of her pretense and of Claude's determined efforts to entice her were wearing her nerves down.

"Relax, *chérie*. There is no hurry." He gave her a wounded-little-boy look. "Don't you like me?"

Jackie laughed uncomfortably. "Of course I do, Claude. You're very charming and attractive. It's just . . ."

"I come on too strong?"

"Yes," she admitted. "We—we've only just met."

He shook his head. "That I will never believe. I know you think I'm handing you a line. I admit I've got something of a reputation for being a lady's man. But this is different, *chérie*. I felt it the minute I walked into the room yesterday and saw you. It was almost a—a presence, a force." He pulled his chair next to hers. "Jacqueline. I intend to make you a believer." He placed his hand on her face, his eyes meeting hers.

Jackie looked away. That was when she saw Peter and Jean-Louis Marigny coming through the front door. Peter waved. Jackie breathed yet another sigh of relief. In all her years in Ohio she couldn't remember a single time she'd had to be rescued from the amorous clutches of a man . . . and here, twice in one day, she'd had exactly that need.

Claude didn't look any happier with the interruption than Philippe had a couple of hours earlier. But he greeted his father and Peter cordially, given no choice but to invite them to sit down.

"Jacqueline and I were just finishing," Claude said, quickly swallowing half a cup of coffee. To Peter he said in English, "Will you excuse us if we don't keep you company? Jacqueline is eager to return to the château."

"Relax, Claude." Peter smiled. "Nothing's happening at the château. We were just there. Troyan was on his way out. An irritating errand, he said. He seemed in a foul mood for some reason."

Jackie and Claude shared a knowing smile that Peter caught and found disturbing. He wondered if Jackie were pleased or annoyed that he'd broken up their little tête à tête. He had thought she was so worried about Claude finding out who she really was; now he wasn't so sure. Either Jackie no longer minded, or she felt more confident about her new persona.

Claude looked over at Jackie. "Whenever you're ready, *chérie*."

Peter's ears perked up at the endearment. Jackie met his gaze, saw his slight scowl, and realized that he felt at least a spark of jealousy. She had an impulse to milk that spark for all it was worth, but she quickly chastised herself for it. She didn't play those kinds of games. Or maybe, she admitted, she was afraid to discover that the spark was all there was. *Damn you, Peter, why can't you believe in fate, believe that we have something special . . . ?*

Jean-Louis Marigny, a tall, well-built man in his early sixties with glistening gray hair, impatient blue eyes, and a complexion darkened by months spent on the Riviera and the Greek Islands, had a formidable manner. He folded his coat meticulously over an empty chair and gave his son a severe look. "Are you forgetting our meeting with Fabert this afternoon?"

Claude's expression made it clear he had forgotten, or not deemed it important enough to consider in the first place. "Surely you can handle that without my help," he said dryly, knowing full well his father was dragging him along to the wine broker as part of a whole indoctrination procedure. Claude made it obvious that he found the plan tedious at best. Especially when it interfered with his own amorous schemes.

"Don't worry about getting Jackie back to the château," Peter said pleasantly. "We have a few things to go over—business, you know." He turned to Jean-Louis Marigny. "In fact, why don't we leave you and your son to prepare for your meeting?"

"Actually, I was thinking you might like to come along," Marigny said. "Alphonse Fabert is one of the leading wine brokers in Bordeaux. He is someone you should meet. At the point you are ready for such services, I cannot recommend anyone more highly."

"Well, I don't know about this afternoon." Peter hesitated, his eyes resting curiously on Jackie.

Claude reached out for Jackie's hand. "That's a fine idea, father. Why don't the two of you have some lunch while I show Jacqueline around the village? Then we'll meet you over at Fabert's at . . . ?"

"Two o'clock," his father said severely. "Sharp."

Claude was already helping Jackie on with her coat, squelching any possibility of her arguing. Peter was not going to be able to rescue her after all.

She felt drained having to play her role of Jacqueline Armand so exactingly in front of Claude. She was also weary of the flirtatious game, the flattery wearing thin. She desperately wanted some time alone, some time to be Jackie Archer for a while.

"We have only an hour to play, I'm afraid," Claude observed steering her toward his shiny red sports car, "before I have to punch in on the time clock. I know just the place to—"

"I'm feeling very tired, Claude. Would you mind taking me back to the château? It was a lovely lunch." She fought off a feigned yawn. "I warned you I'd had too much wine."

"But your partner will be expecting you at the meeting with Fabert."

"He'll manage on his own," she said tersely, looking away as Claude's gaze registered curiosity.

"As will my father. I'm merely going along for the ride." Claude sighed—a very Gallic sigh.

"I have trouble understanding your lack of interest in the vineyards," Jackie said. "There's been nothing I've ever known that's more exciting than this whole way of life."

Claude gave her a provocative smile, but Jackie's frown discouraged it. "I'm not really so disinterested." He opened the car door for her, helping her into the low-slung passenger seat. He looked down at Jackie, his eyes traveling over her delicate features. Then he carefully closed the door, walked around the car, and slid in behind the wheel.

"Perhaps," he mused, his eyes straight ahead, the car keys still in his hand, "I feel some kind of need to keep up a rebellion that began when I was a boy. Typical of strong, domineering fathers and equally strong, unyielding sons." He shrugged. "I always did exactly the opposite of what my father expected . . . by now it's become a habit." He took her hand, bringing her fingertips to his lips. "But you inspire me to be more cooperative. I want to impress you, *chérie.*"

Jackie smiled and pulled her hand from his grasp. "I'm not sure that's going to be a very lasting source of motivation."

"You're wrong, Jacqueline. You are a delicate, beautiful flower. And you are clever and charming—a woman of so many faces." He arched a brow and smiled. "How could I grow tired of wanting to win your affections?"

Jackie didn't say anything. She was relieved when he started the engine and headed for the château. She gave him a thoughtful glance as he sped down the vineyard road. For a brief moment she felt as though he was onto her guise. It was a foolish pretense to keep up now, anyway. It looked as if Marigny wasn't going to invest in the château, so it didn't matter if Mademoiselle Armand from a fine French family was giving Château Cardinet the *Good Housekeeping* seal of approval. But then there were other prospects, investors who already expected to be introduced to Mademoiselle Armand. Once having begun this pretense, Jackie saw that she was trapped in it, at least until Peter got the backing he needed. After that, she'd be out of it. Her end of the deal would be completed and she could return to being Jackie Archer. An odd sensation struck her. Could she really step back into her old shoes again? Did she really want to abandon the exciting, dramatic, luxurious life of a femme fatale?

Staying meant keeping up the pretense. How long could she possibly manage it?

Claude pulled up in front of the château. "I won't walk you in. Philippe is probably in there waiting to crucify me for my little trick. It's just as well I am not staying another night."

"I don't know that I can blame him if he's furious." She laughed.

"Ah, Philippe is used to my tricks. He's very fond of my parents and so he continues to tolerate me."

Jackie opened the car door. "Thanks again for lunch, Claude."

He reached over and stroked her cheek. "I would like to have you come down to Château Maiffret next weekend, *chérie*. It's very beautiful."

"Well, I'm not sure of Peter's schedule," she said hesitantly.

"Does Santiago make you work seven days a week?" He made a clicking sound with his tongue. "I'll have to speak to him about permitting his lovely partner some time for fun."

Jackie got out of the car. "For me work is fun. And I'm supposed to motivate you to begin feeling the same way, remember?"

Claude chuckled. He stuck his head out of the window as Jackie came around. "My father will be thrilled I found you, *chérie*. I'll call you. Give Philippe my best," he said, grinning.

Jackie waved and ran up the broad stone steps to the château. Philippe opened the door for her.

Jackie stifled a groan. She was in no mood to

contend with Philippe Troyan's outraged indignation.

"I see that rogue has slipped off," he said, watching Claude pull around the circular driveway.

He closed the door and looked solemnly at Jackie. "Claude Marigny is utterly disreputable. I hope you know he is not to be trusted." He threw up his hands. "I'm sorry, *ma chère*. He is not worth my upset. I had hoped we could have a nice, quiet lunch together, but Claude saw to it that I was tied up for several hours." He helped her off with her coat and took hold of her arm. "Come, have a drink and warm up. You must be chilled."

"To be honest, I'm exhausted. I came back to take a nap."

Philippe looked at his watch. It was close to two o'clock. "My business manager, Edouard Racine, is arriving at five for a meeting. I have a feeling I'll be tied up from then until dinnertime. Janine will have to serve a bit late tonight anyway, as Gérard St. Jacques left a message that he won't be able to make it here until eight o'clock. Why don't you rest for a couple of hours and then we can meet in the library at four? That will give us a few moments to ourselves."

"That sounds fine, Philippe. Until then." She hurried up the stairs.

Jackie took a quick shower, slipped on her robe, and picked up a magazine from the desk to read. When she stretched out on her bed she had no idea how really exhausted she was. So it came as a shock when, a couple of hours later, she felt herself being gently shaken out of a deep sleep. She groggily opened her eyes.

"It's all right, *ma chère*. Don't be alarmed. It is a few minutes after four."

Before Jackie realized what was happening, Philippe Troyan was stretched out beside her on the bed, his arm snaking out to tightly grab her waist.

"Please, Philippe. Let me go." She wrenched his hand from her hip and practically rolled out of bed, racing directly into her private bathroom. She sank against the door. This was getting ridiculous. Then, catching her breath, she hurried to the sink, washed, combed her hair, and hastily slipped on the dress she'd left hanging on the bathroom hook. When she stepped out, Philippe was sitting patiently at the desk chair.

He smiled warmly and stood up as though nothing had ever happened. "Shall we go down to the library, *ma chère?*"

Peter was coming down the hall toward her door when she and Philippe stepped out of her bedroom. The look on his face was truly priceless.

Jackie couldn't help laughing. "Philippe just came upstairs to get me. I fell asleep."

"Oh," Peter said inanely. He was not used to being caught so completely off guard and found himself at a rare loss for words.

"How was your meeting with Fabert?" she asked pleasantly.

There was still that look of perplexity in his

expression. "I thought you were going to meet me there."

"I was tired."

"And now?"

"Perfectly rested, thanks," she said airily.

"Good." He turned to Philippe. "If you don't mind, Troyan, Jacqueline and I must take a ride over to Château Cardinet to discuss some unfinished business."

Troyan, not given much choice, merely nodded.

Jackie was too surprised to say anything.

"Back in the States this would be known as a white elephant." Peter grinned as Jackie stood in the middle of an enormous foyer that was sadly barren and gloomy.

"A white elephant crying out for some tender loving care," Jackie said, opening one of the wooden shutters to let some light in. The shutter sagged heavily on its hinges. Jackie bent down to pick up a large fragment of stained glass from one of the arched windowpanes.

"What a pity," she said.

"Careful."

Jackie set the shard down and strolled over to a large salon. Here the windows were uncovered, the light streaming in to reveal endless cobwebs, badly crumbling walls, and water-stained antique paneling. The furniture, what little there was of it, was literally on its last legs.

Peter followed her. "I guess the place is in pretty bad shape."

She whirled around to face him. "It needs a great deal of work and cleaning up, but . . . oh, Peter, I think it's magnificent. Absolutely *merveilleux*. Come on. I want to see every single nook and cranny of the place." She grabbed his hand and started for the next room.

"Hold on."

She stopped short.

"You really think it's—*merveilleux?*"

She smiled. "Your French is improving, monsieur. Yes. I do. Now, come on."

Filled with excitement and wonder, they began running up the once elegant, now creaking, chipped staircase, laughing like two kids on a treasure hunt. They wandered about the labyrinth of rooms on each of the three floors, shrieking with delight over the sheer quantity of space and the grandeur that once must have made the château a real showplace. They bemoaned the sadly crumbling walls, broken objets d'art, the handcarved balustrades that had been covered in ugly graying varnish. They thrilled to anything in the château that had weathered the rough waters of time and neglect. More than once they found themselves hopelessly lost and spent long minutes figuring their way through the maze of hallways.

"You'll need to make a map of the place," Jackie said, stepping into an exquisite tiny library back on the main floor. "Isn't this beautiful!" The room was the smallest in the château and the least destroyed. A lovely oak fireplace filled one wall of the room and bookcases lined with old books covered the rest of the wall space. A fine Oriental rug partially covered the floor, and two large, velvet-upholstered sofas faced each other across an inlaid coffee table. None of the furnishings were rare antiques by any means, but they were nonetheless attractive and added to the charm and coziness of the room.

"I guess," Peter said with a teasing smile, "deep down you'll always be a librarian at heart."

"Deep down I'll always be Jackie Archer." She shivered as he walked over to her and rested his hands lightly on her shoulders.

"It is freezing in here. I'll go see if I can scrounge up some wood for the fireplace."

"Okay." She ran her tongue over her dry lips.

Ten minutes later Peter returned with an armload of logs.

"There's a huge pile of wood in one of the sheds out back. It should be enough for the rest of this winter."

Jackie helped him set down the logs and watched from the couch as he tended the fire.

"It will warm up in a few minutes. That's the beauty of such a small room. It was probably the favorite of all the owners. I'd hate to think what the oil bills would be if the château had central heating. The last people who had the place, an elderly couple by the name of Vaneau, used this room, the kitchen, and one of the small bedrooms upstairs as their only quarters. Now I can see why."

"It would be a shame not to restore every square inch of the place," Jackie said. "Just think of the history within these walls. If I close my eyes I can picture what it must once have looked like. Can't you?"

Peter was kneeling in front of the fire. He looked over his shoulder at Jackie and smiled. She looked very beautiful, her head leaning back against the cushion, her long dark lashes brushing her rosy cheeks, her hair loose, tousled from the wind. He gazed at her, unable to turn his eyes away.

Jackie felt him staring. She looked across at him. "What's the matter?"

"We do have some unfinished business to deal with, you know." He stood up, walked to the couch, and sat down beside her.

Jackie closed her eyes again for a moment, her mind flashing an image of the two of them locked in each other's embrace in bed yesterday. When she opened her eyes again and looked at him, she was stunned by the intensity of her own desire for him.

She didn't say anything, but waited for him to gather her in his arms, even though she knew it made no more sense for the two of them today than it did yesterday. But instead of drawing her to him, Peter leaned back, stuck his feet up on the coffee table, and sighed.

"The thing is, Jackie . . . I'm nervous."

"You are?" Her tone of surprise made him laugh.

"Yes. Nervous. I've never let myself get . . . well, you know what I mean." He gave her a knowing glance and then stared down at his hands. "This would be a first. And I wish I knew it wasn't going to be a mistake."

Jackie touched his cheek. "Peter, it's a risk for both of us. I'm nervous too. I think I can understand what's frightening you. You've never really let yourself feel—"

He grabbed her hand, cutting her off. "Okay, Jackie. You win. I need you."

Jackie's heart started pounding, her body experiencing the most astounding rush of arousal. "Oh, Peter."

"I thought about it half the night. What makes sense to me is that you concentrate on the shipping end and take charge of all direct communications with distributors. And first thing tomorrow, I think you ought to start giving me French lessons. If I'm going to become a native son, then I need to start speaking my new native tongue, *n'est-ce pas?*" he grinned, his blue eyes sparkling.

Jackie stared at him, open mouthed. "Handle the shipping?"

He gave her a puzzled look. "I thought you'd like that. Don't forget about cousin Louis in California. He has a big vested interest in helping us with distribution in the States. He may not be my favorite relative, but he's going to be a big help to you. Don't worry about a thing. I have complete confidence in you."

When Jackie said nothing, Peter went on. "Things are really starting to look up, Jackie. Jean-Louis Marigny is going to meet with me next Thursday in Paris. He says he's willing to seriously consider an investment. If he does, we could get started this spring. His endorsement for Château Cardinet wines will immediately give them status. For a while there I admit I was afraid I might never get this vineyard off the ground—at least with me in charge."

Jackie's blank expression puzzled him. "I thought working with me was what you wanted," he said.

She brought herself sharply down to earth. After all, it was certainly a large part of what she wanted. She just hadn't been expecting a job offer at this particular moment. "I'm thrilled. Really. I guess my mind is still foggy from all the excitement of seeing the château. It's wonderful. I don't know what else to say . . . except that you won't be sorry, Peter." She stood up and walked over to the fire. "I love this place. I'll work day and night, I promise. Shipping, distributing, picking grapes—I'll even stomp them if you like." She came to an abrupt stop. "It just hit me that it won't be me stomping those grapes. It's going to be Jacqueline Armand." She sighed.

Peter put his arms around her. "I'm crazy about Jacqueline Armand." As her brow creased, he said, "Don't worry. Once everything is under way, we'll let Jackie Archer out of the closet. My guess is she'll charm this crowd as successfully as Mademoiselle Armand."

She grinned, her eyes shining. "Of course, we still need to see if Marigny will definitely invest. If not, we'll keep at it until we find others. He's not the only fish in the sea."

"I'm not worried. Just remember, though, I'm the boss here. What I say goes."

"A Santiago must reign at the helm of his own house," she said softly. "I understand, Peter. As long as we communicate openly and you're willing to listen to suggestions, even if you don't take them, we'll do fine together."

"Will we, Jackie?"

Her eyes shot up to study his expression. She'd misinterpreted him once already today. Was there really a seductive tinge to that last question? She didn't say anything, not wanting to fall into the trap again.

"Are you warming up?"

She dared do nothing but nod.

"Good." He unbuttoned her wool jacket and slipped it off her shoulders. Then he carefully unwound the scarf from her neck. Jackie's eyes never left his.

He dropped the scarf on the floor. "We still have some other unfinished business, Jackie. Don't you think?"

Again she nodded.

"We should finish it, *n'est-ce pas?*"

"*Oui,*" she murmured as he slipped his hands around her neck and tilted up her chin with his thumbs. He bent low and kissed her softly. Then he released her.

"That was nice." Jackie sighed, eyes closed. "Do it again?"

He smiled. "You mean, *encore?*"

Jackie opened her eyes. "*Encore.*"

"Certainement, ma chère." He kissed her again, this time more deeply.

"C'est bien?" he asked, before sliding his tongue across her parted lips.

"You're learning very quickly," she said, moving her arms around his neck. *"Encore."*

"With pleasure."

Before he met her lips she whispered, "That's *'avec plaisir.'* "

"Now I'll give you some French lessons," he murmured, pulling her tighter. "This is known as a French kiss." His mouth hungrily met hers, his tongue thrusting past her teeth and inside the warm recesses of her mouth. As they kissed passionately, they dropped to the floor. He kissed her again and again, his tongue slipping in and out of her mouth in a provocative, mind-shattering motion.

Peter's hands slipped under her sweater. In an instant he had released the clasp on her bra, tugged the sweater up, and cupped her breasts, his mouth leaving hers to savor first one taut nipple and then the other. He brought the same fiery excitement to her breasts as he had to her mouth. Slowly, erotically, he drew each nipple into his mouth, the tip of his tongue caressing, teasing, nibbling. With his fingertips he stroked her flat stomach, feeling the muscles quiver beneath the smooth, silken flesh.

Jackie pulled her sweater over her head and Peter helped her remove her opened bra. Then he gently lowered his lips to hers again, his hands moving to the snap on her slacks.

"I love undressing you, Jackie." He smiled seductively, drawing her pants down over her hips. "How do you say that in French?"

Jackie, barely conscious of anything but the way her body responded to his expert caresses, unbuttoned his shirt, and pulled it off, thrilling to the warmth of his chest against her palms. *"Je t'adore—"*

Her breathless words were halted by another passionate kiss. "Me too." His lips trailed over her chin, down the soft, tender center of her breastbone to her navel.

Jackie gasped in pleasure as Peter tenderly circled her navel with his tongue and then moved lower, his fingers gently stroking her inner thighs as her whole body arched and quivered under him, her fingers digging into his scalp. The rhythmic, persuasive movement of his tongue made her cry out in soft, whimpering half-words. When at last he returned to her lips, Jackie was trembling fiercely, her whole body raw with a burning need.

Peter rolled over, bringing her with him. Jackie pushed his hands away from her waist, and with a heated urgency tugged his pants off. She bent over him, kissing him, trailing her mouth across his chest and stomach, the tip of her tongue erotic and inviting. As he felt her warm breath and the tickling sensation of her hair against his thighs, he experienced a surge of arousal that took his breath away.

He pulled her up on top of him and pushed steadily inside her. Jackie gasped as they began moving together, driven by his powerful, insistent thrusts. Without even being aware of his shifting her position, she found her back pressed against his thighs, his legs bent to support her. Jackie's head tilted back, her breasts exposed for Peter's passionate exploration. Then, when she felt as though she were on fire, he tugged her to him, her breasts crushing against his chest as she felt herself being swept into the eye of the storm. She gave herself up completely to the sensations, letting herself whirl mindlessly, thrilling to the feel of Peter, hard and demanding, inside her. They clung to each other as they reached that final summit, their cries of ecstasy seeming to echo through the château.

Peter swept Jackie's luxuriant hair from her face and kissed her chastely. *"Merveilleux,"* he whispered. He kissed her again. "You're going to have to teach me more adjectives."

"I'll be happy to oblige," she said with a wicked little smile.

His hands moved languorously over her breasts. "The fire is dying out."

"I'm perfectly warm." His fingers toyed with her nipples. She laughed. "Hot."

"Hot? Mmm." He cradled her breasts in the palms of his hands. *"Chaud?"*

"Very good." She stretched like a contented kitten as his hands left her breasts and slid down to her slender hips.

"See what reading French sink-faucets will teach you?"

"Wait until you see what my instruction will

teach you." She grinned, letting her fingers glide over his chest.

"Class isn't over yet. How do you say, 'I'm crazy to make love to you again'?"

"Encore is all that's needed," she murmured with a soft, seductive smile. As she put her arms around his waist, Peter's lips captured hers once more.

CHAPTER EIGHT

Jackie and Peter just made it back to Château Vauvilliers in time to change into evening wear. Jackie looked smashing in her new black jersey cocktail dress, Peter very debonair in his black tuxedo. They hadn't planned on making a grand entrance, it just worked out that way; all eyes turned admiringly as they walked down the stairs.

Dinner that night was a subdued affair. There were six guests besides Jackie and Peter: Philippe's solicitor, Bernard Léon, his wife, Laurette, and son, André, Philippe's close friends Monsieur Gérard St. Jacques and his daughter, Emilie, and Edouard Racine, Philippe's business manager.

Once again, Philippe placed Jackie at his right. He was less effusive than he had been the previous evening, but then Jackie had been far more attentive at last night's meal. He continued, however, to be quite cordial and charming. Thinking only that she had spent the afternoon engaged in purely business matters, he believed himself still in the running for Jacqueline Armand's affections.

A servant poured out wine for each guest. Philippe lifted his glass. "We shall toast our new neighbors, Monsieur Santiago and Mademoiselle Armand, and wish them the utmost success for the Château Cardinet." He spoke in English out of respect for Peter.

All of the other guests raised their wine goblets, nodded their approval, and sipped. Jackie lifted her glass and beamed across the table at her new partner.

"Here's to you, Professor Higgins." She winked, leaving the others at the table bemused.

"And you, my fair lady," he replied with a grin, tapping her glass.

"So, Jacqueline," Philippe said as they set their glasses down, "what is your impression of the Château Cardinet? *C'est dommage*—a pity"—he smiled over at Peter—"to let such a valuable piece of property fall into ruin. During the war the Vichy government commandeered the château for a hospital. It suffered greatly during that period, I'm afraid. Then, in the fifties, François Dulac put a great deal of money into restoring the vineyard. Unfortunately, several bad years forced him to sell before he could do much about renovating the château itself. Since then, it has gone steadily downhill. I seriously wonder if it can ever be salvaged."

"I fell in love . . . with the château, Philippe. With everything about it, as a matter of fact. Peter and I are going to restore it to its former splendor," Jackie said, full of enthusiasm. Since she and Peter had left the château, she felt as though she were floating on air. Philippe's pessimism didn't begin to touch her.

"That will take a great deal of money, *ma chère.*"

"When the people of France discover the rare pleasure of a Château Cardinet Zinfandel," Peter said, "there will be enough profits to use some for the château. It is only a matter of patience and hard work."

"And we're both hard workers." Jackie smiled over at Peter.

Bernard Léon cleared his throat. He looked exactly like Jackie's idea of a French solicitor; a small man with a sallow complexion, a sharp, beaklike nose, and perpetually pinched lips, who dressed in very formal clothing. He peered through thick bifocals at Peter. "The vagaries of the wine business, monsieur, are countless. As you undoubtedly know, one poor season due to inclement weather, a sudden rainstorm or freeze, the rapid spread of any number of infestations—all of these factors perennially threaten the harvest. But I believe your greatest risks are twofold: introducing a wine that might, as you think, entrance the French consumer, but on the other hand might completely disinterest him; and, as I assume you will also do a good deal of exporting, you must contend with the international shippers and distributors, who have the power to make or break you. A poor distribution of your wines, a delayed shipment—*voilà!*" He spread his arms dramatically. "Zinfandel," he added, with what Jackie took as a note of pleasure, "must be drunk as a young wine. It can't afford to stand idly around."

"There are no gains without risks, Monsieur Léon," Jackie said.

"I understand, mademoiselle, that you are going to be in charge of shipping and distribution," Gérard St. Jacques commented, his expression somewhere between incredulous and amused.

Jackie turned to him in surprise. "How did you know?" She glanced across at Peter.

"Oh, we have big ears in the country. And I am a neighbor of Jean-Louis Marigny," St. Jacques replied. "We met for a short while before I came over here."

"I don't understand. How did Monsieur Marigny—"

"I mentioned it to him this afternoon." Peter shrugged, giving her what Jackie interpreted as a calculating smile.

She arched a brow but said nothing more about it. The issue might have fallen by the wayside, had Emilie St. Jacques not piped in at that moment.

"Claude Marigny is certainly optimistic. We had a drink this evening and I must say, in all the years I've known Claude, this is the first time he's shown such enthusiasm—for work, anyway. Although, I am afraid, Monsieur Santiago, that Claude is not noted for a great deal of—how do you say it—fortitude?"

Edouard Racine, Philippe's business manager, laughed. "True enough, Emilie. But I think Jean-Louis will see to it that Claude works hard. I'm sure he's grown weary of his only son being little more than a playboy."

"I wonder," said Madame Léon, "what it will be like for the carefree Claude Marigny to put in a hard day's work."

"I think you are being too harsh, Madame Léon," Emilie said. "Claude tells me it was his suggestion that he become involved in Château Cardinet. As he tells it, he was a great influence on his father's decision. You are most fortunate to have stirred Claude's interest." Emilie focused her gaze on Jackie as she made the last comment.

"Decision?" Jackie stared straight at Peter.

"Well, the details are still to be worked out, of course. I don't think we need to go into it right now."

Jackie was about to question him further when Philippe took her hand. "I think we've discussed Claude Marigny quite enough. His parents are good friends of mine. I don't know if Jean-Louis was quite fair to foist his son on you, but it will be very good for Claude to learn what it takes to make a vineyard blossom. I hope, though, that this is not another of his whims. The last one was a firm that published romance novels. But it lasted all of a few months before it went under." He laughed derisively. "You would think, with all Marigny's own romances, that he would have at least done well in that pursuit. And before then . . . but there is no point to listing his failures. All I can do is caution you and Monsieur Santiago to realize Claude has never before been seriously interested in the vineyards and therefore has little but his father's backing to offer Château Cardinet. I'm sure you will find a position for him that—will suit his abilities. And now, enough said on that subject. Tell me some of your plans for redecorating the château, Jacqueline. Will you cope first with the grounds or the building itself?"

Jackie was in no mood for discussing interior decorating. Her blood was boiling. So that's why Peter had suddenly decided to ask her to work at the château. The three men had struck a deal this afternoon—and Jacqueline was the door prize. Peter couldn't very well let her leave when Claude was holding the winning raffle ticket, so handsomely paid for by his father. The other dinner guests sensed the tension and everyone, including Peter, became intent on seeking safe topics of conversation. Jackie said almost nothing and her appetite vanished before the succulent *entrecôte à la bordelaise* arrived at the table.

Shortly after dessert she asked to be excused, begging a headache that was quite legitimate. She didn't go up to her room. She went to Peter's instead. She doubted he would seek her out to explain matters, but she had every intention of getting some straight answers before the night was out.

It was past midnight when Jackie heard the last car pull out of the driveway. She stopped pacing and sat down in a straight-backed chair to wait Peter's arrival. Minutes passed.

By twelve-thirty Peter had still not shown up. Jackie's anger set her to pacing again. Finally, she sat down in a more comfortable armchair. By one in the morning she was sound asleep.

Peter, dreading a confrontation with Jackie, fortified himself with several Cognacs before saying good-night and going upstairs to bed. By then he'd come to the conclusion that there was no need to deal with additional problems this evening. He would discuss everything with Jackie tomorrow. After all, he had done nothing so terrible. He'd merely omitted mentioning that Jean-Louis Marigny had already agreed to invest in Château Cardinet. Of course, there was the matter of Claude Marigny. Jean-Louis was thrilled that his son wanted to participate in the vineyard. It had been the factor that had finally swayed him to Peter's court. And Peter knew Claude was thrilled that he would get the opportunity to work side by side with Jackie.

He had some difficulty navigating the steps, but refused to acknowledge that he was more than a little intoxicated. He started for his room, and then came to an abrupt halt. Doing a wobbly about-face he headed straight for Jackie's room.

He threw open her door and shut it securely behind him.

"All right. I've come to confess. It's true Marigny has already agreed to invest in the château. Claude Marigny went on and on all afternoon about how wonderful an experience it would be for him to be involved in the restoring of Château Cardinet. He also couldn't stop raving about you. How clever, hardworking, determined you are and what a great influence you'd be. I know exactly what you're thinking, Jackie," he said loudly, his words becoming slurred, "but it isn't true. Claude and his father had nothing to do with my decision. I'd already decided—after last night. I swear." He tripped over a chair leg. "Well . . . do you believe me, princess?" He sat down on the edge of the bed.

"All right, don't answer. But I swear the only reason I didn't tell you the truth was because I knew if I told you about Claude and then asked you to work with me, you would have immediately jumped to the conclusion that you have jumped to. There." He hiccuped. "Does that make any sense?"

He yawned and rubbed his eyes. "You were the one who said you wanted us to communicate openly. What kind of communication is this? Come on, Jackie. I know you're not sleeping. You're too angry to sleep. Talk to me."

He slipped off the bed onto his knees. His head felt cloudy and he was having trouble focusing. "Jackie, this afternoon . . . making love to you . . . it was so wonderful. I—I've known for a while that I wanted you to stay—to help me. It has nothing to do with Claude Marigny. I swear I would have asked you anyway. Jackie?"

He pulled himself up and reached his arm out over the bed. "Jackie?" He felt all around with his hands. His head cleared long enough for him to realize she wasn't there. Then he felt a sharp wave of dizziness and passed out on the bed.

Jackie woke with a start. Every muscle in her body ached. She carefully unfolded her cramped legs from the armchair, rubbed her stiff neck, and groggily glanced at her watch. She was stunned to discover that it was seven-twenty in the morning. Her eyes darted to Peter's bed. It was empty and unslept in.

It took her less than five seconds to conclude that Peter and his pretty dinner partner Emilie St. Jacques had passed the early-morning hours together. A hasty conclusion, but it made sense, given her growing belief in Peter Santiago's devious nature. After all, he was trying to wangle a big investment from Emilie's father. She would not put it past Peter to assume, as Philippe had suggested, that lovely Emilie might be as persuasive with her father as Claude had been with his. Or maybe Peter was simply up for another little fling.

Jackie shivered as a bitter chill coursed through her. She felt ruthlessly jealous and wanted to strike out at him, but a voice inside her head told her the smartest thing to do would be to pack up immediately, return to Paris, and forget everything that had happened to her over the last two weeks. Hot tears stung her eyes as she started down the hall, still unsure of which course of action she was going to take.

Peter rolled over in bed and stretched. His eyes sprang open when he realized he was still dressed in evening clothes. A sharp pain shot from one side of his head to the other. He groaned and closed his eyes again. Opening them more slowly this time, he glanced around.

Ignoring the piercing pain at his temples, he sat up abruptly. Jackie wasn't there. He walked over to her closet. The black jersey cocktail dress she'd worn last night was missing. He stared absently across the room.

His conclusion took a good ten seconds to materialize, but then his mind wasn't working as fast as Jackie's due to one hell of a hangover. It was obvious that she was dealing with her anger at him by spending the night with Philippe Troyan. Troyan had been making a play for her for the past two weeks, coming on especially hot and heavy this weekend.

Peter remembered Troyan going upstairs early last night, leaving him still sipping Cognacs in the library with André Léon and Emilie St. Jacques. Peter had no trouble picturing Troyan heading straight for Jackie's room. The man had been there only that afternoon. He probably knocked —no, maybe he felt comfortable enough to walk right in. He'd see Jackie was upset and invite her to his room—for a comforting little chat, no doubt. Peter had to admit it seemed wholly unlike her to go along with Troyan's game, but maybe he didn't know Jackie Archer as well as he'd thought.

He considered barging into Troyan's quarters and confronting Jackie, but he refused to give in to such a base emotion as outraged jealousy. Not the cool, independent Peter Santiago. He was damned if he was going to give her the satisfaction of knowing she'd gotten to him. He was having his own troubles dealing with it. How had he let it happen?

Peter had never been in this boat before. He felt baffled, angry, hurt . . . even scared. Alien feelings for someone who'd always thought he was immune to the tumultuous confusions of romantic love. He rubbed his eyes vigorously and tried to clear his mind.

He should end it here and now. Tell Jackie to forget the whole deal—Marigny, too, if it came to that.

Then he thought about Jackie racing hand in hand with him through the halls of Château Cardinet, laughing and joking. He pictured her in his arms, making love before the open fire. He sighed. One thing seemed clear. This golden opportunity of his was starting to dull rapidly.

Peter stepped out of Jackie's room still completely confused about what he ought to do.

"*Bonjour*, Monsieur Santiago. Did you sleep well?"

Peter looked to his right to find an amused Emilie St. Jacques standing in her robe, eyeing him quizzically from her bedroom door. Her gaze trailed down his crumpled black evening jacket as he stepped away from Jackie's bedroom and walked over.

For a moment Peter put aside his anger and let out a small, dry laugh. "No, mademoiselle. As a matter of fact I slept very poorly."

"I'm sorry to hear that," she replied, her amusement deepening.

Peter smiled ruefully. *"C'est la vie."*

His smile faded abruptly as he glanced down the hall to see Jackie, shoes in hand, still wearing that sexy black jersey dress, heading straight for him.

When Jackie saw Peter and Emilie St. Jacques cozily conferring at Emilie's doorway, it was the last straw. She stormed up to him, and before Peter knew what hit him, Jackie's palm had smacked across his cheek.

"Salaud!" she hissed, before storming past them to her room.

Emilie, having realized her mistaken conclusion about Peter and Jackie's having just spent the night in each other's embrace, threw her head back and laughed. "Roughly, she called you a bastard. Shall I translate more precisely for you?"

Peter, rubbing his cheek, shook his head. "No. I think I got the message close enough. Excuse me. I have my own message . . ." He didn't bother finishing the sentence.

Jackie was standing in the middle of her bedroom, her back to him when he stormed in.

"I know how angry you are about Marigny. You think I only asked you to stay on because of him, but that doesn't condone your behavior," he practically growled. "Don't you think it's stooping a bit low to climb into bed with your host only a few hours after you made love to me? Or are you making up for lost time? Prim Ohio librarian turned—"

"Go-go dancer?" She pivoted around and

stared at him, her big green eyes sparkling, a broad smile on her lips. And then she leaned against her bedpost and broke into a peal of laughter.

Peter was completely stunned. For a second he thought she'd gone over the edge into hysteria. He rushed to her and grabbed her shoulders, shaking her. "What the hell is the matter with you, Jackie?"

She opened the palm of her hand and produced his bow tie.

He stared down at it, still not understanding what was going on.

Getting the laughter under control, she tugged free of his grip. "You were here the whole night," she said, as though she had come to some amazing revelation.

"You're damn right I was here. And you weren't. I came in here around one in the morning to straighten out the whole issue about Marigny only to discover the room was empty. I guess I fell asleep." He failed to credit his passing out to all the Cognacs he'd consumed earlier. "I woke up alone in your bed this morning," he said pointedly. "So, how about coming clean, Goldilocks? Whose bed did you sleep in last night?" He glared at her, his voice filled with venomous sarcasm.

"No one's." She smiled innocently.

"I suppose you're going to tell me you wandered around the grounds all night . . . so distraught you didn't even bother to take your coat," he sneered.

"I was distraught," she snapped, forgetting her

relief at discovering that Peter hadn't spent the night with Emilie St. Jacques. "You lied to me. You had no intention of asking me to stay on until after you learned how taken Claude Marigny was with the idea of working with me. If you didn't have me stay, Claude would never have shown the slightest interest in Château Cardinet and you know it. He talked his father into it. Oh, I'm sure Jean-Louis was thrilled to see his son so enthusiastic about the wine business for once. Talk about golden opportunities. I guess this was one you couldn't turn down either—even if it meant having to tolerate my staying on."

"All right," he admitted. "Claude's interest in working at the vineyard, whatever the reasons, helped to hurry along the negotiations with his father. But the old man was enthusiastic about investing before he realized the extra gain of giving Claude some sorely needed on-the-job training."

"On-the-job training? Is that what he thinks Claude's going to get? Ha! That's a laugh. You know damn well Claude's only interest in Château Cardinet is in 'winning *ma chérie*'s affections,' as he so charmingly puts it. He loves the pursuit, but I guarantee he holds strongly to your own philosophy of keeping his relationships brief and meaningless. I suppose you're hoping that he'll grow bored quickly. Then you can dump him, dump me, and have everything come out just the way you wanted. Well, you can take your job, your ten percent, and your—your bow tie!" She tossed it at him, swallowing hard to fight back tears. "I could have dealt with your little manipulation if you hadn't used me." She threw up her arms in disgust. "What an idiot I was! I actually believed you when you said you needed me. I believed that when we made love it meant something. But you, Claude, Philippe—you're all alike. Every one of you charges out and takes what you want. And when you're finished, you wash your hands and walk away. I'm sick of the whole lot of you. Oh, gaining admittance into the aristocracy has been quite an eye opener. I've learned a great deal, namely that I much prefer honest toil and my little garret flat in Paris where I had no one to worry about but myself and Gogo."

She strode over to the closet and began pulling her clothes off the hangers. She dumped the whole armload on a chair and rummaged through them, selecting a pair of gray slacks, a sweater, and a simple beige wool dress. She folded the dress and put it in her overnight bag. "I'll take these as payment in full for my starring role. The rest are yours."

"What are you going to do?"

"First, I'm going to get out of this dress and add it to your collection. And then I'm going back to Paris and find myself a very ordinary, uncomplicated job."

Peter walked over to her. "I don't want you to do that."

She glared up at him. "What's the matter? Nervous because my walking out will blow the deal with Marigny?"

He took the suitcase from her hand and pulled

her over to the bed. "Sit down." He wasn't in the mood to take no for an answer and tugged her down, protesting.

"You've had the floor, princess. Now it's my turn." He expected an argument and was thrown off a bit by her silence. "Okay. Good. Now, first of all, I've known things between you and me . . ." He ran his fingers nervously through his hair. "I've felt something for you right from the start. And I'm going to give it to you straight: I'm not happy about it. I came to France with only one goal in mind, to make Château Cardinet into one of the best vineyards in the world. I had everything planned, knew just what I needed, just what I wanted. I've never let myself get close to anyone, Jackie. I'll be truthful with you. I think I make a real lousy bet. I'm egotistical and stubborn, I like running the whole show. But then you come along"—he smiled tenderly—"not even my type. And look what happens to me. I start thinking about you at all kinds of odd moments, dreaming about you, wanting more and more desperately to reach out and grab you. I made up my mind yesterday morning to ask you to work with me. But I knew long before that I wasn't really going to be able to let you walk out of my life. I do need you. If you didn't mean something to me would I be standing here right now torn with jealousy and rage that you spent the night—"

"I spent the night in your room, you fool," she said wearily. "I waited for you all evening. I woke up this morning in your armchair feeling like a pretzel. When I saw your bed made up, all I could think was that you'd spent the night with Emilie St. Jacques. And then . . . seeing you smiling at each other by her open door . . . I was convinced. It never even crossed my mind that you'd be here until I saw my crumpled bed and your bow tie lying there."

Peter grinned. "So that was what the whopper of a slap was all about." He laughed. "What an insane comedy of errors, Jackie. Here I was, livid that you'd spent the night with Philippe, and you were convinced I'd spent the night with Emilie, Emilie saw me walk out of your room this morning and assumed I'd spent the night with you— that is, until she saw you stomp over and slug me. I bet she's still trying to figure that one out."

Jackie managed a weak smile.

"Don't you believe me yet, Jackie?"

"I need to think about it, Peter. About the whole thing. You said yourself you're a lousy bet. I'm going to head back to Paris, rent a room, and spend some time considering the odds very carefully."

"You have no money."

"I have a plane ticket to Ohio that I can cash in. I've come through this much and survived. I figure I'll do all right . . . one way or another."

"I'll collect my stuff and drive you back."

"There's a bus in town. Just drive me there. You ought to stay around and talk with Gérard St. Jacques. Or his daughter. Philippe says she's the best bet." Her voice was tight, the distrust still evident.

"I've told you all my worst traits, Jackie. Seducing women for personal gain isn't one of them." His own voice was equally tight. Then he strode across the room and walked out the door, Jackie staring after him. She picked up the bow tie that he'd put back on the bed. As miserable as she felt, a tiny smile creased the corners of her lips.

CHAPTER NINE

Jackie stuck one toe gingerly into the plastic bucket of steaming hot water. Deciding it was perfect, she settled herself into the worn flowered armchair, hiked up the hem of her terry robe, and immersed both of her aching feet. She'd almost forgotten what that kind of pain was like. But three straight days of pounding the pavement again had brought it back posthaste, along with an ample assortment of blisters.

Jackie cast a rueful glance around her miniscule hotel room, her eyes resting on the torn, faded wallpaper, the lumpy mattress, and the dismal excuse for furnishings that amounted to the chair she was sitting on, a lopsided bureau, and a metal desk beneath the one window in the room. Quite a comedown from her enormous, elegant boudoir at the Château Vauvilliers.

She'd made up her mind her first day back in Paris to find a job and do her best to forget Peter Santiago, Château Cardinet, and the fictitious Jacqueline Armand. No more games, no more pretenses, no more heartache. Fired as she had been by anger, suspicion, and confusion, it had seemed the only sensible solution at the time.

Unexpectedly, tears slipped down her cheeks. She sniffed in a most unaristocratic fashion, wiping her eyes with the sleeve of her robe. Gogo fluttered about in his cage. He landed on his trapeze and began singing.

"It's useless, Gogo. I'm not in the mood to be cheered up."

She was miserable. As much as she told herself to forget Peter, she couldn't keep him out of her mind for more than a few minutes at a time. She had come to Paris, France, and fallen hopelessly, foolishly, in love. And now it was over, the whole magical, crazy escapade finished. Only, Jackie couldn't end it in her mind. She leaned over toward the bureau and flicked on the radio, hoping the loud music would obliterate her sad thoughts.

There was a light knock on the door, a brief pause, then a firmer rap. Jackie frowned. It was probably the man next door come to complain about the noise. She lowered the volume, hoping that would suffice. She had no desire to step out of the soothing water to answer the door.

Another knock. Jackie was reaching for her towel, resigned to the disturbance, when a low, husky voice speaking in French on the other side of the door made her freeze in utter panic.

"Jacqueline? I know you are in there. Please, I must talk to you."

Claude Marigny? How the hell had he found her? Jackie looked around the room frantically. She couldn't let him in. She couldn't let him see her looking like . . . like a washed-out hausfrau. She stared mournfully down at her bathrobe, her feet still stuck in the bucket of water. She ran her fingers distractedly through her tangled hair.

"Jacqueline. Open the door."

"Oh, God," she muttered, praying he would grow weary of standing there and go away. But he kept knocking persistently and calling her name. She stepped out of the water and stared toward the door, at a complete loss what to do. Gogo didn't help matters any, his singing taking on new gusto.

She considered the window, but remembered it was jammed shut. She was having trouble thinking straight. What did he want? What was he doing here? How had he tracked her down?

Then, just as she was trying to decide between hiding under the bed or throwing on her clothes and facing the music, the knocking ceased and Claude's footsteps moved down the hallway. She let out a loud sigh and fell back into the chair.

That was exactly the position she was in when, two minutes later, the key turned carefully in the lock and Claude stepped into the room, the curious concierge hovering in the hallway. Claude closed the door in the man's face and stared into Jackie's astonished green eyes.

"I told him you might be ill and he was kind enough to let me in," Claude said casually.

Jackie gaped at him, unable to get her vocal cords to work.

"You shouldn't have run off like that." He

switched to English, which was Jackie's first clear confirmation that the jig was up.

"You know who I am, then." Her expression turned to one of resignation and she did away with the phony French accent.

He smiled. "Shall I tell you a little secret, *chérie?*" He walked over and knelt down beside her, hastily shifting his position upon finding his knee resting in a puddle of water. He slid the bucket out of the way. Jackie could do nothing but stare at him.

"I knew all along."

Jackie's mouth fell open. Then she muttered, "I don't believe you."

"It's true. Oh, don't get me wrong. You were magnificent. It was I who was the fool. I should have been more observant all those weeks you worked for me at *Toujours Amour, ma petite.* When I saw you at Troyan's château, it hit me like —how do you say it in Ohio—a ton of bricks, what an extraordinary woman you were."

"You're lying. You were fooled. What about that line that we were lovers in a past life? Why would you pretend not to know the truth? Why not simply confront me, reveal me as an imposter?"

He laughed. "Because, *chérie*, I fell madly in love with Mademoiselle Armand. If I had told you I knew the truth, she would have vanished. It was a charming pretense. I thoroughly enjoyed chasing after the enchanting French temptress from Lausanne."

Jackie was speechless. Not to mention feeling exposed and humiliated.

"But," Claude said tenderly, "I will gladly chase after Jackie Archer as well."

"How did you find me?"

"I hired a private detective. He had little trouble tracing you, especially as I guessed you'd be registered as Miss Archer. And I doubted you'd be staying at the Ritz."

He glanced around the room and smiled at her. Jackie bent her head.

"Please go away, Claude. I feel dreadful. I look dreadful."

He tilted up her chin. "Nothing that a good meal in a fine restaurant won't fix. How about the Côte d'Or?"

"No," she wailed, breaking down completely.

Claude was stunned. "Please, *chérie*. It's all right. We can go somewhere else. Only please stop crying. Jacqueline. Jacqueline, please tell me what I can do."

"Stop being so nice to me. I deceived you. Peter deceived you. You should be furious."

Claude laughed. "I'm not furious in the least. You know me, I like a good joke. You were wonderful. And, as a bonus for all of this, Santiago pulled out of the deal with my father and I have a reprieve from the vineyards for a while. We can stay in Paris together and—"

"Peter pulled out of the deal?" Jackie stared at Claude in amazement.

Claude shrugged. "He came over on Sunday . . . quite agitated. He told my father he would prefer to look for other investors. I guess he did not feel I would be a great asset to his company. Which, I assure you, *chérie*, did not offend me in the least. We both know Santiago is a hard taskmaster and I doubt we would have done well together. Besides, if you stay in Paris, I'll come up with some plan to stay with you."

Jackie smoothed her hair distractedly, no longer concerned about her disheveled appearance. "I've got to speak to Peter." She stood up. "Will you give me a lift to his apartment? I'll only be a few minutes getting ready. Why don't you wait downstairs for me?" She was already ushering him to the door, oblivious to his look of consternation.

"But *chérie*, we were going to have dinner. I want to—"

"I appreciate the invitation, Claude. Perhaps another time." She opened the door. Then, as he was stepping out, she caught his arm. "Does your father know?"

"Know what?"

"About me?"

Claude grinned. "Peter did mention something about it."

Jackie narrowed her gaze. "So that's how you—"

He raised his right hand. "No, *chérie*. I swear I knew all along about your charming pretense. You'll have to trust my word."

Jackie laughed. "I suppose I'll never know the truth. Not that it matters anymore. I'm just glad the act is over."

Claude started out the door and paused. "Oh. I should warn you that Philippe Troyan knows the truth as well. My father felt it only right to tell him. I'm afraid he's not as taken with practical jokes as I am. He went quite apoplectic there for a while. I think he was counting on Mademoiselle Armand's funds to help him out of debt."

"I suppose all those alimony payments to his former wives must keep his pockets quite empty." Jackie grinned. "He should count his blessings that he didn't sweep me off my feet. My dowry would have really given him apoplexy. Besides, I've no doubt saved him from struggling to come up with yet another alimony bill." She started to close the door, but Claude stood his ground.

"I'll wait for you, *chérie,* but I must admit I am not pleased to deliver you into the arms of another man. Unless it is purely business?"

Jackie didn't answer. She only smiled.

Claude shrugged. "I don't discourage easily, *chérie.*"

She laughed. "That I believe, Claude. My present appearance would certainly have discouraged many a determined suitor."

His smile was seductive. "Perhaps I can talk you out of . . ."

She shook her head.

"Very well." He sighed. "Another time."

Jackie closed the door after him and flew around the room getting dressed. She opted for the charcoal wool slacks and the teal blue sweater, having stained her one good dress with

Poupon mustard at lunch that day. She ran a comb through her hair, dabbed on some lipstick, and tugged on her boots. She winced as a blister on her ankle rubbed against the leather, but she didn't stop to hunt for a bandage.

Twenty minutes later Claude reluctantly pulled up in front of Peter's apartment building.

"Are you sure I can't talk you into having dinner first, *chérie?*"

But Jackie was already out the door. She leaned down for a moment and threw him a kiss. Then she rushed off to the entrance.

She had left her key in Peter's apartment on Sunday when she returned for Gogo and her few belongings. That meant if Peter wasn't home, she would have to sit about the lobby and wait for him. It suddenly struck her that he could very well still be in Bordeaux.

The doorman told her Peter was out, but that he had been in the apartment a few hours ago. The usually taciturn guard was in a magnanimous mood tonight. When Jackie said she'd misplaced her key, he generously offered to let her in.

She stepped into the darkened apartment and switched on the light. As she stood in the small foyer, it belatedly dawned on her that she wasn't really certain why she had come. Or what she wanted. When Claude had told her Peter had turned down Marigny's deal, her immediate thought had been that it was because of her. But what if Peter had gotten a better deal—one that was unencumbered? Claude had been right about one thing: Jackie couldn't imagine him and

Peter getting along in a work situation. They were on opposite ends of the pole, Claude always exerting himself to put in the least effort possible and Peter willing to go to any lengths to achieve what he wanted.

She walked into the living room and poured herself a Cognac. It was odd to be back here. A strange blend of feeling as if she didn't belong, yet feeling at home. She wondered what Peter's reaction would be when he walked in and found her there.

Jackie carefully pulled off her boots and sat down on the sofa. She slowly sipped her drink, trying to relax. But she continued to feel tense and keyed up. Perhaps she shouldn't have come. After all, Peter, unlike Claude, hadn't gone looking for her. Maybe he was just as happy to have put an end to the whole foolish game, to be rid of Claude and her.

She gulped down the drink, then quickly realized it would go straight to her head on her empty stomach. She hadn't had any dinner, and in an effort to stretch her meager funds, hadn't eaten particularly well for the past few days. Not that she'd had much of an appetite, she'd felt too depressed.

She heard the front door open while she was munching an apple in the kitchen. Quickly chewing up a large chunk, she padded across the floor on bare feet and stepped back into the living room.

Peter stared at her from the other end of the

room, while she hastily tried to swallow her food. She set the apple down awkwardly on the bar.

"Hello," she said cautiously.

Peter continued examining her.

"The doorman let me in."

He nodded. "He told me."

"Then why do you look . . . so surprised?" Her hand went to her hair. "Were you expecting the carefully groomed Jacqueline Armand? I'm sorry to disappoint you, but I've decided to return to my true self."

He walked over to her, his gaze curious. Confused by his expression, she stiffened. "I guess I shouldn't have come." The apple, perched at the edge of the bar, fell to the floor. She started to bend down for it, but Peter caught her elbow.

"I had a meeting with St. Jacques this afternoon," he said, a glimmer of a smile curving the corners of his lips.

Jackie didn't know what to say. His remark threw her further off balance.

Peter, still gripping her arm, continued. "As it turns out, he's a member of a consortium that is willing to consider a sizable investment in Château Cardinet."

"That's wonderful," she murmured.

"They would prefer that I stick to Médoc wine and forget about the Zinfandel. They feel it's too risky."

"What did you tell them?"

"I have another meeting tomorrow with the whole group. I intend to convince them of the merits of my plan." He studied her heart-shaped face, her small, upturned nose, her delicately shaped cheekbones, the soft, natural flush on her cheeks, and those large eyes shimmering like rare emeralds. "I sure could use some help."

"You could?" She gave him a swift glance.

He bent down, brushed the hair from her forehead, and kissed her tenderly. "I could."

"But if Jean-Louis Marigny knows about me," Jackie said, "so must St. Jacques. I won't be able to woo the group as Jacqueline Armand."

"He's expecting to meet with me and Jackie Archer."

"But . . ."

Peter slipped a piece of paper out of his pocket. He showed it to Jackie. Scrawled across it was her address at the Hôtel Delambre. He grinned at her. "We almost had another of our crazy mishaps. I finally tracked you down this evening. Which was fortunate, since I'd told St. Jacques the two of us would be in his Paris office tomorrow at three P.M. A half hour ago I was standing in one of the most dreadful little dumps in all of Paris. I would have spent the night there waiting for you, but I figured out, after a hefty bribe to the concierge, that you'd gone off with Claude. I was furious and stormed out."

Jackie laughed. "I asked Claude to take me here. And I was determined to stay put until you walked in that door."

"We're going to have to do something about these farcical mixups. You'd better move back here with me."

Jackie hesitated. "What about your being a lousy bet?"

"That's still true, princess," he admitted with a smile.

She turned away, not sure her mind was clear enough to pursue this shift in the conversation. "How does St. Jacques feel about the fact that I'm not Mademoiselle Armand?"

"He's a businessman, Jackie. He decided we both had a lot of guts, which he feels we'll need to pull Château Cardinet out of oblivion. Besides, Emilie found the stunt very amusing and softened the initial shock for her father."

"I see."

Peter grinned. "We both have a very jealous streak running down our back, princess."

"I wish I believed I had as little cause for mine as you have for yours," Jackie retorted. "I think we ought to move a little more slowly this time, Peter. I'll go with you to the meeting with St. Jacques tomorrow, but I'd better head back home tonight."

"You can't be serious, Jackie. I wouldn't call your fleabag of a room at the Delambre home if it was the last place left standing in Paris."

"I'm the person who spent three months in that cold-water flat, remember? Anyway, it's romantic to suffer in Paris. I wouldn't dream of missing out on that opportunity." She grinned.

"How much suffering do you need to do?"

"I'm not sure yet." She bent down and picked up the half-eaten apple.

"Are you hungry? Or are you into suffering starvation as well as deprivation?"

She laughed. "I've suffered enough starvation. I'm famished."

"Stay put. I'll run down for some sandwiches."

"Peter—" she started to protest.

"Jackie, we should spend some time going over our strategy for tomorrow's meeting. St. Jacques and his associates are tough cookies." He walked across the room, picked up his coat, and grinned at her. "Besides, you look lousy. But I'll fix that up," he added with a wink and headed out the door.

Jackie poured herself a second Cognac to try to stop the trembling sensation in her body, but she had little chance to sort through any of her feelings, as Peter was back from the charcuterie in record time. He set the thin plastic bag down on the coffee table and unloaded an exquisite loaf of French bread, a large round of Camembert cheese, and a bottle of Château Maiffret Haut-Médoc.

He laughed as she eyed the label. "Jean-Louis Marigny's vineyards produce a fine wine. And I picked the bottle as a show of trust. Claude Marigny isn't your type anyway."

"I'm not your type either," she reminded him.

"That was before I discovered you go beyond a type." He took the bottle from her hand. "You are a one-of-a-kind model, princess."

Jackie's heart took a little skip. She smiled. *"Merci."*

He kissed her mouth, her cool lips trembling

beneath his. She gently pushed him from her, surprised at the undisguised look of sadness on his face.

"I meant what I said about moving slower this time." Her voice was soft, tender. "We've been too impulsive. It's gotten me in some awkward difficulties—and some painful ones."

He started to speak, but she cut him off. "I know what you're going to say. It was my daring to be impulsive that brought me to Paris in the first place. That much I don't regret for an instant." She hesitated. "But I don't want to spend my time here nursing a broken heart. And you, Monsieur Santiago, have a very strong hold on this heart of mine. One wrong move and you could do some serious damage."

"Okay." His expression softened. "I'll handle you with care, princess. We'll take things one step at a time."

"Good." She smiled. "Then feed me before I pass out from that second glass of Cognac I drank to steady my nerves while you were out."

She sat cross-legged in the armchair, accepting a large wedge of cheese and a piece of bread from Peter. She was determined to keep a safe distance while they ate, afraid that the nourishment might weaken her own resistance. Peter had never looked more handsome. She watched him unobtrusively as he concentrated on opening the bottle of wine. His dark hair fell jauntily over his brow as his head tilted forward slightly. She noticed that his eyes seemed a deeper blue this evening, more hypnotic, with tiny creases radiating from the corners. His lips struck her as more sensual, his cheekbones stronger, more defined. And his body . . . she couldn't keep her mind from drifting back to their lovemaking in the château, remembering with an almost painful clarity how his flesh had felt against her hands, her lips, the tremor of his muscles in response to her caresses.

She took an overlarge swallow of wine, her face, already warm, turning scarlet as she burst into a fit of coughing. Peter rushed over, took the glass from her hand, and thumped her several times on the back. "Take it easy, princess. Small sips. Did you forget everything I taught you?"

That was just the problem. She hadn't forgotten anything. The coughing subsided, but as he sat perched on the arm of her chair, his palm gently massaging her back, she felt an almost irrepressible urge to pull him down to her. Peter squeezed her shoulder.

"Are you okay?"

She managed a little nod.

He bent down and kissed her ear. Jackie felt her body move against him.

"You'd better eat something." He stood up and walked back to the sofa.

Peter had noticed her subtle movement and realized it would not take much to manipulate the situation in his favor. But, despite his own needs and desire for her, he had to agree with Jackie's decision to take things a bit slower this time—for both their sakes.

These past three days had been dreadful for him. When he'd left Jackie at the train station on

Sunday, he'd tried to comfort himself with the notion that her leaving was for the best, silently arguing that he had been right in the first place about running the show all alone. He didn't need these complications. He didn't want any commitments or obligations to anyone. It had been a foolish moment of weakness that had made him ask her to stay on. He had let his emotions get in the way of his better judgment. It was just as well that she'd fled, believing his only reason for asking her to work with him had been because of that fool Claude Marigny.

Then, driving back from the station, he'd felt an overwhelming sense of loss that made his hands tremble on the steering wheel. He'd had to pull the car over and get a grip on himself. The sadness quickly switched to anger, anger at himself for letting Jackie get under his skin so thoroughly. Imagine, he told himself, what she could have done to him if she'd stayed. She would have started by suggesting changes, insisting she have her say, then end up making demands and trying to wrench control out from under him. Yes, he'd insisted, it was good riddance.

He'd spent hours driving around, trying to resolve his feelings. In the end he'd gone back for his bags at Troyan's, fighting against the sadness as he folded in Jackie's clothes along with his own. He knew what he had to do. He drove over to see Jean-Louis Marigny and canceled the deal. Monday morning he was back in Paris, and by Tuesday he'd built up his courage to start searching for Jackie, knowing he had to try to convince her he did need her, even though he was scared as hell. He was at his wit's end when he finally discovered she was registered at that sleazy hotel on the rue Delambre; and then the raw anguish when he'd thought she'd gone off with Marigny. He'd practically hugged René, the doorman, when he said he'd let Jackie into the apartment. Seeing her again had forced him to acknowledge how totally vital she had become to him.

"Why is St. Jacques so opposed to the Zinfandel?" Jackie asked, trying to ignore the intense study Peter was giving her from the sofa.

He rubbed his eyes in an attempt to clear his mind of the enticingly erotic thoughts that had begun to surface. He took a deep breath and tried to focus on business. "For one thing, he's concerned about the vines Morgan is prepared to ship us. St. Jacques believes they present too big a risk. I've talked to Louis on the phone. He agreed to insure the shipment for its full replacement value. If worse comes to worst, we'd have the insurance money to try again, or we could give up on the Zinfandel and focus solely on Médoc."

"Will that satisfy St. Jacques?"

"I don't know. I think his underlying worry is that I'm an American vintner who's brash, impulsive, and filled with a bunch of newfangled ideas that will turn Château Cardinet topsy-turvy. His fear is that I'll turn out to be indiscriminating and that I'll sacrifice quality for quantity. Not to mention stirring up animosities among fellow vintners in the area by breaking with tradition and cultivating a variety of grape known best in the States." Peter smiled. "Shall I go on?"

"Are you trying to tell me it isn't going to be an easy sell?"

They laughed, a low contented laugh, and for the first time in days they both felt terrific.

CHAPTER TEN

Peter was doing his best to move about the kitchen as quietly as possible. He drew the shades up a few inches to let in enough morning light to find the small package of coffee in the cupboard. Running the tap water at a bare trickle, he slowly filled the coffeepot with water and set it on the stove. There were a couple of eggs in the refrigerator, which, along with the leftover Camembert cheese and bread from last night, would make a fine breakfast. Not that Peter was a big one for hearty morning meals. Back in California, mornings were usually solitary, rushed times—a quick cup of coffee and a doughnut stuffed down on the way to the winery.

His cousin Louis could never complain about Peter's hours or diligence. His life had revolved around the business ever since he'd graduated from college. And since the time he was a small boy watching his father at work, the winery had always held a fascination for him. It was in his blood. Now, at last, he was close enough to reach out and snatch his dream. All he needed was to get St. Jacques and his associates to see the light.

Louis had been in a great mood on the phone the other day. He hadn't even balked when his daughter grabbed the phone for a couple of minutes of small talk before he got on the line. Amazing what a few thousand miles of distance could do. Louis thought the consortium sounded like a promising possibility. He was eager to get things under way, since at this point his investment in the château was nothing but a drain. Once the operation got started, he would be turning his share over to Peter in exchange for exclusive distribution rights to Château Cardinet Zinfandel in the States. If Peter couldn't get the winery going, he knew Louis would more than likely sell off his share of the château.

Peter had made up his mind that no matter what happened at today's meeting, he had to come up with some way to buy Louis out. When he'd first agreed to the deal with his cousin about the property, he was filled with bitterness. Jackie had called it right when she had accused Peter of feeling entitled. Louis owed his father and he was collecting on the debt.

But something was happening to him. For one thing the bitterness was giving way to a new sense of purpose, a need for fulfillment achieved solely on his own merits. He hadn't lied to Jackie when he'd told her his arrangement with his cousin had nothing to do, at least on his part, with Louis's daughter. But that issue hung in the air. Louis believed he'd bought Peter off. Pam probably did too. Peter didn't want that hanging over him.

He felt the need for a straight, unencumbered deal with his cousin. Louis would supply the Zinfandel vines needed to get the vineyard started and provide his shippers for exporting the wine in exchange for exclusive United States distribution rights.

The coffee started boiling over. Peter turned off the knob and grabbed the pot handle, then let out a yell as the hot metal burned his hand. Jackie appeared in the doorway.

"Are you all right?" she asked with a sleepy yawn.

Peter was running his hand under cold water. He nodded. "Sorry. I was going to let you sleep until I had a fabulous breakfast feast laid out on the table."

"You tricked me." She lifted a potholder out of the drawer and removed the coffee from the burner to pour two cups.

"You fell asleep on the couch. It was all very proper, I promise."

"I fell asleep because you talked nonstop until dawn. I can't remember half of what you said."

He wiped his hands on a dishcloth. Jackie walked over and looked at the burn on the palm of his hand. He flinched as she touched it lightly.

"You'll need some cream on that," she said.

"It's nothing. I'll be all right."

"Don't be stubborn. You must have some kind of ointment around the place."

He scowled. "I'm fine. Forget it. Don't start looking after me, okay?" His tone was light, but Jackie sensed his irritation.

"Sorry," she said in the same light tone. It didn't mask her irritation, either.

"I was about to scramble your eggs just the way you like them," he said, intentionally changing gears. "You sit down and I'll take care of everything."

Jackie leaned against the counter. "That is your style, isn't it?"

Peter sighed, aware they were about to get into a subject he had hoped to skirt. He carefully set down the eggs and walked over to her. Resting his hands on her shoulders, he said, "You've got my number, princess. Not that I've done anything to conceal it. I'm a take-charge kind of guy. And I don't like having to be taken care of. I got enough of that growing up. My whole family was into being looked after."

He dropped his hands to his sides and looked away. "I always used to blame my cousin Louis for putting my family in a dependent position all of our lives. But"—he shrugged—"I'm beginning to understand that neither one of my parents had the courage to break away. My father couldn't handle the prejudice against him, so he built a safe little nest among family. And when he died, my mother was afraid to face the real world, so she clung to her cousin and taught me to do the same thing. Oh, she used to give me endless lectures about how Louis used my father, about how he owed us, and I believed her. I guess if I hadn't I would have become very bitter toward her. I would have expected her to pick herself up and make a life for the two of us."

He turned back to Jackie. "I never want to feel that kind of dependency again. I've decided to buy Louis out rather than accept his share of the château as a gift when I get the vineyard in full swing. No favors. We'll have a clean business arrangement, nothing more."

She put her arms around him. "That sounds wonderful, Peter."

He smiled. "I'm going to stop feeling entitled, princess. But I'd better warn you, I intend to be hard as nails when it comes to business. I'm either going to sink or swim. No lifesavers or rubber rafts. I have to make it on my own, and I have to play it my way. It's not going to be any picnic."

"Lots of blood, sweat, and tears," she said softly.

He looked into her brilliant green eyes, a look that combined intimacy and intensity. "Some of mine . . . some of yours."

She captured his hands, holding them firmly. "Oh, Peter, I feel like we're both embarking on a new beginning."

He kissed her cool lips. "What do you think? Can a small-town librarian from Middle America and a hotshot Mexican-American find success and happiness at a château in the wine country of France?"

"Ever since I was a little girl I knew happiness was exactly what I would find here. I kept clinging to that dream. Nothing, no one, could get me to shake it." She laughed. "For ages I drove everyone in Middleton Corner crazy by talking to them all in French. My mother would give me a grocery list and I'd name off each item in French for George Olson at the corner store. My teacher would ask me to read a page from a book and I'd do it in French. In desperation one day, my mother made me promise to stop on threat of canceling my subscription to the *Le Monde.* But in my head I kept translating everything until, finally, my thoughts no longer came into my mind in English. A big part of me has always been here. And now I feel complete."

Peter smiled tenderly, his hand gently caressing her neck. "I feel more complete right now than I ever have before. And being in France is only one part of it."

Peter's eyes reflected passion, but Jackie had come to understand him well enough to know that his fears about commitment could not evaporate that easily. Right now they were both filled with a newfound sense of hope and spirit, but she was not going to let those feelings fool her into believing in make-believe happy endings. No, the road ahead was going to be rough and bumpy. She and Peter were strong-willed people, intent on making their dreams come true; along the way they were bound to have some head-on collisions. She had no idea how either one of them would come through those clashes.

"We'd better eat, and then you can prep me again before the meeting," she said matter-of-factly, aware of the flash of disappointment in Peter's face.

A moment later he began beating the eggs vigorously.

There were four men waiting as Jackie and Peter were ushered into St. Jacques's office. *Office* was not quite the right word, as the space resembled a formal drawing room straight out of an elegant château far more than a place of business. Even the men, all in their late forties to early fifties, casually seated about the room, seemed to be awaiting cocktails rather than a contest of wills.

St. Jacques, wearing a fine camel's wool jacket, dark-brown twill pants, and a Paisley cravat tucked into the collar of his ivory-white shirt, stood up from the sofa and greeted them with a pleasant smile, then introduced them around. The three other men shook hands with Peter and, with suave European flair, lightly kissed Jackie's hand. St. Jacques went over to the bar and poured six glasses of his best estate-bottled wine for the group and offered Jackie and Peter seats close to the blazing hearth. The message was clear that this meeting was expected to be a civilized, polite affair, one in which St. Jacques's group designed to get their way.

Whether it was out of discomfort or a need to jump in and take the offensive, Peter was the first one to speak. He got straight to the point.

"Gentlemen, I'm eager to get going this spring, as you know. My associate in California, Mr. Morgan, is ready to ship the Zinfandel vines. I am prepared to cultivate whatever Médoc vines on the property can be revitalized, although I doubt many of them can be saved without undue expense—money I see more profitably used for the establishment of the Zinfandel. If the plan I laid out to Monsieur St. Jacques is amenable to the rest of you, I suggest we spend our time now negotiating the terms of the contract. . . ."

As Peter talked, Jackie watched the faces of the four men. If her partner had thought St. Jacques was worried that he might be too brash and impulsive, he was presently giving all four of these men good cause for those beliefs. Peter's forthright style was definitely not the style of this cultured crowd. They did things slowly, methodically, conservatively. Peter didn't know it, but he was fast destroying any chance of getting the consortium's financial support.

St. Jacques's shrewd smile did not mask his growing impatience as Peter continued his steamroller approach. The other three men's smiles were barely polite. They had obviously been less inclined all along to participate in this investment and now felt duly justified in their reluctance. They were hardly paying attention as St. Jacques finally broke into Peter's sales pitch.

"Monsieur Santiago, please do not take it as an affront when I say that there is simply no comparison between the princely Médoc and the pleasant, though simple, Zinfandel. The Haut-Médoc region has a reputation to uphold, a tradition. Château Cardinet must be part of that tradition. If not, I think it best to leave things as they are. You might consider selling the property to a vintner schooled in the great traditions of our art, someone whose capable management will restore Château Cardinet Haut-Médoc wines."

"Someone of your own circle, no doubt," Peter said testily.

He'd begun by digging his grave and now he was pulling the dirt in over his body. Jackie felt her stomach muscles tighten as she looked at the cool, hostile faces of the four men. No one was bothering with polite smiles anymore. For a moment everyone sat frozen.

Jackie broke the ice by standing up and walking over to the hearth. She stretched one hand out to the fire, her back to the group. She took a sip of her wine, then turned around with slow drama. She smiled at each of the men in turn—all except Peter, whom she very much wanted to fade silently into the background. In her lyrical French she complimented St. Jacques on the glass of wine she was drinking.

"I can understand your deep appreciation for and love of the Haut-Médoc. It is a wine of legendary excellence. My fondest hope would be to produce wines from Château Cardinet that would even come close to the rich, harmonious ones you so successfully produce. All of you, I understand, are involved in only the finest, most esteemed vineyards in France. You have obviously chosen very wisely. In my eyes that makes you all visionaries. You can see the promise in each of your investments, and your success speaks for itself."

The four men, warmed by Jackie's flattery, her charm, and her exquisitely fluent French, smiled appreciatively. St. Jacques walked over and poured her some more wine. She thanked him demurely. Then she moved to the couch, positioning herself near the other three men. St. Jacques hung back for a moment, then went and sat down beside her.

Jackie continued talking. The consortium continued smiling. Only Peter, who had difficulty picking up more than a few of Jackie's words, maintained a sullen expression.

After a few minutes St. Jacques turned to Peter. "Your partner has a good head on her shoulders." He gave Jackie a swift smile. "And a very pretty one, I might add. She understands our position perfectly."

"Of course," Jackie said, switching to English, thus including Peter in the conversation once more, "the restoration of the Château Cardinet Haut-Médoc vineyards may create some problems for the other vintners in the region. There is nothing better for business, I realize, than healthy competition. But too much of a good thing . . ." She let the sentence hang, allowing the group to absorb her point.

After a moment she continued. "I found my weekend down in Margaux a fascinating and enlightening experience. I learned, for instance, that there are an increasing number of wine growers operating nonclassified vineyards in the region. Monsieur Pierre de Borie, in particular, has put together a collection of parcels from a group of châteaus and, from what I understand, is producing a first-rate wine. So, certainly Château

Cardinet would not be the first vineyard to break with tradition by introducing a new wine. And I needn't remind you that it will not upset the balance of profit within the region for the vintners of the Haut-Médocs."

"Yes, I agree you make some solid points, mademoiselle," Michel Sardon, the portly gentleman on Jackie's left, responded. "But de Borie maintains very high standards and produces a supple, full-bodied wine that far surpasses those of most other nonclassified vineyards. Our group must uphold a standard of excellence. The vineyards we are involved with produce only wines of great quality, wines full of grace and breeding that can come only with age. The Zinfandel is a perfectly pleasant young wine, but it lacks the finesse and subtlety that are hallmarks of the fine Médocs."

"Gentlemen, I'd like to propose a toast," Jackie said, surprising the group, who felt a celebration would be the last thing she would call for, considering that they were gently but firmly turning down Peter's proposal.

St. Jacques, openly flustered, tried to explain more directly, but Jackie cut him off. She walked over to the small wicker satchel she'd brought to the meeting that was now resting at Peter's side. "More accurately"—she turned to the four men with her most charming smile—"I should call it a wine tasting." She produced two bottles of wine from her case, both of whose labels were concealed by a taped piece of paper.

"You see, my friends, one or both of these bottles contain a Zinfandel wine. I propose a little contest. All I ask you to do is to select which is the Zinfandel."

"I assure you, Mademoiselle Archer, we are all connoisseurs and will have no trouble making that selection," St. Jacques said a bit impatiently.

"Then we will not have to detain you much longer," Peter replied, bringing over clean glasses from the bar. He took one of the bottles from Jackie, uncorked it, and poured four small portions of wine. Jackie, acting the hostess, handed them out.

René Verger, the most pompous member of the consortium, held his glass up to the light, studied it thoughtfully, and sipped. As he watched his companions, he wore a smug smile.

The four men gave each other knowing glances. "This is a Zinfandel," St. Jacques said, speaking for the group. "I must admit it is quite a lovely young one, but it cannot compare to the classic French Haut-Médoc."

Jackie nodded pleasantly while Peter wiped each glass with a cotton cloth and poured from the second bottle.

The four men, taking their sips this time, seemed much less sure of themselves. Alain Briand, the oldest member of the group, a lean, soft-spoken man with neatly combed black hair graying at the temples, tugged at his goatee, his nostrils flaring. St. Jacques set down his glass, idly rubbing one hand against the sleeve of his jacket. René Verger's smug smile had vanished. The heavyset Sardon looked to the others for enlightenment.

Jackie glanced at Peter, who gave her the barest hint of a smile. They had them.

"Well, messieurs, do we have here another Zinfandel? Or perhaps a vintage Bordeaux? I will confess," Jackie said, "that I was fortunate enough to purchase several fine wines this past weekend in Margaux."

"It is too rich, too subtle, to be a Zinfandel." It was St. Jacques who spoke first. "I would guess either a Lafitte or a Latour."

"Yes," declared the pompous Verger, "definitely not a Zinfandel. This particular wine has character, grace. I would wager a guess that it is a Mouton-Rothschild. There is a full-bodied quality here—"

"Well, mademoiselle," Sardon interrupted, "I think we all agree"—observing Briand's nod of confirmation—"that only the first wine was a Zinfandel."

"You feel the second wine is a far superior wine?" Jackie asked.

They nodded.

"A wine befitting a Château Cardinet label?"

"Certainly," St. Jacques said, "if your vineyards could produce a fair amount of wine of this quality, we would have no complaints. That has been my point all along. The Haut-Médoc wine has an aristocratic complexity that a Zinfandel cannot begin to compete with."

"But messieurs," she said in French, a devilish glint in her eyes, "Peter Santiago's point all along has been that you do not appreciate the potential of the Zinfandel—both as a young wine and as one that ages quite nobly. A wine, in short, that can produce early profits, curb further competition in the region, and, with proper aging, offer vintage quality." She removed the label of both wines and handed the second one to St. Jacques. It was a 1973 Morgan Zinfandel.

They were standing in bright sunlight, in the middle of the Champs-Elysées. Peter lifted Jackie in his arms and whirled her in a wide circle.

"You were brilliant, *chérie. Magnifique! Merveilleuse!* Quick, give me some more French adjectives for *wonderful,*" Peter shouted, giving her a hearty bear-hug.

"You deserve the credit. It was your idea to bring the wine. I merely carried out the plan."

"A plan only someone of fine breeding, subtlety, and aristocratic grace could pull off."

"Don't forget full bodied." She giggled.

Peter's blue eyes flashed seductively. "Definitely full bodied enough for me."

The wind was blowing hard. Jackie pulled up the hood on her jacket.

Peter hailed a cab. "This calls for a celebration. Where to, princess? The sky's the limit."

"The sky it is, then," she grinned. "Take me to the top of the Eiffel Tower."

"Are you serious? It's awfully windy outside," he said as they entered the warmth of the taxi.

"Just for a couple of minutes. I want to look out on Paris as the sun goes down. I want to revel in the thrill of success as we watch the lights in the city burst upon the darkness." She leaned her head back against the seat and closed her eyes, her lips curved in a full smile.

Peter put his hand over hers. "It's very hard for me to imagine you were ever standing behind a pile of books in a library in Middleton Corner, Ohio."

"It's getting harder and harder for me to remember that's where I spent the last eight years of my life. More than that, counting all the years I worked part time while going to school. I was the perennial dreamer. What better place to lose myself in fantasies? And then one day I realized that was all my life would ever be unless I did something drastic. Claude Marigny's job offer rescued me. At least long enough to leave Ohio and get my feet wet in Paris." She turned her head to Peter and touched his cheek. "And then I met you."

"Amazing how quickly you fell for me," he teased.

Jackie laughed softly at the memory of their calamitous first encounter. "I thought you were the most infuriating, egotistical man I'd ever met. But then you went and baffled me, climbing up that rickety fire escape and saving Gogo. . . ."

Peter leaned over to kiss her.

"Tour Eiffel," the cabdriver announced, squealing his tires to a stop along the curb and interrupting Peter's kiss just as his lips touched hers.

Jackie kissed him quickly. "Hurry. The sun is going down."

She hopped out of the car and rushed to the tower. Peter paid the driver and hurried after her. They made the last trip up of the day, riding the elevator to the middle observation deck, since the top one was closed due to the high winds. When they stepped out they were alone on the platform. Peter put his arm around her and they huddled close together against the strong winds and looked out over the Seine, the gardens, the heartbeat of Paris. As the sun dropped over the horizon, he gathered her in his arms and they shared a warm, tender kiss.

The first lights twinkled on in the city. Jackie leaned against Peter, feeling sweeping waves of happiness and excitement wash over her along with the bracing wind. They had to hurry to catch the last elevator ride down. The elevator operator regarded them as if they were mad. Indeed, they felt a bit wild and crazy at that moment.

Jackie didn't argue as Peter hailed another cab and gave the driver his address. Their eyes met in understanding, and during the short drive to his apartment they sat together in quiet contentment.

Ten minutes later Peter unlocked his door and, holding Jackie's hand tightly, led her inside. They barely got their coats off before he swept her into his arms, brushing her cheeks, her neck, her mouth with his lips. Then he kissed her hard, all the passion and intensity of desire he'd forced himself to hold in check last night and all day today bursting through the floodgates. His hands and mouth moved over her in hungry yearning.

A deep moan escaped Jackie's lips as all of the turmoil and fears of yesterday evaporated. She knew this was what she wanted, why she'd come back to Peter. His touch was intense and familiar. A rush of arousal burst inside of her as he moved against her, demanding, fiercely passionate.

He practically tore at her clothes as he undressed her. When they were both naked, he carried her to the bed, smothering her with hot, hungry kisses. He pressed his lips against the hollow of her throat, his cool hands cupping her breasts, feeling the strong, rapid beat of her heart.

Jackie trembled, her hands moving down over his body, exploring, caressing, feeling him yield to the sensations she created with her touch. She slid her fingers up along his inner thigh. He shivered, his hand moving over hers as she softly stroked him.

His breathing grew raspy as her lips traveled down his chest with possessive tenderness. She had never really made love to a man before Peter, only been made love to. Now she felt an urgent, fiery need to know him as deeply, as intimately, as he knew her.

Peter lifted her to him finally, crushing her warm lips with his, his hands slowly sliding over her body, cupping her buttocks, then trailing down the backs of her thighs so that she cried out in pleasure. He ran his mouth over her breasts, tugging gently at the nipples. Jackie moaned, her body shuddering in ecstasy as the warm, wet tip of his tongue slid lightly down her ribcage and over her stomach, gently insistent as he pushed her onto her back. Jackie arched her neck, yielding completely, nearly swooning over the intoxicating sensations flooding her body.

When he entered her she could not wait, her hips moving, her fingers gripping his buttocks until she cried out with sudden, astounding release. Peter enclosed her in his arms, his breath hot against her ear as he lost himself to the mounting, quickening pressure carrying him into a whirlpool of oblivion.

They lay together afterward, Jackie's cheek pressed against Peter's chest, her arm slung comfortably across his hips. Peter idly toyed with her silky hair, slipping his fingers through the chestnut strands. He truly did feel complete now.

Jackie stretched, then fell back against him. She looked up into his smiling, contented face. "I did promise myself when I returned to Paris on Sunday"—she sighed wistfully—"not to let myself get into this position again."

They both laughed. Then his expression grew serious and tender. He cupped her chin, then ran his fingers over the delicate contours of her small, lovely face. *"Je t'adore* . . . how do you say 'in this position'?" Then, before she could answer, he shook his head. "Never mind. Let's just leave it at that."

CHAPTER ELEVEN

Jackie was setting another log on the fire in the cozy library at Château Cardinet when Peter walked into the room. He set down his overnight bag by the desk.

"You look exhausted," Jackie said, watching him wearily remove his jacket and tumble into the gold-brocade armchair.

He rubbed his temples and sighed. "You know you're in the wine business when you spend half your nights counting corks instead of sheep," he muttered, then leaned his head on her shoulder as she came over and sat on the arm of the chair. She stroked his brow soothingly. "I hate going back to Paris without you." He sighed. "I never sleep well anymore when you aren't beside me."

"It's impossible for us both to go in for those meetings with St. Jacques's group. There's so much to do here at the château. I have to show you something." She started to get up, but Peter grabbed her and tugged her onto his lap.

"Not now," he whispered into her hair. "Mmm. You smell good. I missed you."

Jackie laughed softly and kissed him tenderly.

These past six weeks had been the happiest and most exciting of her life. To be adored, to be a part of Peter's world, to find a place that felt so right . . . it was all happening for her. Jackie's only fear was that somehow, something would go wrong and she'd lose everything. That feeling cropped up whenever she and Peter got caught up in an argument over business.

Peter had such set ideas about how to run the vineyard that, whenever Jackie so much as broached another concept or approach, she could literally see him bristle. He kept his temper for the most part, choosing instead simply to disregard her comments. Then she'd bristle. It hadn't happened too often. Jackie kept many of her ideas to herself, realizing how little she knew about most aspects of the wine business. But she was learning. She spent a large chunk of each day visiting vineyards, talking with the owners, the cellar masters, and the workers. Every night she read until Peter dragged the book from her hands.

Their arguments were short lived, Peter always making the first advance. He'd be funny, sexy, teasing. Jackie would play along. She knew what he was doing, and although his manipulations bothered her, she wanted peace as much as he did. There were times, though, when she wondered if she shouldn't be more assertive. Love, she concluded, was a very powerful force.

"Tell me about your meetings with St. Jacques," she said, catching hold of Peter's hand as he began unbuttoning her blouse.

He grinned at her, planting an intentionally wet kiss on her nose. Then he began doing the same thing to her cheeks, her eyes, her chin.

"Peter . . . stop." She tried to squirm out of his grip, but he held her fast.

"That's what you get for trying to discuss business at a time like this. Be quiet now"—he slipped her hands behind her back—"and let me make proper love to you." His blue eyes sparkled, his deep baritone voice rumbled with sensuality. "Didn't you miss me?"

"I've been so busy," she teased, "I didn't really notice you were gone. Now, let me see, was it two nights or three?"

He wrestled her to the floor and began tickling her mercilessly.

"Stop," she pleaded between fits of laughter. "I'll admit it. I will."

"Tell me." He was fully on top of her now, his hands gripping her wrists against her hips.

Jackie gave him a long, sultry look. "Have I told you that you are a very stubborn and demanding man?"

"Very stubborn and demanding," he agreed with a wicked grin, one hand leaving her wrist to glide down her thigh until he came to the hem of her skirt. A moment later his fingers slid underneath, moving upward until he came to the waistband of her pantyhose. His other hand released her, trailing up her ribcage to grasp her breast.

Jackie's breath caught as he ran his fingers back and forth over the thin silk blouse until her nipples grew hard and erect. "Please, Peter," she murmured, her hands tugging the edge of his shirt from his waistband, her fingers tracing the line of his backbone.

His lips brushed hers. "Tell me," he murmured back, his fingers continuing their mesmerizing movements as his other hand tugged down the pantyhose just far enough for his palm to press against her naked hipbone.

"I missed you." She kissed him hard on the mouth. "I missed you every minute of the seventy-two endlessly long hours you were gone." He rolled off her and deftly began unbuttoning her blouse with one hand while the other worked at the clasp and zipper of her skirt. "Oh, Peter," she whispered in a throaty voice of joyful surrender.

Ravenous with need for each other, they made love with a hot, burning urgency. They might have been apart for weeks, months, instead of a few days, for all the passion pent up inside of them bursting for expression.

Afterward, Peter lay on his back on the carpet, a full, contented smile on his face, his hands cupped beneath his head. Jackie studied him thoughtfully. "What are you thinking?"

Peter pulled back her hair so that he could kiss her cheek. "For such a fragile little thing you never fail to astound me."

She laughed. "Was I too rough with you?"

He nuzzled her neck. "I can take it."

"Oh, you can, can you?" Her large green eyes flashed seductively.

Peter ran his fingers idly down her neck and

across her shoulders. "I love you, Jackie." His eyes shot up to catch her expression.

She was smiling tenderly. "I see."

He turned over on his side. "I've never said—" He caught the suspicious glint in her eyes and laughed softly. "Okay, but I never meant it before. Do you believe me?"

Jackie tilted her head to the side. "I think I do. I want to believe you. At moments like this . . . it's hard not to."

"What does that mean?" His tone had a slight edge to it.

She sat up and reached for her blouse. Peter grabbed it, preventing her from putting it on. "Tell me," he demanded.

Sighing, she released the blouse, letting it fall over her thighs. "There," she said. "You're doing it now."

"What am I doing?" He stared at her, puzzled.

"I told you I found you very stubborn and demanding."

"It didn't sound like those were traits that bothered you." His tone was decidedly defensive now.

"Sometimes they're very appealing. Other times . . . they're infuriating."

Peter let go of her blouse. "If you're referring to the argument we had the other day about the stainless-steel vats—"

"It wasn't any one argument, Peter. It wasn't even the whole batch of them. It's your attitude toward me."

"My attitude? What the hell is that supposed to mean? I just got finished telling you that I'm in love with you and you're down on my attitude? I don't get it, babe."

Jackie ran her tongue over her dry lips. She really hadn't wanted to get them started on another argument. She wasn't even sure how things had escalated so rapidly.

Peter was pulling on his pants. He zipped them up and tossed her skirt over to her. "You better get dressed. The fire's going out." His tone had gone from irate to nonchalant in seconds.

"You know what I'm talking about. And this is typical of how you choose to handle it. You ignore the issues, ignore the fact that I'm a second-class citizen when it comes to discussing the least little thing about the vineyard. You either humor me or cast me a look that very blatantly states you don't think I have the right to offer my opinions."

"Offer all you like," he said smoothly, slipping on his shirt.

Jackie tugged her arms angrily into her blouse and started looking around the floor for her bikini panties, a frown of frustration marring her smooth features.

She was searching under the couch when Peter knelt down beside her, dangling the silky underwear from his fingers. She snatched them from him. He caught her hand. "This is definitely not the afterglow I expected," he said gently. "I'm sorry, princess. You're right. I do have a hard time listening, but it's not just you. Don't take it personally. You should have seen me this afternoon. I had four men about to pull their hair from their heads. And believe me, a couple of them can't spare it. By the time we work everything out, I guarantee you they'll all be as bald as bowling balls."

Jackie's lips turned up into a tiny smile. Her eyes searched his face. "I want so much to be an important part of—"

He stopped her words with a tender kiss. "You are important, Jackie. More than I can tell you. I'm not used to having somebody in my life who matters so much to me. You—you're almost an obsession. I can't imagine being without you. I wasn't lying when I said I find it intolerable when we're apart. Sometimes it scares me."

She touched his cheek. "I know."

Their eyes met in tender understanding. But then her expression turned wistful. "I just wish you could see me as a real business partner, not only a lover."

"I think it's better to separate the two as much as possible. Anyway"—he kissed the tip of her chin—"you've got your work cut out for you handling the distributors. Which reminds me, we've got to get a flight for you to San Francisco next week so you can meet with Louis."

"I thought you found it intolerable for us to be apart. Why can't you come with me?" she asked, a bit petulantly.

"I'm too busy, princess. You know that. I promise to hate every moment you're away . . . but you're the one that wanted to work with me."

She gave him a wry smile. "You've got me there."

He watched her get dressed, his eyes gleaming with appreciation for her lovely, ethereal figure.

She looked over at him as she zipped up her skirt and slipped her feet into her slippers, not bothering with the discarded pantyhose. "I'm nervous."

"About meeting Louis? Don't be. He's going to be very charming and hospitable. He likes women."

Jackie narrowed her gaze. "In business?"

"My mother used to do the books for him."

"That's not the same thing. I'm not going to meet with him as a clerk. Or have the two of you worked everything out already and this trip is just to humor me?" Her brow furrowed in suspicion.

Peter shook his head. "I can't seem to win with you. First you accuse me of not giving you enough of a say in the operation, and then, when I do, you immediately become suspect." He raised his right hand. "I swear that you and Louis will work out the shipping and distribution arrangements. Afterward—"

"Afterward, you'll decide whether or not they will get your seal of approval."

He shrugged. "I'm the man at the top. I get the final say. If that's not something you can live with . . ."

"Yes?" she challenged.

But Peter was not about to step into the battlefield again. He fell onto his stomach, reached for her legs, and sent her tumbling down over him onto the floor.

"If that's not something you can live with," he

repeated, sprawling on top of her, "then I'll have to occupy you with less mundane tasks . . . like making passionate love with me every single moment of the day. That should keep you in your place," he said with a provocative gleam in his eye.

"Why you . . . *salaud!*"

"Calling me a bastard will only make me more demanding and stubborn." He dipped his hand under her blouse.

"Stop," she protested. "This is another ploy to get me off the subject."

But he wouldn't stop until Jackie grew breathless, her murmured sighs punctuating the stillness. Then he rolled off her. "Okay, I'll stop. Let's get back to arguing," he announced with aplomb. "Where were we?"

"Salaud," she whispered, pulling him back to her.

The fire had died down completely by the time they dressed again. While Peter got it going, Jackie headed for the kitchen to check on dinner. She was halfway down the hall when she heard the shrill ring of the ancient doorbell.

"I'll get it," she shouted out to Peter.

When she opened the heavy wooden door, she was greeted by a warm kiss on the lips from Claude Marigny. *"Bonsoir, chérie.* Ah, you look particularly lovely tonight." Smiling broadly, he touched her cheek and stepped inside. Jackie was feeling decidedly nonplused.

Peter appeared in the hallway. Claude glanced

at him, and the Frenchman's smile turned wistful. He walked over and shook hands with a somewhat begrudging Peter.

"Did Jacqueline not tell you she'd invited me for dinner tonight?"

Jackie shut the door. The late afternoon's activities had made her forget about the invitation herself.

She walked toward the two men, Claude smiling charmingly, Peter's lips drawn in a tight grimace.

"I met Claude in town today and he was an enormous help with the printer. I invited him for dinner to show him my gratitude." She gave a nervous little laugh as Peter's expression remained sullen. "I can't promise my *boeuf bourguignon* will be just reward, but my cooking is improving steadily. Before I check on it, come into the library." She grabbed Peter's hand. "Peter, I meant to show you these label ideas from the printer when you came back this afternoon. It slipped my mind for a while." She gave him a devilish smile that Claude observed as well.

She led Peter over to the desk, Claude following them into the room at a leisurely pace. Peter looked up at Claude. "I thought you were still in Paris."

"I haven't been there in days. It must be the country air that agrees with me. Lately, I find myself wanting to spend more and more time here. My father is quite pleased at my new interest in the vineyards. Perhaps you shouldn't have turned down his offer."

"Things are working out quite nicely with St. Jacques," Peter said tightly.

"That's good to hear. My father was under the impression that you were having some difficulties."

"None," he snapped.

"I'm pleased," Claude said pleasantly. "I must admit I like the idea of the Château Cardinet coming back to life. But then, I like competition." He gave Jackie a subtle wink that Peter was quick to spot as well.

Jackie could see Peter's temper start to flare. He should realize, she thought, that Claude was only baiting him, but she knew his jealous nature was getting in the way of his common sense. She pulled out a sheaf of papers from a large envelope. Out of the corner of her eye she watched Claude walk over to the sofa. She spotted her pantyhose on the corner of one of the cushions at the same time Claude noticed them. Jackie flushed scarlet as she watched Claude pluck them up. Before she could say or do anything, he tucked them neatly into the pocket of his jacket. Peter, who had been concentrating on the preliminary wine-label renderings, looked up instantly as he heard Jackie's sharp intake of breath. "Are you all right?"

She turned away abruptly, knowing she was red as a beet. "I'd better go check on the food," she mumbled, hurrying out of the room, but not before she threw the amused Claude a stinging glance.

"Wait, *chérie.*" Claude came up behind her.

"I'll help you. *Boeuf bourguignon* happens to be a specialty of mine."

As soon as they were out of earshot of Peter, Jackie hissed icily, "Give them back to me."

"You are *très belle* when you're angry, *chérie*."

"You are only trying to embarrass me, Claude. And I don't like it." She marched ahead of him, swinging the kitchen door so hard that he had to grab for it so he wouldn't get smacked in the face.

He walked into the kitchen and took hold of her arm. "I'm sorry, *chérie*. But I'm very jealous. You think it's easy for me to accept that you have taken a lover?"

"Oh, Claude, stop being so—so French," she said in frustration. "I've never led you on. I'm in love with Peter and you know it. You've known it almost from the beginning. Now, give them back." She started to reach into his pocket.

Claude took the opportunity to put his arms around her. "But I love you, Jacqueline. I can't help myself. Every time I see you I can barely restrain myself. Give me a chance, *chérie*. Santiago—he's not the man for you."

Jackie stuck her hand in his pocket to retrieve the stolen pantyhose. At that instant Peter walked into the kitchen. It made quite a picture, Claude's arms wrapped around Jackie, her hand half in his pocket clutching her undergarment.

She pushed Claude away, the pantyhose falling to the floor. Peter's complexion went white. Jackie's was bright red. Only Claude seemed perfectly at ease as he let his eyes drift to the floor.

"Now, how shall we explain this *petit faux pas, chérie?*" He pressed a finger to his lips.

"This is ridiculous." Jackie glared at Claude and then moved toward Peter. But as she took a step, Peter did an abrupt about-face and stormed through the swinging door, forcing Jackie to jump back so that she wouldn't get the door in her face this time.

Claude gave her a contrite smile. "He has a bad temper, *n'est-ce pas?*"

"You are *un enfant.*" She started for the door.

Claude clasped her wrist. "I apologize again. Let me explain to him."

"I think you had better go, Claude. I'm afraid this is not a good night for the three of us to dine together."

He refused to release her. "Do you forgive me?"

She gave him a rueful grimace. "You really are a child, you know."

"Only because I am so very infatuated with *une belle petite femme* from Ohio. It makes me do crazy things, *mon amour.*"

"Claude, you have to stop saying things like that. It's only your ego talking. You simply can't stand to think your charm is failing you with even one woman."

"No, *chérie.* You are wrong. I will prove it to you."

Jackie shook her head vigorously. "Please, don't. You're wasting your time and I don't want any more embarrassing mishaps. Give me your word, Claude."

He shrugged languidly, then brought her wrist up to his lips. "I cannot give my word, Jacqueline, only my heart."

"Oh, you're impossible. Go home, please." She wrestled free of his grasp and went running down the hall after Peter.

He was in the library when she came bursting into the room. "Will you let me explain?"

He watched her walk up to him. "I've already figured it out," he said slowly.

"You have?" Her tone was wary.

But then Peter smiled. He pulled her to him and she let him support her weight completely. He buried his face in her hair.

Jackie slipped her arms around his waist. "He only did it to upset you . . . and to strike back at me for rejecting his advances," she said softly.

Peter kissed her full on the mouth. "I love you, Jackie. The very thought that someone else—" They heard a loud bang as the front door slammed shut.

"Sshh." She pressed a finger to his lips. "There's no one else."

He held her at arm's length. "Claude Marigny is a rich French aristocrat. And the bastard has to be good looking to boot. He's already made it clear he loves competition, and we both know exactly what he was referring to. He intends to keep pursuing you."

"I've made it clear to him that he'll be wasting his time. Do I really need to make it clear to you as well? After all we've shared—all I want us to share in the future?"

She expected him to take her in his arms. Instead, he let go of her and walked over to the fireplace, idly prodding a log with the poker.

"What's wrong?" Jackie asked softly. "Don't you believe me?"

"I believe you." His back remained to her.

"Then what is it?"

He turned around slowly and gazed at her for a long time. "You'll want to get married at some point, I suppose."

Jackie felt her muscles tighten. "That doesn't sound like a proposal . . . or even a proposal to propose," she said, trying for lightness. Marriage was a topic she'd admittedly thought a lot about recently, but it was one Peter had never brought up before.

"I don't want to get married," he said evenly. He had trouble meeting her gaze. "It's just not something that's ever been in my plans. I want us to go on together like this. . . ."

"You mean without any real commitment, is that it?"

"I don't think we need a marriage certificate to feel a commitment." He turned back to the fire.

"Marriage would complicate things, I suppose," she said sarcastically, "especially if they have shared property rights in France."

"That isn't the point."

"Oh, I think it's one of the points," she replied, a hard edge to her voice. "You're afraid I might gain too much power, that I might interfere with your precious position of authority." She walked over to the desk, staring down at the wine labels bearing Peter's name. PETER SANTIAGO, PROPRIÉTAIRE.

Peter sighed. "Why are we starting to fight like this, Jackie?"

She reeled around to face him. "Because we're getting close, dammit. And you're terrified."

"That's crazy. I'm in love with you. I'm insanely jealous."

"You're afraid Claude might ask me to marry him one of these days. Oh, you wouldn't want that, but on the other hand you feel obliged to let me know you would never consider proposing yourself."

"Look, Jackie, my parents didn't have a good marriage—"

"Oh, do spare me that timeworn line. It's almost as pat as 'my wife doesn't understand me.' Let me tell you something, Peter, my parents were divorced when I was six years old. My mother remarried twice after that—which accounted for all the eligible bachelors in Middleton Corner at the time—and neither one of her new husbands lasted more than a couple of years. So my mother had three lousy marriages. That was her misfortune, not mine. I'm my own person, dammit. I am certainly not going to replay somebody else's life. And I'm not going to use my mother's failure to find happiness as an excuse not to go looking for some myself."

Peter didn't know what to say. He stared at her awkwardly.

"Oh, don't worry about it, Peter. I'm far from considering marriage at this point—to you,

Claude, or anyone else. You can stop looking like a scared rabbit," she said in a flat, weary tone. She sat down behind the desk, her hand still clasping the illustrated wine labels. "What did you think of these?" she asked, a resigned expression on her face. Her eyes moved from the papers to Gogo swinging merrily on his trapeze. The cage was perched on a special brass stand beside the desk. Love, Jackie reconsidered, was for the birds. She gave Gogo a sad smile.

Peter walked over, took the papers from Jackie's hands, pulled her up out of the chair, and put his arms around her. He pressed his lips against her ear. "Don't give up on me, princess. This is a whole new ball game for me . . . I just don't know how to play it very well yet."

Jackie pushed aside her hurt and met his gaze. "I'm just as new at the game. I'd be happy if we could learn to play together."

CHAPTER TWELVE

It was three weeks before Jackie could spare the time to take that flight to San Francisco to meet Louis Morgan. During those three weeks she met with over a dozen French distributors and local shippers. Several firms were willing to take on the Haut-Médoc's from Château Cardinet, but the Zinfandel was another story. A couple of the larger, more reliable companies turned them down flat. Another prestigious firm agreed to take on a limited quantity of Château Cardinet Zinfandel, but demanded sizable up-front money. The smaller companies were, for the most part, even less willing to take chances on trying to distribute the new wine. The shippers were equally cautious, concerned about the viability and thus the profits of the burgeoning vineyard. Jackie was well aware that one of the big issues behind the concern of distributors and shippers alike was that Château Cardinet was not only planning to produce a wine heretofore grown solely in the States, but that the vineyard itself was being run by a California vintner.

The suspicion toward an American penetrating

their stronghold generated resistance at every level. While Jackie struggled daily with lining up the distributors and local shippers, Peter was having his own problems coping with the seemingly endless regulations and legal bottlenecks that had to be deciphered and resolved. He was also having difficulties hiring a staff, especially a *maître de chaix* who had the experience and qualifications to supervise such a major undertaking. The most desirable cellar masters were either happy where they were, or loathe to work under an American owner.

Tensions were running high during those three weeks, but Jackie and Peter put an all-out effort into keeping their tempers under control. Their last blowup on the night Claude Marigny had come for the *boeuf bourguignon* dinner that no one ended up eating, had shaken them both. They did not want a repeat performance. And during these trying times they knew that they only had each other for support and comfort.

It wasn't until the night before Jackie was to fly out to San Francisco that the walls of Jericho started shaking again. Jackie had just returned from another depressingly unproductive meeting with a local distributor. She was becoming more and more convinced that they were not going to be able to find French buyers for the Zinfandel.

"I think," she said at dinner that night, "that we should settle for exporting the Zinfandel to the States for now and concentrate on distributing the Haut-Médoc here and abroad. I have two reputable local companies agreeable to handling the Haut-Médoc. With Louis taking on the Zinfandel we should do all right."

Peter set down his knife and fork. "All right isn't good enough, Jackie. Besides, sending all the Zinfandel overseas completely defeats my whole plan. Unless the Zinfandel can be established as a French as well as an American wine, no one in the States is going to be particularly interested in it. Oh, some will try it out, but most of the bottles will remain on the shelves. How long do you think somebody as established as Louis Morgan is going to back that kind of an operation? No. We don't need a huge local market, but we must have a share in it. I've decided we should go with Grillet. He's a topnotch broker and he's got a shipping company already lined up."

"But he wants a four percent cut, Peter. Don't you realize that's double what other brokers get —what he gets from other vineyards? It's highway robbery."

"It's also the only way we're going to accomplish our goals. St. Jacques and his buddies are willing to loan me the money I need to buy Louis's share of the château from him by late spring provided I line everyone up. Right now Morgan holds the title on the property even though I've put in almost half of the down payment. However, it was his connection that got us the deal. But I don't trust Louis not to hold on to the ownership until he's sure of the profits. I could be under his thumb for as long as two years, during which time he could pull the rug out from under me anytime he chose."

"But you told me a long time ago that he had agreed to turn the title over to you once you were established."

"Don't be naive, Jackie. We don't have a signed and sealed contract. He can define 'established' any way he damn well pleases. Meanwhile, I'm little more than a puppet on his long string."

Jackie took a deep breath, deliberately busying herself with buttering a piece of bread. For over a week now she had been nurturing a plan in her mind, a plan it was going to be hard to talk him into considering.

Peter, already familiar with Jackie's tactics, gave her a long, hard look. "Okay, spit it out, princess."

She grinned, trying at the same time to relax. She set the bread down, but held on to the butter knife just for something to grip. "Peter, why can't we act as our own shippers? I mean locally for starters and then, as soon as we can branch out, internationally. Several of the châteaus in the area have their own shipping concerns. It makes so much sense. I know I'm still a novice, but you'd be amazed at how much I'm picking up each day. I had a long talk on Tuesday with Jean-Louis Marigny." There was a nervous edge to her voice, especially when she brought up the name Marigny. Peter had an almost allergic reaction to that particular surname, even though he had nothing against Jean-Louis. The problem was that Claude Marigny had been assuming more and more involvement in Château Maiffret over these past few weeks and Jackie knew Peter didn't like the idea of her having contacts with him.

She hurried on. "Jean-Louis has offered to assist me—"

"Assist you?" His tone had a definite bite to it.

"Is it the 'assistance' that troubles you, or is it the 'me' part?" she asked impatiently.

"Both."

"I see."

"No, you don't see. Will you stop being so damn sensitive for a minute? What I'm saying is that we have enough to handle getting the vineyard under way. You have no idea of the red tape, the costs, the hassles, I'm going through. Now you offer this ridiculous idea that, on top of everything else, you want to start a private shipping company? It's crazy."

"It isn't crazy or ridiculous. If you would stop being so hotheaded, so adamant about keeping every ounce of control in your tight little fist, you would realize it makes complete sense."

"Just tell me one thing. Where does Claude Marigny fit into the picture? No, wait, let me guess. The grapevine has it, he's taking over that particular branch of the business at Château Maiffret. How convenient that the two of you are in the same line."

Jackie shoved her barely touched plate of food away. "You call my ideas crazy and ridiculous. Well, if you weren't so jealous and so threatened—"

"It has nothing to do with jealousy," he

shouted, both fists pounding the table. "The man is a complete incompetent. He'll have that shipping company in bankruptcy before the year is out. Just like he sat back and let his publishing house go down the drain. You should know his ineptitude better than anyone else. And you want me to go along with his help and advice?"

Jackie was angry at Peter's reaction, but she wasn't surprised. Refusing to lose her temper or give up, she said in a calm voice that took a great deal of effort, "All right, we don't need to get assistance from him or his father, if that's your main concern. Even though you are wrong about Claude. He isn't inept. And he's changed. According to his father, he's working very hard and he's doing a good job." She saw Peter's frown and hurried on. "Still, we don't have to turn to them for assistance if the idea is so repugnant to you. I've made several other contacts—"

"No." He cut her off sharply. "Forget it, Jackie. It's too big for us to handle."

"You mean it's too big for me to handle."

"Dammit, are we going to start that again? Do you think if it were feasible I wouldn't say go ahead? I'd love to cut all ties with Morgan and all these local shippers who are giving us such a hard time. But do you have any idea what it would cost to put that kind of operation into the works?"

"As a matter of fact, I do. We would have to start small, but by cutting the costs of the middlemen, we'd come out way ahead in the end."

"If we made it to the end, which I seriously doubt."

She threw up her hands in frustration. "You don't want to consider the plan. That's the bottom line. It's too much of a threat to your supreme ego, your need to control everything."

Now it was Peter who was trying to rein in his temper. He knew they were venturing into dangerous territory. And tomorrow Jackie would be leaving for San Francisco. He didn't want her going off with the two of them in a raging feud.

Reaching across the table, he took hold of her hand. "How about giving me some time to think about it?"

She threw him a suspicious glance.

"No. Honestly," he said, "I'm not rejecting the idea outright. You took me by surprise, that's all. I've been up to my ears in problems these past few weeks and then you come out with a new one for me to digest."

"It doesn't have to be a problem. I see it as a solution—the best solution," she said, desperately wanting to believe Peter meant what he was saying about considering the plan.

"Maybe. But don't forget, Jackie, that Morgan isn't very likely to supply the Zinfandel vines if he isn't going to get the shipping and distribution rights."

"There might be some kind of a deal I can work out with him. We probably couldn't get our own company into full swing for overseas export for at least a year. We can give Morgan full rights until then and after that work out a percentage in the operation. If we're successful he might be willing to accept a cut rather than nothing at all. Maybe it's time you held the strings and he did some of the dancing."

Peter lifted her hand to plant a warm kiss on her palm. "You are a shrewd woman, Jackie Archer."

She gave him a captivating smile. "I'm also a jealous woman. I like the idea of you having as little involvement with Morgan and his pretty daughter as you want me to have with Jean-Louis and Claude Marigny. Of course, we must also be practical. We can't afford to let our personal feelings interfere with business. Still, if I could get Louis and Pam Morgan out of the picture without hurting the vineyard, I wouldn't mind in the least."

He grinned. "You don't have to be jealous of Pam. It's been months since I've seen her, weeks since we've even exchanged so much as a casual hello on the phone. She hasn't been staying up in Napa Valley lately. Last I heard, she'd started a new boutique in San Francisco and spends most of her time in her apartment there."

"Do you think she's still in love with you?" Jackie tried to keep her tone casual, but she could hear the slight tremor in her voice.

"Shouldn't the question be, am I in love with her?"

"That's a good one," Jackie said with a light tone both of them knew she didn't mean.

Peter looked hurt and insulted despite the fact he'd asked for it. "I never loved Pam. I found her attractive and for a while we . . ." His face was taut. "I love you, Jackie."

For a few moments she said nothing. Finally, her muscles relaxed and she gave him an apologetic smile. "I'm sorry, Peter. That was a dumb question for either of us to bring up. I'm feeling on edge tonight. I guess it's this trip to San Francisco, being away from you for so long, and being back on home turf again."

"Are you sure you want to stop in Ohio on your way back here?"

"I'd like to visit my sister, a few friends—stop at the cemetery and leave a bouquet of lavender on my mother's grave. They were her favorites. I need to go back for a lot of reasons. Maybe I want to show off a little, prove to everyone in town that I'm different now, that I'm making it here. I'm sure that's part of it. But I also don't want to forget my roots. Middleton Corner will always be a part of me. So will that plain little librarian who used to dream big dreams. When I left Ohio I felt so desperate to get away. At first I thought I'd never go back, never chance getting drawn into that narrow little world again. Now I feel more confident." She smiled. "But not enough to keep from feeling a little nervous."

Peter pulled her over onto his lap. "You'd better come back to me. If I find out that you've decided to become a librarian again, I'll show up in Middleton Corner and grab you right out of that dreary little building."

"It isn't dreary. It's a perfectly nice-looking library. Very sunny, bright, cheerful. And I had a very pleasant boss," she teased.

"I have my pleasant moments, don't I?" Peter asked, gently kissing her hair.

"Occasionally," she whispered, slipping her hands around his neck as he stood up and carried her out of the dining room.

Louis Morgan was a large man with a thick neck, broad shoulders, and strong, square hands. The comfortable paunch around his middle was well concealed by a handsome tweed jacket and well-tailored gray slacks. His light-brown hair was flecked with gray and he wore it combed straight back, making no effort to hide his receding hairline. For a man in his early sixties his face was remarkably smooth, the only wrinkles being a few lines at the corners of his eyes and one slash on either side of his mouth, giving him a somewhat grave expression even when he smiled.

The smile was only one of the things that disturbed Jackie about Louis Morgan. His whole demeanor reminded her of an oversized Napoleon. As they walked through the busy airport, she had the feeling he expected the crowds to part for him like the Red Sea. He took immediate command of everything, including the decision that they spend the night in town at the St. Regis and drive up to Napa Valley in the morning.

As it turned out, he had made that decision before he met her at the airport, two rooms already having been booked that afternoon at the hotel. He had even reserved a table there for dinner.

Jackie, exhausted from the flight, first into New

York the day before and then this evening into San Francisco, was too tired to argue. She also admitted to feeling a bit intimidated by the compelling Mr. Morgan, but she promised herself that after a good night's sleep she'd feel more in charge. As it was, she allowed him to usher her into the quiet, elegant dining room at the St. Regis and didn't make a peep when he ordered dinner for the two of them.

"I'm sure you'll want to make it an early night. I know how tiring the trip from abroad can be. Especially if you're not used to it," Louis Morgan added.

Jackie fought back a yawn. Maybe she was reading too much into his manner and the little remarks he kept dropping, but she got the distinct feeling Morgan wasn't thrilled with her participation in the business. She tried not to form any firm judgments until she knew him a little better. Over the next week she was sure she'd know exactly where she stood with Louis Morgan —and where he stood with her.

"I'm sure it will get easier with time," she said, pushing her disquieting thoughts from her mind. "Fortunately, the trip gave me a chance to catch up on some paperwork and go over some of the preliminary arrangements you and Peter have talked about on the phone."

"How are things going for Peter? Last we spoke, he was having his hands full finding a decent wine master."

"Did he say that?" Jackie was sure the last person in the world Peter would confide his problems to would be his cousin.

Morgan fixed his mild blue eyes on her. "I've been in this business for a long time, Miss Archer. I know what Peter's up against starting a vineyard on foreign soil. And, knowing Peter as well as I do, I can read between his lines, if you know what I mean. I told him it wasn't going to be easy, but he was determined and I'm willing to support his efforts. I believe in helping family, Miss Archer."

Especially when it's in your own best interest, she reflected, but was careful to keep her thoughts to herself.

"Peter has had his problems, Mr. Morgan, but things are working out just fine. The St. Jacques's consortium has been a big help. And on the day I left, Peter had just hired an excellent *maître de chaix*—a wine master," she quickly translated.

Morgan looked insulted. "I know the term."

"Yes, of course you do. Sorry."

"How's Peter's French coming along? He mentioned you were teaching him the language. Fortunate he found somebody who could do some of the translating for him."

"Yes," she said curtly. "I think we've both been fortunate."

Morgan gave her one of his grim smiles. "It's a big job the two of you have taken on. Don't get me wrong, Miss Archer, I'm rooting for you. I want to see Peter make out over there."

"You also have a fair investment in his success," she couldn't resist saying.

"True." He nodded pleasantly. "Why not come out ahead of the game while lending a helping hand? Anything wrong in that?"

"No, I suppose not," she said cautiously, realizing that Morgan was manipulating the conversation very adeptly.

The waiter delivered their dinners, perfectly crisp capons filled with chestnut stuffing on a bed of wild rice. For a few minutes they both concentrated on their food, although Jackie found her appetite affected by the growing tension she was feeling.

"I suppose," Morgan said, after swallowing a sip of wine, "that you have gotten to know Peter quite well over the past couple of months, working with him so closely and all."

"Is there a particular question in your mind, Mr. Morgan?" she asked bluntly, the effect of the wine loosening her tongue.

He chuckled. "Direct. I like that. Well, to be equally direct with you, not so much a question as an observation."

Before he continued he took another sip of wine. "Peter's a real heartbreaker, Miss Archer. Always has been, since he first learned about the birds and the bees—from me, I might add. Girls used to fall all over him in school. His mother had to orchestrate his phone calls and his dates. Finally, I talked her into sending him to a boy's military prep school. Turned out to be a big mistake. Peter didn't go for authority. He broke every rule in the place and got himself thrown out before the first term was up."

"Why are you telling me this, Mr. Morgan?"

"Do you know about Peter and my daughter Pamela?"

"Do I know what?"

"Don't be cagey with me, Miss Archer," he said impatiently. "I think you are a very pretty, very bright young woman who knows some of the score. You ought to be pleased I'm here to fill you in on the rest of it."

"Why should I be pleased?" she asked tersely.

"Because, just like most other women, including my own daughter, Miss Archer, you've probably fallen head over heels in love with my young cousin. Correct?"

"You make it sound like a crime."

"Look, you came here to do business with me. Peter tells me he's cut you in for a fair share of the vineyard because of all your help and because he says you're real talented. I don't believe in beating around the bush, Miss Archer. Peter is as likely to break your heart as he has Pam's, and that is going to complicate business matters. I don't like unnecessary complications."

"I assure you, Mr. Morgan, that Peter and I are perfectly able to keep our personal and business relations separate."

"Bull."

"Furthermore," she went on, "from what I understand, you were the one that saw to it that Peter's relationship with your daughter didn't get too serious."

"Too serious?" he exploded. "Pammy was looking at bridal magazines. But I knew damn well

Peter wanted to marry the Morgan Winery, not my daughter. Just like his father married my cousin Helene so he'd have his future secure. When I told Peter I'd disown Pam if they got married, he started cooling real fast. Unfortunately, my plan backfired. Pam blamed me for keeping them apart. She wouldn't speak to me for weeks—until I offered Peter the château in Labarde and he took off without a minute's hesitation. That brought the picture into sharper focus for her. Not that she isn't still a little in love with him, but at least now she knows the score." He took a big bite of chicken and, when he finished chewing it, aimed the prongs of the fork at Jackie. "And now you know it too."

"I know your version of the score," she replied coolly, refusing to let his message penetrate the trust and belief she had in Peter. She didn't like Louis Morgan and she didn't put it past him to manipulate the facts as well as the people he dealt with.

"I like that, too, Miss Archer." He gave her a quick pat on the hand. "You're a gal who doesn't jump to conclusions too fast. That's fine. Believe me, the only reason I'm telling you this little story is to help you understand that, first and foremost, Peter Santiago is an opportunist. I say that without malice, since in business that's probably the best kind of person to have on your team."

Jackie flinched. If she had anything to do with it, the team was going to be disbanded as expediently as possible. But for the time being she had no choice but to play along. From even these few hours with Morgan, Jackie knew he would never cooperate if he thought she and Peter were going to set up their own shipping company a year or so down the line. And the more time she spent with Morgan the more convinced she was that it was the only way to go. Now all she had to do was convince Peter they could manage it.

She finished her dinner quickly, using her exhaustion to good advantage by bidding Morgan an early good-night. They walked together into the lobby.

"I hope I haven't said anything to disturb you about Peter, Miss Archer. I'm very fond of him despite our somewhat tempestuous relationship. Actually, I'd like to see him settle down, get married to the . . . right girl. But I don't think Peter has his heart set on marrying for love alone."

"I can't help noticing, Mr. Morgan, that as much as you profess such strong feelings for your cousin, you certainly have very few positive things to say about his character. But then," she said with an airy superiority as she watched the elevator door open, "perhaps that's just your nature."

Although her voice was light, the undertone did not escape Louis Morgan. The doors slid apart and Jackie stepped inside the elevator. She stared into Morgan's grim face. *"Bonsoir,* Monsieur Morgan."

He gave a short nod of his head, but this time he made no effort to smile. Not that it would have altered his expression much anyway. For the ride up to the fifteenth floor Jackie felt better. Morgan

231

might be a good Napoleon, but she'd had some solid practice playing the aristocratic Mademoiselle Jacqueline Armand. She intended to put everything she had learned about dealing with men such as Louis Morgan to good use. By morning she would be well rested and ready for round two.

CHAPTER THIRTEEN

The next morning Jackie received a message from Louis Morgan. In bold, authoritative script, he wrote that he had an early appointment in town and he would pick her up at the St. Regis at one in the afternoon for the drive up to Napa. Jackie was irritated at herself for feeling relief at the temporary reprieve. But she couldn't deny the strain of relating to Morgan, now that they had both revealed a flashing glimpse of their hands. Yes, Jackie reflected, the cards were already dealt and now she had to figure out which ones to hold on to and which to let go. She was pretty certain Morgan was astute enough, even given their brief encounter last night, to begin sorting through his options as well.

She wandered into the coffee shop at the hotel, ordered a blueberry muffin and coffee, and skimmed through the *San Francisco Chronicle*. Somewhere close to the middle of the newspaper she spotted a fashion ad that caught her attention. It wasn't so much the hand-woven mohair sweater that attracted her, though it was quite lovely; it was the name *Morgan Designs*. Peter had told her that Pam Morgan had opened a boutique in San Francisco. Jackie figured the odds were with her that Morgan Designs was Pam's new shop. She tore out the ad, finished her muffin and the last swallow of coffee, paid her tab, and left.

Jackie knew as soon as she spotted the newspaper ad that her curiosity about what Pamela Morgan looked like would have to be sated. She admitted to herself that the thought of dropping into the boutique had crossed her mind more than once before she ever saw that ad. What did she want to do? Check out her competition? But Peter had insisted Pam Morgan wasn't any competition. He didn't love Pam Morgan, never had —or so he said. Well, maybe he'd told Pam he loved her in the heat of . . .

Jackie's pace quickened as she walked out of the hotel, her conversation with Louis Morgan drifting back into her mind. Morgan's version of the relationship—the version she'd so cavalierly tossed aside last night—was that Peter had not only been seriously involved with Pamela, but that he'd actually proposed. According to Peter, it was Pam who had done all the talking about marriage. He was the one who had told her he had no desire to marry her or anyone else. Jackie shivered. She'd probably gotten the same speech from Peter about his feelings on marriage as Pam had heard a few months ago. She wondered ruefully if Pam had bought the spiel about his parents' rotten relationship as an acceptable excuse for Peter to be so turned off to the idea of wedded bliss.

Last night Jackie had been so sure she'd finally come to trust Peter's feelings for her. Last night she was put off enough by Louis Morgan not to want to give him the satisfaction of arousing her suspicions. In the light of a new day Jackie found herself struggling with the two different versions of the story, wondering which one was true. Although she chided herself for opening old wounds, she started remembering the doubts and suspicions that had cropped up all during her tumultuous relationship with Peter Santiago.

She walked over to a cable-car stop, joining the early-morning residents and tourists already forming a casual line. A few minutes later she climbed into the colorful red-and-yellow trolley with the crowd, too preoccupied to do much more than note that this was her first experience riding one of the newly refurbished, world-famous San Francisco cable cars. The first precipitous climb up one of the steeper hills of the city, however, made her sit up and really take notice.

For a brief while Jackie allowed herself to play tourist, thrilling to the exhilarating open-air ride that clickety-clacked noisily up and down incredibly steep inclines. A couple of times Jackie literally held her breath for fear the cable car would give out halfway up a hill. She was amazed at the nonchalance with which San Franciscans hung out into the street, one hand grasping a leather stirrup, some of them actually reading newspapers as they held on.

By the time she got off at Union Street, a fashionable strip where many of the classier shops and boutiques were located, Jackie was disappointed at not having more time to explore the breathtakingly lovely city. Perhaps one day she and Peter would come back here for business—or pleasure. The thought brought her full circle to her earlier concerns.

Exactly what she hoped to gain by dropping in at Pam Morgan's shop, she had little idea, other than satisfying her curiosity about Pam's appearance. She certainly didn't intend to ask Pam for the true account of her past involvement with Peter. Chances were, she'd have a version all her own.

It was close to ten in the morning when Jackie started down Union Street, her eyes searching for Morgan Designs. She decided to stop trying to sort out her motives. If nothing else, maybe she'd buy that sweater advertised on the slip of newspaper in her pocketbook.

Most of the shops were just opening and the street was still relatively empty, making it easy for Jackie to spot Morgan Designs across the street. Hesitating, she ended up walking on past, feeling suddenly foolish about her decision to catch a glimpse of the attractive Miss Morgan. Did she really need to assure herself she was just as attractive, just as appealing?

She came to an abrupt stop a few stores down and turned around. Okay, so she did want a little reassurance. Pam Morgan had obviously been someone Peter considered his type—for a while anyway. Jackie, he'd claimed so romantically, was beyond type, a one of a kind. That should have made her feel more secure. At the time it had. But now, a few thousand miles away from Peter, Jackie found herself feeling vaguely anxious. She hated to face how much Louis Morgan had gotten to her. Well, she was going to make damn sure he was the last to know.

She walked into Morgan Designs acting like an ordinary shopper dropping in to check out the new fashions. There was a subtle scent of fine perfume about the place—a touch fruity, tinged with a hint of musk. A striking abstract sculpture, almost as tall as Jackie, stood close to the entrance. On closer examination she realized it was an expressionist's imaginative and somewhat grandiose fantasy of a female form. Draped over the voluptuous stone figure were a few well-placed, handmade sweaters and shawls, all done in soft shades of lilacs, blues, and creamy tans. Jackie recognized one of the sweaters as the one in the ad. It was even lovelier in person. She made up her mind to buy it, until she took a casual glance at the price tag. Morgan Designs was definitely not a place to grab a bargain. She decided this was going to be a browsing excursion after all, her budget clearly not up to the purchase of two-hundred-dollar sweaters.

"May I help you?" A slender young woman appeared from behind a curtained area in the back of the shop. She was tall, expertly made up, her reddish-blond hair cut in a short, almost mannish style that in no way detracted from her strikingly feminine features: full lips, warm chestnut-brown eyes, and a perfectly chiseled nose that was too fine to call pert. She was wearing a slightly different version of the sweater Jackie had coveted. Jackie was glad she'd decided against it, feeling she could never carry it off with the same panache. Depressing how quickly she had slipped back into feeling like plain Jackie Archer, librarian from Middleton Corner, Ohio. She doubted at that moment that she could dredge up even a remnant of the stylish, aristocratic Jacqueline Armand. Fortunately, she didn't have to try.

Five minutes later Jackie found herself in the peculiar position of feeling undeniable relief and yet, at the same time, vague disquiet. It turned out that the chic young woman who had momentarily posed such a threat to Jackie's self-confidence was not Pamela Morgan, but merely one of the saleswomen who worked for her. Pamela Morgan, it seemed, was not in town at the moment. She'd left for Paris three days ago on a buying trip.

Paris was not a hop, skip, and a jump to Labarde and Château Cardinet, but it wasn't a few thousand miles away, either. Was Pam planning on paying a friendly visit to Peter while she was in France? Jackie might not have found the notion so threatening if she weren't halfway across the world. Here she was, struggling all morning about Peter's trustworthiness, and now she was being handed another item to fret over.

Jackie idly fingered a mohair shawl as she

chided herself for being unreasonably suspicious. Even if Pam did stop by to say hello to Peter, what did that mean? They were relatives, after all. Distant relatives. Her fingers gripped the mohair fabric. As long as they stayed distant, everything would be all right.

"That shawl would look wonderful on you," the saleswoman was saying.

Jackie released her grip, completely unaware that she'd been holding it, and stepped back. "Thank you. Perhaps another time." She started for the door. "I'll drop in again."

"Did you want to leave a message for Pam? Or your name?"

"No. That's all right. She doesn't know me. I just wanted to compliment her on her exquisite taste."

Jackie hurried out of the shop feeling a bit foolish and more than a bit depressed. She had to face a week of the smug, opinionated Louis Morgan, and as if that weren't going to be tough enough, now she had to worry about her lover's impending reunion with his old flame.

Jackie spent the rest of the morning taking a cable-car tour around town, trying to recapture the carefree excitement of feeling like a tourist. But she had little success, and by the time one o'clock rolled around she was relieved to begin battle again with Louis Morgan, deciding it was better than battling her own unsettling thoughts.

Morgan was right on time, pulling up at the entrance of the St. Regis in his sleek silver BMW sports car. He looked very dapper and well rested this afternoon, greeting Jackie with a friendly smile, one that was much less austere than any he'd bestowed on her last night. Swinging his body easily out of the car, no small feat considering his large frame, he walked around and helped Jackie into her seat while the doorman worked at stuffing her two small suitcases into the tiny trunk.

"You look very lovely this afternoon," he commented magnanimously as he started the engine. "I hope you had a good night."

"Yes, thanks." She observed his ruddy complexion, his eyes sharper and brighter in daylight, his youthful appearance even more apparent. "It looks as though you had a good rest too."

He gave her a broad grin. "Actually, I was up until three this morning going over a very lengthy prospectus. Probably got no more than four hours of sleep, but I feel great. Just settled a sweet deal, which never fails to perk me up, no matter how little sleep I've had. Peter has probably told you I'm a workaholic. I like to have my fingers in lots of pies—although, of course, the wine business comes first. Morgan Winery goes back close to seventy-five years. It's one of the best. I only deal in quality, Miss Archer." He gave her a sly glance. "And I'm not just talking wine now."

"Sticking to wine, Mr. Morgan, I think you've definitely got a quality investment as far as Château Cardinet is concerned. But I'm sure that's small potatoes compared to some of your other vested interests," she added, hoping to feel him out a little. Before she could come up with a game plan to present to Peter, she needed to know how important Château Cardinet was to Morgan.

"I have plenty of bigger potatoes"—he chuckled—"but some of them were real small when I started up with them. If Peter plays his cards right, he could have a real gold mine out there. As long as he doesn't get too greedy." This time his glance was very shrewd. "I don't believe in biting the hand that feeds you, Miss Archer."

"What do you mean?" she asked cautiously.

"Did I mention that my shipping company has started to import Château Vauvilliers wines? You do know Philippe Troyan, don't you? I thought Peter mentioned a while back that the two of you were guests of his out in Margaux. Fabulous place he's got. And with my help he'll probably be able to hold on to it. I'm sure you'll keep it to yourself, Miss Archer, but Troyan is a lousy businessman."

"I'm having trouble following you, Mr. Morgan," she admitted. "What does Philippe Troyan have to do with your worries about Peter getting greedy?"

Morgan didn't answer at first. Jackie wasn't sure whether it was for effect or because he was trying to get around the traffic bogs. Finally, he said offhandedly, "You're living in a tight little community over there, you and Peter. Like small towns in this country, pretty soon everyone learns everyone else's business. I end up being in the grapevine, too, especially since I started working with Troyan. The man is a natural-born gossip. Of course, you have to take some of what he tells you with a grain of salt."

He suddenly looked older, the crease lines about his eyes more pronounced as he squinted into the sun. Jackie cringed, her imagination running rampant about all the tidbits Philippe Troyan had shared with Louis Morgan.

Ever since he'd found out about her impersonation, Philippe had been blatantly cool and unfriendly toward her and Peter. The fact that both St. Jacques and the Marignys seemed undisturbed by the masquerade had only increased Troyan's irritation. Whenever he saw either Jackie or Peter at a dinner party or in town, he went out of his way to snub them. Until now it had never bothered Jackie in the least.

She could feel herself growing increasingly tense. But, as uncomfortable as she felt, Jackie was not about to sit there in agony during the hour-long drive and risk spending the next week fretting over what Morgan knew or thought he knew. Unless she confronted him directly, she sensed that Morgan would not mind keeping her squirming.

Giving herself a couple of minutes to relax, she said lightly, "Tell me what you've heard over the grapevine."

"Well, now," he answered slowly, "I heard, for instance, that you pulled the wool over Troyan's eyes for a while there . . . Mademoiselle Armand, was it?"

Jackie heard the humor in his voice and laughed. "I guess Philippe will never forgive me for that one." She felt herself relaxing a little more. It lasted less than a minute.

"He also mentioned that you spend a lot of time at the other châteaus, pumping people for information."

Jackie bristled. "Most of the château owners are exceptionally gracious about helping me learn about the business. I certainly wouldn't call it pumping them."

He pursed his lips. "I hear you're particularly interested in learning all about how some of the vineyard owners run their own shipping companies."

She felt an invisible hand clutch her stomach. "I want to learn every aspect of the business. Especially everything to do with shipping and distribution. That is one of my major responsibilities at Château Cardinet."

"The way I hear it from Troyan, you and Peter seem mighty interested in forming your own shipping concern, Miss Archer. Which leads me to wonder where I'm going to end up in this deal."

Jackie felt a thickening in her throat. She'd thought she was holding her trump cards close to her chest and the whole time Louis Morgan had already seen and memorized them.

"I have been investigating the idea on my own." Her voice sounded raspy. She wished she had a glass of water. "I only presented it to Peter the day before I left, and he was opposed to it," she said truthfully. "I wasn't thinking so much about our exports when I started exploring the possibility. I was focusing on local distribution of our wines. It's proving both difficult and costly to get companies to handle the Zinfandel. I thought having our own company would get around the problem altogether."

Morgan made no comment at first, concentrating on maneuvering the car over to the right-hand lane as the sign for Napa Valley appeared overhead. He exited off the ramp and turned left onto Route 29, a road lined with boutiques, restaurants, motels, and wineries. There were even a couple of shops advertising hot-air balloon rides.

"That's a load of bull, Miss Archer."

Jackie gave him a look of mild shock.

He chuckled. "Pardon my French," he said with a wink. "Maybe I should have said full of hot air. I've been in this business too long not to figure out your scheme, honey. And let me tell you straight from the shoulder that I never end up with the short end of the stick. While you're here we'll work up a nice, tidy contract assuring me exclusive shipping rights for a substantial period of time."

"Are you also prepared to work up a neat contract granting Peter full title to the property in exchange?"

"Peter knows he's going to get title. But not until I'm assured that he's got a viable business under way. I'd be a fool to give up that property only to see it go down the drain. He needs my backing. Unless, of course, he can come up with the cash to buy me out. But I doubt he's in any position to have that kind of money lying around right now." He swung into a gravel driveway. "Ah, here we are. Home sweet home. Relax, Miss Archer. You're new to the game. It seems to me you're already doing all right for yourself. You can't expect to win against the big guys just yet." He gave her a supremely demeaning smile.

If he was anticipating her feeling intimidated, he was in for a shock. Jackie burst out laughing, Morgan's smile reminding her so strikingly of Henri Bouchard, the arrogant maître d' at the Côte d'Or. And remembering him brought back other memories—Peter tripping her that first night, the soufflé landing in de Ternaux's lap, the escapade at her apartment building when the factory worker absconded with Peter's coat and most of her worldly possessions, her masquerade as Jacqueline Armand, and the comedy of errors at Troyan's château that first weekend.

Morgan was right about one thing. In some ways it was a game. But he was wrong about her being a novice. Jackie may not have been playing the game very long, but she'd played it with an intensity that more than made up for that shortcoming.

"Sorry," she said airily when Morgan stared at her as if she had gone mad. "You just reminded me of someone for a moment. It struck me funny." Another little laugh escaped her lips and she pressed them shut.

The ride up to Napa with Morgan had turned out to do wonders for her spirits. Their little battle of wits had pushed worries about Peter and

Pamela completely out of her mind, at least for a brief while.

Morgan showed her around his stone castle like a true lord of the manor. It was a lovely old building with a rough-hewn charm, but for Jackie, who had been a guest at some of the most lavish châteaus in France, it did not compare. Still, she was very complimentary, if not gushing, and Morgan seemed satisfied that she was duly impressed. She was sure he felt a need to gain ground after she'd deflated his ego so soundly in the car.

"Tomorrow, I'll give you the grand tour of the winery," he said as they returned to the main hallway, one of the darker, more somber rooms in the house due to the heavy drapes covering the windows. "I'll spare you the gift shop and the tasting room. It's usually mobbed with tourists. We'll have plenty of opportunities for private tastings while you're here."

He called out for his housekeeper, a kindly looking, middle-aged woman to whom Morgan had introduced her when they arrived.

"Anna will show you up to your room. You might want to freshen up or rest. We'll dine at seven. It will just be the two of us tonight. I'd hoped Pamela would join us, but she's in New York on a buying trip."

"New York?"

Anna walked into the hallway. "For her boutique," Morgan explained. "Every couple of months she has to fly into New York for stock.

She's doing very well, so she tells me," he said proudly.

She obviously doesn't always tell you the truth, Jackie reflected, the disquiet she'd managed to shove aside for the past few hours returning with a rush.

After six days of intense, head-on meetings with Louis Morgan to negotiate the shipping and distribution arrangements, coupled with meetings with dealers, other winery owners, and several dinner parties where Jackie played hostess for the widowed Morgan, she was too worn out to worry much about infidelity at Château Cardinet. Besides, she'd spoken to Peter twice this week, and other than sharing worries about Morgan's trying to tie them to an exclusive five-year contract, they'd spent the rest of the time on the phone telling each other how lonely they were.

It was late afternoon; Jackie and Morgan were sitting in his library ironing out some of the last-minute details of the agreement before she left for Ohio the next day. For once Jackie was glad that Peter had the ultimate say over any contract arrangement she and Louis worked out. That allowed her to stall Morgan on any final terms until she returned to France and Peter had a chance to go over the thick sheaf of papers accumulated during this long, tiring week. When she'd talked with him on the phone yesterday, Peter had seemed less hostile to the notion of setting up their own shipping company. And Jackie, after spending almost a week with the manipulative, self-aggrandizing Louis Morgan, was more certain than ever that it would be the best thing she and Peter could do. Of course, they'd have to figure out some way to break ties with him as soon as possible, but Jackie had several ideas about how that might be accomplished.

Louis Morgan lit his pipe and leaned back in his chair.

"I think that covers the whole deal. Don't you, Jackie?"

"We've dealt with everything but the kitchen sink." She smiled wanly. "Let's call it a wrap." She began gathering the scattered papers on the desk, slipping them into her leather briefcase.

"What's the matter? You look kind of pale. Are you feeling homesick for that château across the Atlantic?" He leaned forward a little. "Or is it just that young heartthrob of a cousin of mine you're missing?"

"Both," she said lightly, having spent the week honing her skills at keeping Louis Morgan from getting her riled.

"Well, I have a visitor coming over for dinner tonight that should cheer you up. Claude Marigny. He tells me he's a good friend of yours."

"Claude? What's he doing in California?" Morgan had managed to get a rise out of her after all.

He leaned back. "He's got some meetings with wholesalers. I guess now that he's taking over his father's shipping concerns he wants to get to know everyone on this side of the world. He was real pleased to learn you were staying with me this week." He grinned, watching Jackie's mouth set into a firm expression. "Something tells me he already had a pretty good idea you'd be around. Like I told you the other day, you're part of a small community over there."

Jackie looked sharply across the desk at Morgan. She was sure his spies across the sea had informed him of Marigny's hot pursuit. And from the looks of it Morgan was thoroughly enjoying the possibility of stirring up trouble. But she was not about to play into his hand after doing so well up to now.

"Claude is a good friend—and my former boss. It will be lovely to visit with him tonight." She checked her watch. "I ought to go up and get ready. It's close to six."

An hour later she was offering her cheek to the debonair Frenchman. With aplomb Claude tilted her chin and moved the kiss to her lips, his free hand skimming the sleeve of her black wool dress. He seemed not to notice her pulling back, but merely stepped closer and put his arm around her, letting a smiling Louis Morgan lead them into the sitting room.

"You look beautiful as always, Jacqueline," Claude said, accepting a glass of dark-red wine from Morgan.

"I feel real bad, Marigny," Louis said with a broad grin. "I've been working the poor girl to the bone. But she's real bright, takes everything in . . . a tough negotiator, I don't mind admitting. My cousin's found himself a real winner." Morgan dug his hand into his pocket and took out his pipe.

Claude's expression clouded. "I wonder if he appreciates that," he said, locking eyes with Jackie for the briefest moment.

It was long enough for her to feel a distinct wave of anxiety. What the hell did he mean by that? Or was this just another of his lines to convince her Peter wasn't worthy of her?

"Why don't you two relax and catch up on gossip," Louis said lightly, "while I go check with Anna on the dinner."

As soon as he had walked out the door, Jackie turned abruptly to Claude, her eyebrows quirked in puzzled suspicion.

Claude held up a hand to forestall her question. "I don't think we want to talk about this now," he said in a languid, mysterious voice.

"Talk about what?" Jackie demanded, her anxiety moving from her stomach to her throat. "What's going on, Claude? What was that remark about Peter not appreciating me all about?" Her tone was glacial.

"*Chérie*, don't be upset. I did not want to come as the bearer of bad tidings. You must know by now how deeply I care for you. I don't want to see you get hurt."

"Claude, the one who is going to get hurt is you if you don't tell me what's going on." She was demanding answers, but deep inside she already had a good idea what Claude was hinting at. Pam Morgan had gone down to visit Peter in Labarde. Word got around easily, just as Morgan was always saying.

"I find myself in an awkward predicament,

chérie. I very much want to speak plainly to you, for your own sake, but I have been sworn to keep a confidence." He bowed his head in regal fashion.

Jackie felt a cold, sickening chill attack her body. In a voice that she barely recognized she said, "Then I'll tell you. That way you won't have to break your promise. Pamela Morgan and Peter both know that if her father heard she'd gone to be with him in Labarde, he'd very likely call off the whole vineyard deal. She's there with Peter now . . . isn't she?"

Claude looked over at her sympathetically. "She arrived early this week and has been staying at the château with Santiago. One day I went over to talk with him about business. He was out. Miss Morgan came downstairs and introduced herself. I mentioned I'd be leaving for the States, that I'd be stopping in California. She was very concerned that no word get back to her father about her presence there. If he knew, there would be repercussions, as you say." He reached out for her hand, but she pulled it away and stood up. "I'm sorry, *chérie*." He got up as well. "I know you think that inside I am gloating—a jealous man who feels if he can't have you, he wants no one else to—but you would be wrong, *mon amour*. My feelings for you are purer than you think."

"Peter never said one word on the phone," she muttered in a small, sad voice.

"Maybe he wanted to tell you in person. I have a feeling Miss Morgan never mentioned meeting me to Santiago. And I didn't tell him that I'd be coming to the States this week. As far as he knows, you are in the dark."

"I am in the dark," she said, a flash of fury washing over her features. "Completely in the dark when it comes to understanding anything at all about Peter Santiago." She started for the door, but Claude grasped her wrist.

"What will you do now, *chérie?*"

"Now?" Her large eyes grew wider. "Now I'm going upstairs to pack. Then I'm going to Middleton Corner, Ohio."

"For good?" He gazed at her, honestly distraught.

"I don't know, Claude. Right now I don't know anything." She bit her lower lip to prevent the floodgates from opening. "Please give my excuses to Louis. I—I won't be joining you for dinner. Tell him I'm sick. It's true enough."

CHAPTER FOURTEEN

Jackie heard Gwen's station wagon pull into the driveway and come to her typical grinding halt inches from the garage door.

"Everybody out. That means you, too, Topper," Gwen's voice rang out, high pitched, with the authoritative tone of a weary mom back from a two-hour jaunt at the supermarket. "Danny, don't let Topper get his dog food until you bring it in the house. Come on, Sarah, it won't kill you to carry two bundles in at one time."

"My nails," Sarah moaned. "You know I just did them this morning for the party tonight. All I need is to break one of them now. You were the one who always told me, 'Sarah, don't bite your nails. It's so unattractive.'"

Gwen, struggling with two overstuffed bundles and dangling a one-gallon container of bleach from her fingers, shook her head, eyes cast to the sky.

"Oh, all right," the sixteen-year-old Sarah relented, carefully taking hold of the bleach container.

"Can I help?" Jackie stepped out of the kitchen door.

"Grab a hold of Topper, will you, hon?" Gwen asked, a grateful smile on her face. "Danny, let Jackie deal with the dog. You bring in the rest of the bundles."

"Come on, Topper," Jackie called out, the sheep dog giving her a quizzical look, then loping over to her side. "That's a good boy. See, you do remember me after all." She gave Topper a friendly scratch on the head, then caught hold of his collar and led him through the gate to the fenced-in yard.

Sarah met her at the kitchen door. "Aunt Jackie, don't forget you promised to help me with my hair tonight. And makeup. I'm dying to try some of those French creams and shadows. God, they're fabulous. I still can't believe how absolutely beautiful you look. If Paris does that to women, I'm leaving as soon as I graduate from high school."

Gwen grinned at her lovely, intense daughter, giving her almost carrot-colored hair a gentle tug. "Let's make that after college, my pet. And then I think I just might tag along with you. I could use a glamorous makeover myself. Now, get your brother and tell him he'd better clean up his room and you go do your homework. I am in desperate need of a moment of peace and quiet, a cup of coffee, and a nice chat with this little sister of mine." She gave her daughter a less-than-gentle shove.

Sarah started out the door to the dining room

and paused. "I'd love to cut my hair the way you have it, Aunt Jackie. If you're going to be staying for a while, maybe you could come down with me to Muriel's next week. I've got an appointment for a regular trim, but if she sees your hair, maybe she could copy it."

Jackie smiled. "I'd be happy to go with you. I should stop in and say hi to Muriel anyway."

A delighted smile flickered across Sarah's face. "Terrific." Seconds later her voice screeched out from the bottom of the stairs. "Danny! Mom says you better clean up your pigsty or there'll be hell to pay."

Gwen grinned and walked over to the kitchen door, shutting it firmly. "They're great kids, but there are days . . ." She moved to the counter and stuck the coffeepot on the stove to heat up the morning's brew. "Want some?"

"Sure," Jackie said, unloading the groceries.

Gwen leaned against the counter and watched her sister work. "Well, since you returned two days ago, Middleton Corner hasn't stopped buzzing. You should have heard everyone down at the market. 'Doesn't Jackie look wonderful? . . . I'd never have recognized her. . . . So sophisticated. . . . She looks like a movie star. . . . I never would have dreamed. . . .' Honey, your homecoming is as close to receiving royalty as Middleton Corner is ever likely to see."

Jackie stuck the container of bleach under the kitchen sink. "To be honest, I feel a little like a freak." She turned to her sister, taking the cup of coffee from her outstretched hand. "Do I really look all that different, Gwen?"

Gwen laughed low in her throat. "It's not just your looks, hon. I think people around here aren't only picking up on the new hairdo, the smart clothes, the great makeup, and heavenly French scent . . . everything about you seems different. You relate differently. There's this sexy, mysterious quality about you that's got everyone entranced." She walked over to Jackie, who was perched on a stool at the counter. "But what I don't think they're picking up—which I am—is that you're very upset about something."

Jackie smiled wanly. "Am I that transparent?"

"Only to someone who knows you as well as I do. Are you going back to France, Jackie?"

"I don't know. I keep asking myself that question. I just don't know what to do."

"Problems with Monsieur Santiago?" Gwen asked gently.

"Endless problems." And then, in a rush, she added, "He's opinionated, opportunistic, controlling, he doesn't believe the least in binding commitments, and—and he's presently having a grand old fling with an old girlfriend of his. He thinks I don't know what's going on, so what the hell. Peter Santiago is not what you'd call your trustworthy, loyal Boy Scout kind of guy."

"You mean he's a rat-fink, as Sarah would say."

"Of the first order," Jackie confirmed.

"And you're wild about him," Gwen said softly.

"But I'm not crazy. Or at least I wasn't until I got involved with Peter on a cold wet night in

Paris. Since then, my life's taken one mad leap after another." Jackie blinked away an errant tear. "And I've loved almost every minute of it." She took a large swallow of coffee, then sniffed.

The doorbell rang. Gwen pressed her hand over Jackie's. "Sarah will get it. It's probably one of her girlfriends coming over to work out their strategy for the party."

But it wasn't one of Sarah's friends.

Sarah appeared in the doorway, an impish smile on her face. "A beau of yours is calling, Aunt Jackie."

Gwen and Jackie both looked up, puzzled. "Who?" Jackie muttered.

"Tom Coopersmith," Sarah whispered. A giggle burst out. "I think he's brought you candy."

"Oh, God," Jackie moaned softly.

Gwen laughed. "I guess old Tom is still pining away for you, hon. He must have heard you were back and looking like a million bucks." She gave Jackie's shoulder a little squeeze. "Keep in mind that he remains Middleton Corner's most eligible bachelor."

Jackie grinned. "If it's up to me, he's going to stay that way." She sighed. "Well, I guess I'll have to make an appearance." She grabbed her sister's hand. "Come on, I can't do it alone."

Gwen tagged along reluctantly. Tom was waiting in the hall, looking slightly uncomfortable. His discomfort blended with pleasure as Jackie walked over and gave him a friendly kiss on the cheek.

Tom Coopersmith was a man who admirably

exemplified all of the Boy Scout virtues that Peter Santiago so blatantly lacked. And he was perfectly nice looking in a collegiate sort of way; tall, on the thin side, sandy-blond hair cut sensibly short, nice hazel eyes, and a warm, easygoing style. On an occasional Sunday he still wore his college sweater with his basketball letter. There was nothing wrong with Tom—except that he was about as exciting as a Saturday night church supper.

"Hi, Tom. Come on inside the living room. Gwen and I were just having coffee. Can I get you some?"

"I could go for a nice hot cup of tea." He smiled at Jackie, then glanced over at her sister. "If it wouldn't be too much trouble, Gwenny."

Jackie held back a laugh. She knew her sister hated being called by her childhood nickname. But Gwen and Tom had gone straight through high school together and he never called her anything else. Gwen had given up correcting him years ago.

"No trouble. You two go on inside and relax. I'll join you in a few minutes."

Jackie gave her sister an admonishing grimace, then led Tom into the living room. He didn't sit down. He placed the box of candies on the mantel. "For you. They're from France." His grin was a little lopsided. "You sure look great, Jackie. I swear I wouldn't have recognized you if I passed you on the street." He came closer, his eyes traveling down the soft gray cashmere sweater and the beautifully tailored slacks that accentuated her slender, shapely legs. "I missed you."

Jackie smiled. She didn't know what to say. It would certainly not have been honest to tell him she'd missed him too. The truth was, she hadn't given Tom Coopersmith a second thought since the day she flew off to Paris.

"Are you home for a visit or are you back to stay?" He asked, ignoring the lack of response he'd gotten to his last remark.

"I haven't decided yet."

"Oh." He took her hand and led her over to the couch. "I was hoping you had gotten France out of your system. But I guess living in a big château and starting a vineyard is a hell of a lot more exciting than stamping books down at the library." His smile turned wistful. "Not that you'd have to spend your time doing that kind of thing if you decided to stay, if you decided to reconsider . . ." He let the sentence hang, sensitive to the uncomfortable expression on Jackie's face. He shrugged. "I've been in love with you for a lot of years, Jackie. I guess it takes time to wear off."

She took his hand. "You are a very nice man, Tom."

He laughed dryly. "Not exactly the words of a lovestruck woman. But you never really were in love with me, were you?"

"I was very fond of you, Tom. I still am. Some lady is going to be very lucky to nab you."

"C'est dommage." He smiled, his cheeks flushing. "See? I've been practicing . . . just in case."

Jackie felt a little wrenching of her heart. She

put her arms around Tom and pressed her cheek against his well-shaved jaw. "Oh, Tom. It is a pity. And you're very sweet. I forgot for a while just how sweet." As he gently rubbed her back, she started crying quietly.

"You're very sweet, too, Jackie," he said softly. He didn't know what was the matter, and he sensed that Jackie didn't want to be asked. Yet she didn't pull away.

"Thanks. Thanks, Tom." She rested her head on his shoulder and closed her eyes, selfishly letting herself be comforted by Tom's soothing embrace.

Gwen was on her way into the living room with Tom's tea and a new cup of coffee for Jackie when the doorbell rang again. On Saturday afternoons the Turner residence was a madhouse of activity. Between her ten-year-old son's pals and Sarah's friends, the doorbell rarely got more than a moment's rest. Gwen checked her watch. Maybe John had finished early at the hospital and, as was often the case, forgotten his key. She always wondered how her absentminded husband could make such a fine obstetrician. "It's amazing," she always teased him, "that once you deliver those babies you don't set them down someplace and forget where you've put them."

It wasn't John or one of the kids' friends at the door, however. Standing on her front step was probably the handsomest, most dashing man she had ever come face to face with in her thirty-six years of life in Middleton Corner.

Her eyes reluctantly left his finely chiseled face

to trail down his elegant, European-cut suit. The man bestowed a charming smile on her, his eyes radiating amusement. Then he took Gwen's hand, pressed it gallantly to his lips, and introduced himself.

A minute later Gwen stepped into the living room, her cheeks still rosy. She stared in surprise at Jackie, who was sitting with her head resting on Tom's shoulder, his arms wrapped around her.

"You've got some more company," Gwen said. She had an impish grin on her face very similar to the one her daughter had sported earlier.

Jackie pulled away abruptly from Tom, giving her sister a questioning look of dismay. Tom smoothed his hair and let one arm rest across the back of the couch.

"Bon jour, ma chère."

Jackie's eyes darted to the living-room entry, her jaw dropping as she stared into the seductively smiling face of Claude Marigny.

"What in heaven's name are you doing here, Claude?" She stood up and hesitantly walked over to him as though she thought he was a figment of her imagination.

"I have decided, *chérie*, to follow you to the ends of the earth," he said in a thick accent, his eyes sparkling. "Which is where we must be at this very moment, *n'est-ce pas?*"

"You are crazy," she exclaimed. And then she started to laugh. Claude Marigny looked so utterly incongruous standing there in Gwen's all-American living room that she couldn't help herself. Meanwhile, Gwen looked on, puzzled by her sister's strange reaction. Tom stood up, appearing painfully ill at ease.

Claude put an arm around Jackie. "Am I that foolish?" He laughed good-humoredly.

She shook her head, still unable to stop laughing. "I'm sorry, I—" She took a deep breath. "It's just that you're the last person I'd ever expect to see in Middleton Corner." She caught her sister's bemused expression, then met Tom's awkward gaze. She quickly introduced everyone, and Tom made a very hasty exit right afterward.

Jackie walked him to the door. He gave her a wistful kiss on the cheek.

"Thanks for coming by, Tom. It really was good to see you again."

Tom squeezed her shoulder. "Take care, Jackie."

When she closed the front door and turned around, Claude was a few feet behind her. They were alone in the hall.

"I was worried about you, *chérie*. You were so distraught when you left California. I finished my business and decided I had to make sure you were all right."

She swallowed. "I'm all right." She smiled wryly. "I have remarkable resiliency."

"Have you spoken with Peter?"

"No. I need to figure out what I want to say first."

Claude moved closer. "Why don't you tell him" —he pressed his large hands to her waist—"that you are going to marry me?"

Jackie stared at him, dumbfounded. "Claude . . ."

"Je t'aime, ma chère. Je voudrais te marier."

"Marry you," she whispered, still stunned by his sudden appearance now followed by his equally sudden proposal. "But, Claude—"

He pressed a finger to her lips. "You don't love me yet, I know. I understand that. I truly do. But, I believe *avec tout mon coeur* that you will love me one day. I want to marry you, Jacqueline, and take you back to my château—or Paris, whichever you prefer. We can get married there—or here—whatever you say. As long as you say yes, *ma petite, ma belle, mon amour.*"

Gwen peered out of the kitchen, then quickly popped her head back in as she saw Claude pull Jackie passionately into his arms. *Boy,* Gwen thought with a modest twinge of envy, *first Tom swooning all over Jackie, now this positively gorgeous Frenchman.* And here she'd been worrying all these years about her plain, shy little sister.

The phone rang. "I'll get it," Sarah shouted from the top of the stairs. Jackie, wrapped in Claude's embrace at the bottom of the stairs, pushed away from him at the sound of her niece's voice. Sarah, her eyes wide, stared down at the two of them in open astonishment. "Oh, I thought you were with Tom, Aunt Jackie," Sarah said, her eyes fixed on the sublime Claude Marigny.

"Hadn't you better get that phone?" Jackie grinned.

"Oh . . . right." She stepped backward, having trouble wrenching her gaze from Claude.

"Never mind," Gwen shouted through the kitchen door. "I'll get it."

Jackie took Claude's hand. "Come on inside. I need a drink." She gave him a beguiling smile. "It isn't often a lady gets proposed to twice in one day."

Claude pouted charmingly. "I hope I am still in the running."

Gwen walked into the living room from the kitchen just as Claude and Jackie entered from the front hall. She looked a little like the cat that ate the canary.

"What's the matter, Gwen?" Jackie asked, at this point accepting the fact that any strange, bizarre event could happen at any given moment. She was right.

"Phone call for you. You might want to take it in the den." She gave Jackie a long, meaningful look. "It's long distance. Long, long distance."

"Peter?"

Gwen nodded.

Claude gripped Jackie's hand. "Let your sister tell him—"

"No. I have to talk to him," Jackie said resolutely, disentangling her hand from Claude's. "Excuse me."

Jackie walked into the den and closed the door. She picked up the receiver. The phone connection was eerily clear, and Peter's voice sounded unnervingly close. So close, in fact, that the first thing Jackie asked was "Where are you?"

"Where am I? I'm in Labarde, of course. Waiting to hear from you, as a matter of fact. What's going on? You were supposed to call yesterday."

Jackie took a careful breath. "I've been busy. How about you?"

"Busy isn't the word for it, princess."

"No, I guess it isn't."

"What did you say? Hey, talk up. Your voice sounds . . ." He paused. "What is it, princess? Tough being back in Middleton Corner? How about cutting your visit short and taking the next flight back here? I miss you. And I need you. I've started talking to a few people around here, Jean-Louis Marigny in particular, about getting my own shipping company started. Aren't you proud of me, princess? I've decided to grow up and separate my personal feelings from what's best for us professionally. Guess what? . . . Are you there, babe?"

"I'm here."

"Jean-Louis thinks we ought to consider going in with his company. That means more money, and St. Jacques's group is already suffering a serious case of apoplexy. Then, of course, I'll need to buy out Louis as soon as possible so we're free and clear. What do you think?"

"Since when did you want my say on serious business matters?"

"What the hell is bugging you, Jackie? Is it the Ohio air, or are you still unwinding from a week of Louis?"

"I'm unwinding from a lot of things, Peter."

"Look, Jackie . . . whatever is bothering you,

let's talk about it face to face. When are you coming home?"

"I am home." Pain, anger, and self-pity turned the corners of her mouth down. She fought back the explosion struggling to erupt.

"Will you please tell me what's going on?" Peter's voice was a blend of frustration and irritation.

Jackie's throat thickened. "I'm . . . thinking about getting married."

"You're thinking about *what?*" Peter's frustration rose to new heights.

"Claude Marigny is here. He's traveled all the way to the end of the earth, you might say, to ask me to marry him." Her voice was hoarse, brittle. Her hand unconsciously clutched her stomach. "I thought . . . maybe you were reconsidering a proposal yourself."

"I wasn't aware I'd made one to you in the first place," he said, anger giving way to fury. "Since when have you and Claude moved from pals to lovers?"

"We haven't . . . yet." She gripped the desk, her knuckles white. "And I wasn't talking about a proposal to me. I was referring to a distant relative of yours. A relative who, from what I hear, isn't so distant anymore."

"So that's what this is all about?" The light was beginning to dawn. "Claude rushed all the way from France to tell you Pam Morgan showed up at the château—"

"Showed up and stayed," she interrupted bitingly. "Maybe she's still there, keeping a spot warm for you. I remember how cold you could get on those chilly nights in Labarde."

"I ought to be furious at you—"

"You furious at me?" She cut him off again, no longer making an effort to keep her voice low so that those in the next room didn't hear her every word. At last she exploded. "You have yourself a revolting little fling while I'm off struggling with your self-righteous, repugnant cousin. Trying, I might add, to come up with some way to get you out from under his clutches—which I may have done—and which you can damn well forget about now. I wouldn't help you if you were the last man on earth, Peter Santiago. Since the calamitous day I met you I've—I've let myself suspend reason, sanity, and common sense. Well, those days are over. You are deceitful, unfaithful—"

"You jump to conclusions pretty fast for someone who's a few thousand miles away," Peter snapped. "Okay, Pam did show up. Uninvited I may add. And she stayed a few days—"

"Also uninvited?" Jackie threw back.

"No. I invited her to stay."

"And to prance around in her negligées in the mornings? How chummy."

"That's just Pam."

"You . . . you bastard! I just made that up about the negligée. I see my vivid imagination is more accurate than I'd thought. Well, that may, as you say, just be the way your cousin is, but this is just me." She started to slam the phone down, but changed her mind. She had a couple of other things to get off her chest. "Furthermore, Monsieur Santiago, you already made it very clear that you never intended to marry me. Well, I've discovered, being back here in Ohio, that I really am a simple, small-town girl. And I want all the small-town simple things . . . like a long white lace gown and a romantic church wedding. I want a man who isn't afraid to share, to go to the ends of the earth for me. A man who doesn't use excuses as to why he could never make a 'binding' commitment."

"Dammit, if that's what this is all about, we can get married tomorrow. Although I ought to tell you I don't like your way of snaring a guy."

Jackie sniffed haughtily. "Frankly, monsieur, out of the three proposals I received so far today, yours gets my vote for the worst." When she slammed the receiver into the cradle, it rocked violently several times from the impact, mirroring precisely how Jackie was feeling at that moment.

CHAPTER FIFTEEN

"Hold still," Gwen mumbled, a slew of straight pins pressed between her lips.

"Ouch."

"Sorry, Jackie. Just another few minutes." Gwen took in three more tucks, dropped the pins from her mouth into her palm, and surveyed her handiwork. She scratched her head. "Did anyone ever tell you that it isn't easy to transform a size twelve wedding dress into a size six?"

Jackie studied her reflection in the mirror. She had to agree that she didn't look much better than she had in that ridiculous costume at the Côte d'Or. But then she was only a waitress; now she was going to be a bride. She rubbed her cheeks, trying to give them some color. "It will be all right. I have confidence in you, Gwenny," Jackie teased.

"I guess so," Gwen said slowly, her eyes moving up to her sister's pale face. "But will you be all right?"

Jackie started to give an airy comeback, but she remembered how well her sister saw through her pretenses. "You think I'm doing the wrong thing, don't you?"

Gwen stuck the pins one by one back into the pincushion. "You don't love him, Jackie."

"He says I will in time. Maybe he's right."

"What if he's wrong?"

Jackie leaned back against the bureau, letting out a small scream as a pin jabbed her.

Gwen turned her around and unzipped her, helping her out of the eighteen-year-old wedding gown. She threw the dress over her arm, studying it thoughtfully for a moment. "God, it's faded over the years. I hope Evans will be able to bleach out some of the yellow when I bring it in for a cleaning."

"It doesn't matter," Jackie said, slipping her arms into her robe. "It will do fine."

"I still wish you'd go into Cleveland and buy yourself something really special, hon."

"No, it will take too long. Claude and I want to get back to France on Monday. If I want a church wedding with family and friends, Sunday is the day. Don't you think you can get the gown ready in four days?"

"I've performed a few miracles in my time. Like the day Sarah came home and told me two days before the Junior Prom that Garry Lester had finally asked her and I had to whip up 'the most heavenly' gown so that she would be the belle of the ball. I guess we'll make a bride out of you for Sunday." She set the dress on her sewing-machine table. "But being a wife is something you are going to have to manage on your own."

"Claude's . . . a wonderful man, Gwen. Don't you like him?"

Gwen came over and placed her hands on Jackie's shoulders. "Honey, whether or not I like him isn't the question. I'm old fashioned. I believe in marrying for love." She pursed her lips together. For the past three days, since Jackie's momentous announcement, ten minutes after that phone call from Peter Santiago, that she had decided to accept Claude Marigny's proposal of marriage, Gwen had vowed to mind her own business and keep her mouth shut.

But this was her sister. Maybe less innocent, more worldly, than a few months ago, but still locked inside a fantasy world. Gwen knew Jackie was hurting, just as she knew her sister was creating a new fantasy, determined not to give up on all her dreams, hopes, and desires. Only, Gwen knew, as well as she knew anything at all, that Jackie was making a dreadful mistake.

Finally, exhaling a long puff of air, Gwen gripped Jackie's hand. "Don't do it, Jackie. You're in love with Peter. He's the one you should be walking down the aisle with. Claude's perfectly nice and I'm sure he's a great catch, but you don't love him now and I'm willing to wager all of John's fees for the next ten years that you never will. He's not your type, honey."

"Types don't mean a damn thing. I've learned that much. And as far as Peter is concerned, he hasn't the slightest interest in getting married . . . except under duress or when he thinks that there's something in it for him. Peter must have finally come to the realization that I'm too valuable to let walk out of the vineyard, so he figured that push had finally come to shove. Well, dammit, I'm not shoving anybody down the aisle." She sat down on the edge of the bed. "Maybe I don't love Claude, but I do care for him. I admit I'm being selfish . . . opportunistic, just like Peter. But I've been very honest with Claude. He knows I'm marrying him because he can give me the kind of life I want. But I'm not just taking, Gwen. I intend to make Claude a good wife, and to work with him at the vineyard. We can be a team. And that's something Peter would never allow."

Gwen sat down beside her sister. "I'm sure you have been honest with Claude, but he strikes me as the kind of man who is very sure of his own charm. He may believe that he can make you love him, but he could end up very bitter when he comes to realize it's an impossible task."

"I'm not going to let that happen. Claude loves me and I am not going to hurt him." And then in a small voice she added, "At least, I hope not."

"You know that Peter called again last night. Sarah followed your orders and told him you had no desire to speak to him again. I think she's gone and gotten herself a first-class crush on your fiancé."

"So I noticed. She seems to be the only one who's really excited about the wedding. How lucky to be sixteen years old and filled with nothing but beautiful, romantic notions. I remember when I used to feel that way myself. Unfortunately, in my case it lasted well past adolescence. Now I'm all grown up and I realize that stars don't always twinkle in your eyes and sometimes the wrong Prince Charming shows up on his white steed." Jackie rubbed her head. "I could use some aspirin."

Gwen patted her back gently. "I'll get you some. But don't forget that Claude said he'd be over to take you out to lunch. And then at three we're all meeting with the pastor to go over the final plans for the ceremony." She headed for the door. "Are you sure you don't want something more elaborate than a small reception back here afterward?"

"I'm sure," Jackie said, stretching out on the bed and flinging one arm over her forehead.

Five minutes later, when Gwen returned with the aspirin, Jackie was already sound asleep.

Very quietly Gwen tiptoed up to the bed and carefully placed her heirloom afghan over her sister. For another few moments she stared down at Jackie, sadly shaking her head. With all her dreams of someday being her sister's matron of honor, she felt decidedly unhappy about finally getting the opportunity this coming Sunday.

"What's the matter, *chérie?* Are you getting last-minute jitters?" Claude put down his soup spoon and studied her warmly.

"Are you?"

Claude laughed. "Not in the least. I admit I'm eager to have the ceremony finished so that we can get back to . . . civilization. I cannot fathom how a woman like you could actually have grown up and lived in this godforsaken place all those years."

Jackie bristled. "I'm also the woman who worked for you for over nine weeks and never received more than cursory interest. It wasn't until I masqueraded as Jacqueline Armand that you sat up and took notice."

Claude smiled, ignoring her irritation. Reaching his hand across to hers, he said softly, "It was when you became Mademoiselle Armand that your true self was revealed, *mon amour.*"

Jackie stared down at her hand in his. "Is that what you think?" Her eyes grew misty. "I wonder." Then bringing herself back to earth, she squeezed Claude's hand. "Sorry, I guess brides-to-be are always emotional."

Claude pulled his chair closer. "Listen, *ma chère,* once we get back to Paris, everything will be perfect. I guarantee to put the bloom back in your lovely cheeks."

"Paris? But I thought we'd go straight down to the château."

"And share our honeymoon with my father and the whole staff at the vineyard? Nonsense, *chérie.* I am going to show you Paris as you have never seen it before. Ah, wait until we stroll down the Tuilleries in the late spring, all the flowers—"

"How long a honeymoon are you planning, Claude?" Her voice had a sharp edge to it.

Again, either Claude was ignoring her note of concern or he hadn't picked it up. "As long as we are both having fun." His voice grew warmly seductive. "I intend for us to have a great deal of fun, *chérie.*" His eyes held a promise of what was to come.

Jackie's eyes only reflected the continued watchful tension. For the hundredth time she asked herself if she were doing the right thing. And for the hundredth time she told herself she was.

While they ate, Jackie kept the conversation focused on the Château Maiffret and the vineyards, those being the only topics that she could immerse herself in and feel relaxed. Claude was duly attentive, although he spoke little. Jackie told herself that was Claude's way, but that she'd soon fire him up with the same enthusiasm and excitement that she felt for the life.

Then the clawing thought hit her: Claude, too, had great expectations of making changes. Was she really going to spark him with a passion for wine making anymore than he was going to turn her fond feelings for him into a deep, abiding love?

Gwen zipped up the wedding dress, admiring her skill as a seamstress while fretting over her ineptitude as a sister. She'd thrown every argument at Jackie that she could think of as her sister morosely went about making her wedding preparations. She fully expected Jackie to back out. More and more these past four days Gwen was convinced that her sister had come to realize it would be a drastic mistake to go through with the wedding. Yet, here she was, standing in front of

Gwen's full-length mirror, a smile as phony as a three-dollar bill plastered across her face, telling Gwen she'd done a great job.

"You do look beautiful," Gwen conceded; then her ire took over. "In fact you look just like one of those exquisite Gothic maidens being sacrificed at the altar. Which, to my way of thinking, couldn't be more accurate."

Gwen waited for Jackie to give her a dirty look or attack her as she usually did when Gwen refused to keep her mouth shut. Only, this time Jackie smiled wanly.

Gwen turned her around. "You don't have to go through with it, honey. Claude wouldn't be the only man or the last one left at the altar. Better now than later. I'll stick by you all the way."

"I love him, Gwen," Jackie moaned, falling against her sister's chest, letting the tears fall despite the newly applied mascara.

Gwen was baffled. "You love Claude?"

Jackie was crying too hard to answer. She just shook her head vigorously for a few moments, her carefully upswept hairdo tumbling down.

"Hush, baby. It's okay. It's okay," Gwen whispered, half carrying her sister toward the bed and easing her down on the edge.

Jackie continued crying, but she managed to talk at the same time. "I love Peter. I can't help it. I hate myself for loving him. He—he's not worth it, the bastard. He's even stopped calling."

"You made it pretty clear you wouldn't talk to him, hon. He probably got exasperated."

"Well, damn it, if he loved me half as much as Claude does, he could have at least blown a few bucks on the phone bill and kept trying! He doesn't care. That's the part that hurts so much. He doesn't love me. He gave me a line just like he gave the others. He told me I was the first woman that he'd ever said he loved and meant it. What a laugh! What a fool I was." Fresh tears filled her eyes.

"Are you so sure he doesn't love you? Maybe you were wrong about him and Pam Morgan."

"It was Peter who admitted that the tramp spent her mornings prancing around in her underwear, or pretty close to it," Jackie said petulantly.

"That's still not proof positive that anything went on."

"You never met Louis Morgan. If Pam is anything like her father, I guarantee you she got her way. And probably without much coaxing. You don't know Peter Santiago, either. He's . . . he's . . ."

"I know." Gwen smiled tenderly, wiping Jackie's mascara-smudged cheeks with a tissue. "He's opportunistic, devious, and untrustworthy—in short, a first-class cad."

"Right."

"So tell me something," Gwen said slightly combatively. "If he's such a cad, how could you fall so madly in love with him? I wouldn't have thought a bright, sensitive, intuitive gal like you would have let yourself be taken in by a con artist."

Jackie stopped crying and pulled herself together. "I've thought about that myself. I can't figure him out, Gwen. There were times . . . so many times that I thought he was the most tender, loving, compassionate man in the world. I even thought for a while there that he was growing less afraid of making an honest woman of me." She laughed dryly. "I guess I must have been all wrong."

John, mercifully freed from delivering babies for one whole day, rapped lightly on the door. "I know how it takes you ladies forever to get ready for a shindig, but this is one time I don't think you two want to be late. I've got a nervous groom downstairs who I'm about to drive to the church. Get a move on, girls."

Jackie jumped up and went over to the mirror. "We'll be ready in a few minutes, John," she said in a strangled voice. "Oh, God, just look at me. I'm a mess!" She opened up a jar of cold cream, coated a ball of cotton, and began cleaning off her cheeks.

Gwen came up behind her and grabbed Jackie's wrist. "Don't go. I'll hurry down and tell John. He can break it to Claude."

"No. I can't do that," Jackie said, attacking her hair, forgoing the upsweep to let it fall simply around her shoulders. "Help me with the veil, will you Gwen?" She gave her sister a sharp, no-nonsense look.

Gwen sighed and lifted up the veil from the bed. "I feel like I'm an accomplice to a crime instead of the sister of the bride," she grumbled, setting the white satin headdress on Jackie's hair.

One of the altarboys motioned to the organist as Gwen's station wagon pulled up at the church. John was waiting outside, ready to take Jackie's arm and walk her down the aisle. His best friend, Mike Burke, had happily offered to stand up with the groom, as Claude obviously knew no one in the tiny town of Middleton Corner.

The pretty little white church with the requisite steeple was filled to the rafters, everyone excitedly waiting to see their own Jackie Archer get hitched to a real French aristocrat. A regular storybook wedding—for everyone but the bride.

Jackie's complexion was so pale against the blush she'd haphazardly applied at the last minute that, when John helped her out of the car, he gave her a physician's squint. "Are you going to pass out, Jackie?"

She shook her head from side to side. "I'm fine," she murmured, her eyes resolutely focused straight ahead at the large wooden church doors being slowly opened.

Gwen gave John a despairing shrug. It was too late now. The die was cast. All she could do was cross her fingers that somehow it would work out all right for her sister. Just how that was going to happen, she honestly had no idea. Especially considering the fact that fifteen minutes ago Jackie had professed undying love for another man. Boy, would she like to get her hands on that bastard Peter Santiago.

John had to grip Jackie's elbow tightly to keep her from swaying. Slowly, carefully, they made it up the entry steps to the paneled double doors. He still wasn't convinced she wasn't going to pass out on him. John saw a bead of perspiration break out across Jackie's brow, but her jaw was set, her gaze determined.

They were flooded with the clear and sharp strains of the organ music as they stepped inside the church. All heads turned toward them. John felt Jackie's step falter for a moment. She gave him a little nod of reassurance, reassurance she no longer felt. But what could she do now?

Her vision grew slightly blurry as she tried to make out the faces of her dearest friends. She could feel her palms grow sweaty inside her white lace gloves. And before John started to escort her down the aisle, she was sure she was actually beginning to hallucinate.

A tall man stepped into the aisle several feet in front of her. Jackie blinked as he started walking toward her, then she gasped.

The music stopped abruptly; a low din of whispered words broke out after a shocked silence.

"What the hell do you think you're doing?" Peter Santiago's voice was so low even John, who had come to a stunned halt, couldn't hear.

Jackie's whole body began to tremble. "I'm . . . I'm getting married."

"Like hell you are," he hissed, scooping her up in his arms just as she started to go into a dead faint.

Peter turned around at the gaping faces

around him. "Sorry, folks. You'll have to carry on without her. We've got other plans." He paused for a moment, then added, "Oh, if you want to meet here same time next week, you'll get to see her make it down the aisle."

John was just about to swing at Peter when Gwen grabbed his arm. "It's okay, honey. I can't believe it"—she gave Peter a broad grin—"but everything is really all right now."

"Thanks, sis." Peter gave her a devilish wink.

Having finally gathered his wits about him, Claude came storming up the aisle. But just as he got to Peter, Jackie came to. Oblivious to anything but the fact that she was, at last, in Peter's arms, she gave Peter a dazed look and whispered breathlessly, "It's about time."

Claude stopped in his tracks, a deep frown across his brow, his shoulders slightly hunched in hopeless resignation.

Still holding Jackie, Peter turned to Claude. "I'm sorry, *mon ami*, but I can't live without her."

Claude managed a pained smile, the true aristocrat up to the bitter end. Then, without saying a word, he continued walking out of the church.

A few moments later Peter, with a half-dazed Jackie in his arms, followed Claude out. The congregation burst into a clamorous uproar.

"Never in my day . . ."

"Can you imagine . . . ?"

"I can't believe . . ."

"That poor man . . ."

"Did you see the way she swooned in his arms?"

The pastor closed his prayer book and calmly left the podium. This was for God to fathom, not him.

Sarah was frantically tugging on Gwen's sleeve. "Oh, God, mother, that was so romantic!" She took a deep breath. "Poor Claude."

Gwen grinned at her wide-eyed daughter. "Maybe he'll wait for you to grow up."

Sarah giggled.

John looked awkward and embarrassed, but Gwen put her arms around him, kissing him ardently on the mouth. He pulled her to him and the two of them began to laugh. He swung his arm around her waist and they started out of the church, Danny and Sarah tagging right behind. Then Gwen turned around and addressed the still stunned townsfolk.

"Remember everyone. Please be here, same time, same station, next Sunday. Let's show our Jackie how much we love her. Now that she's had a little practice, she's sure to get it right the next time."

Jackie came to her senses halfway down the street. She made quite a sight being carried down Marion Avenue in her long white wedding gown, her veil precariously tipped to the side of her head.

"Put me down."

"Never," Peter said, gripping her more tightly. "Let you go for a minute and you might go off and pull some other totally dumb stunt."

"You're pretty damn good at pulling stunts yourself."

"Pamela Morgan wasn't one of them, you idiot." He gave her his most endearing smile. "I told her the day she showed up that I was planning to get married and she didn't stand a chance of changing my mind. She went off riding with Philippe Troyan the next morning, figuring she'd find somebody to console her, and ended up twisting her ankle. That was the only reason she stayed on for a few days. I had a feeling she was putting one over on me, but I was too busy to pay any attention to her. I was working my tail off all day long . . . and dreaming of you all night long."

"Why didn't you tell me?"

"Because you got me so damn mad throwing Claude's proposal in my face. I'm really mad as hell at you for this last little stunt."

"It wasn't a stunt," she admitted. "Just a crazy, insane mistake."

"Good thing I got there in the nick of time. I made a stop in California first to have it out with Louis. If I'd known the church bells were going to be ringing today I would have gotten here sooner. I only found out when I arrived in town twenty minutes ago."

She put her arms around him and kissed him full on the mouth. Then she narrowed her gaze. "What happened with Louis?"

"I told him to go to hell. There are plenty of growers in Napa Valley willing to sell me Zinfandel vines."

"Peter . . ."

"I know. I've got a ten-day buy-out clause before I lose the château to Louis. If I don't come up with some brilliant idea—pardon me, princess—if *we* don't come up with some brilliant idea we're going to have to start figuring out some altogether new stunts."

Jackie kissed the tip of his nose and grinned. "I've got an idea or two up my sleeve. Just stick around, Monsieur Santiago."

"I've got to stick around, princess. I just invited a church full of strangers to our wedding next Sunday."

"Oh, Peter, I love you."

"Then how about turning down any other marriage proposals that happen to come your way before I make an honest woman of you next week?"

"*Je promets.* I promise."

"I love you, Jackie. And I still swear I've never felt that way about anyone else."

"I'll never doubt you again, Peter."

They stood in the middle of the street, Jackie in her flowing white bridal gown, Peter in a black leather jacket, his face unshaven, his eyes slightly bloodshot from the early-morning flight. Arms around each other, they kissed with utter abandon, ignoring the stares of all the people who had followed them out of the church. When they finally broke apart, they were met with a round of hearty cheers.

The following Sunday's wedding went off without a hitch. Everyone agreed that Jackie made an exquisite bride . . . they'd thought much the same thing only seven days earlier. There were those who argued that Claude Marigny was a better catch, while others held steadfast to the romantic belief that love will out. But everyone did agree that Peter Santiago looked divinely handsome and dashing in his cutaway tuxedo.

Gwen cried for joy all the way down the aisle. John was relieved that Jackie's coloring was good and that he didn't have to support her as he walked her down the aisle. The minister seemed just plain glad to get the ceremony over with before some other trial was sent from heaven to test him.

Jackie was radiant. It was the happiest moment of her life when the pastor told Peter he could kiss his bride. It was a heart-stopping, spine-tingling kiss. Then Peter scooped her up in his arms and ran up the aisle with her, everyone following after them throwing rice and cheering.

Peter decided, in the short ride from the church to Gwen's house, that even though nothing seemed to have come from whatever vineyard-saving idea Jackie had said she'd had, he didn't give a damn. Now that he had her, now that he knew how wonderful loving and being loved was, he'd come up with some other plan . . . find some other dream. It would be okay now that she was his at last.

Everyone crowded into the small living room for the reception. As soon as Jackie was sure they were all there, she grabbed Peter's hand and dragged him to the middle of the room.

"Okay, everybody. Announcement time." They quieted down immediately. She turned to Peter. "You know, in all this time, you've never once inquired about my dowry, Monsieur Santiago."

He gave her a puzzled look. "Dowry?"

"The thing is, my family wasn't very rich. But I have grown up in a town where, in a special way, everyone here is family to me. And they got together"—her voice faltered, tears brimming in her eyes—"and decided I ought to have some sort of a dowry. And I . . . well, I decided, since there will always be a part of me here in Middleton Corner, Ohio, why not bring a part of Middleton Corner with me to France? So take a look around, darling. You're looking at seventy-four part owners in a château."

Peter stared dumbfounded as Gwen presented him with an envelope, inside of which was a cashier's check for the exact amount of money he needed to buy out Louis Morgan.

Peter sniffed, rubbing furiously at his eyes. "I . . . I don't know what to say. This is just . . . just unbelievable." He stopped bothering to erase his tears. "I think the whole batch of you are the best damn group of partners a guy could ever ask for." He drew Jackie into his arms. "And you, my love, top the list." He dug into his pocket. "I've been carrying this around since the day you left for California." He handed the rectangle of paper to her. "Up until this moment I thought we'd never get a chance to use it."

It was a label for Château Cardinet Zinfandel. And printed across the bottom were the words, PETER ET JACQUELINE SANTIAGO—PROPRIÉTAIRES.

Jackie pressed the paper to her lips. Then she turned to Peter and circled her arms around his neck. "I love you, Monsieur Santiago."

"I love you, Madame Santiago."

A shocked cry came from the kitchen. It was Gwen.

"I'll see what's wrong," Jackie said, hurrying off.

Gwen was standing at the kitchen table, staring down, mortified, at the exquisite three-tiered wedding cake.

"I can't believe it. The idiots."

Jackie walked over. In ornate pink lettering across the top of the cake appeared the words: JACKIE AND CLAUDE FOREVER. She burst out laughing.

"It isn't funny, Jackie. Peter will be terribly upset."

There was a devilish twinkle in Jackie's big green eyes. "Don't worry about a thing. I've got just the solution."

Jackie carefully lifted off the top layer and set it on a cake plate. Gwen ran ahead to open the kitchen door. When Jackie appeared at the entry the whole group broke into a rousing rendition of "The Bride Cuts the Cake." Peter was led to the head of the main table as Jackie drew near.

He saw that special gleam in her eyes as she came closer.

"Jackie . . . you wouldn't . . . you—"

"Remember the Côte d'Or? I owe you one, Santiago." And with that she dramatically stumbled forward and dumped the cake squarely in the middle of his lap. While everyone stared aghast, Jackie broke into a fit of laughter. Peter jumped up, pulled her into his arms, and they laughed loudly together. The wedding party got as much of the joke as they could—it did make a funny scene—and soon every last person in Gwen's living room was laughing hysterically along with the happy bride and groom.